WILD BOLTS
ELECTRIC

WILD BOLTS
ELECTRIC

ADAM DOMPIERRE

SMILODON SUN
PUBLISHING

First published by Smilodon Sun Publishing

This book is a work of fiction. Names, characters, businesses, organizations, places, events and incidents either are the product of the author's imagination or are used fictitiously. Any resemblance to actual persons, living or dead, events, or locales is entirely coincidental.

Printed in the United States of America.

For more information, or to book an event, contact:
adamdompierre@gmail.com
http://www.adamdompierre.com

Book design by Marissa Lete
Cover design by Tim Gould

ISBN - Paperback: 979-8-9890122-0-6
Library of Congress Control Number: 2023917586

First Edition: October 2023

To Paul and Julie,
sine quibus non

I

Strangely enough, it started with a game. Or a competition maybe; with each other, with themselves... with the way minutes and hours are stretched to their breaking points and then made to crawl uphill, especially when it's summer and the job requires working with people. It was impersonal and judgmental but harmless fun through the eyes of bored young men. A game.

Logistics: James Chandler worked as a building manager for an on-campus gym and had many duties. Among them he sometimes had to sit at a desk and scan ID cards, make sure everyone entering the gym was a member in good standing, sell day passes, that sort of thing; they weren't exactly splitting the atom. The check-in desk was roughly fifty feet from the gym entrance, and that allowed the workers a sizable window between when people entered and when they reached the desk. The employees gave life to this aspect of the job, made a joke of it, being approached like kings and queens by the provincials who made the way to their illusory thrones.

In that time—the time between the door-chime announcing the next unveiling and when they were in earshot—James and whoever would quietly hold their own private roasts about the latest oblivious patron who had the temerity to come through those doors. That particular day found him stationed alongside his coworker Brent. Brent was a clown, but a good guy. Fun guy. And the chime rang.

Back up. The first half of the game was the jokes. They would see this person from a distance and have about ten seconds to size them up and construct their one-liners. It wasn't high art. They fell back on lazy stereotypes. The slow-witted jock, the spacey sorority girl, old men and women fighting an unwinnable battle against time and consequence. They could find fault in anyone and, like archers, they felt rewarded to hit their targets with increasing degrees of accuracy.

Second half was verification. How to validate the shots from the first half. Here, against time, James was in his element. A complete psychological/life profile compressed to less than a minute, any faint clue the potential difference between victory and defeat. The search for the incidental heightened the senses, which was about all he could hope for during some of those longer, monotonous shifts. More than once he had been redeemed simply by looking up the visitor's car on the parking lot security camera, though this sort of easy mode came at the cost of some self-respect. Like bowling with bumpers.

Back to the door-chime. It sounded two notes, high then low, euphonious and sterile. There were times James resented it before the invention of the game—another potential headache—but in these moments it was his lifeblood. Brent was right there with him.

"Gentlemen, place your bets." He nudged Brent with an elbow. "What's this guy's deal?"

"He is," Brent began softly, "an eccentric hundredaire."

"Dozenaire," James added, softer still.

Their visitor was surprisingly swift and upon them before they could take it any further. Unusually tall, with a slight frame of lean muscle and sinew, he wore a black full-cover jumpsuit in spite of the heat, dirty to the point of looking like it had never been new. A red ring, not much hair, and wild, deep blue eyes, searching. Another punchline seen from far, James was uncomfortable in the man's proximity. A body warped by wrinkles that spread across it like fault lines. Forty, maybe, or sixty? Hard to tell. Face too... like a mask. On edge, no question, but unnervingly comfortable there, the familiar sea he swam in. The stranger eyed them quickly but comprehensively, and settled on James. The tone of the room had changed, the air newly electric. And they began.

An awkward silence everyone waited for someone else to break before James realized the move would need to be his. "What can I do for you, sir?"

Without taking his eyes off James, the man wordlessly slid a piece of paper across the desk in response. James unfolded it and couldn't make sense of what he found there. Letters, yes, but not words. A phone number on the reverse side, Charlottesville area code. He passed it to Brent with a raised eyebrow, and Brent had to turn away to keep from laughing. James couldn't empathize; he was agitated since this specter fixed his stare upon him, and no break felt forthcoming.

He noticed Brent abandoned him, bolting into the back somewhere. Nowhere to go but forward. He met the man's eyes—mentally traced the dark red blood vessels that stood out like highways, never blinking—and felt all the more alone.

"I'm not sure what you want," he managed.

The man smiled, an act of malevolence. "I'll see you," he said, raspy but matter-of-factly, tapping his fingers on the desk. The fingernails were long, unbroken, like curved bones. Claws protruding from skin stretched nearly to the point of translucence. He turned away then, eternity in an instant, and James took the opportunity to do the same, retreating to join Brent. Out of view. Anywhere but there. Away from that.

Brent was laughing. "That was an all-timer! I never answered your questions, let me see..."

"Forget it," James said. "Doesn't matter now."

"What a weirdo, man, what an absolute bizarre jackass." He walked around swinging his shoulders in an exaggerated mimic of the visitor's mannerisms. "What does that guy drive? I have to know what he drives. A decommissioned tank? A hearse. Tank that doubles as a hearse, but creepier and less practical. Powered by misunderstanding of social norms."

"Go and see," James said, still trying to shake the trance. "Go and see." *I looked and saw, and behold, a pale horse. And the name it said on him was Death. And Hell followed with him.* A bit much. He shook his head.

Brent exited the room and returned soon after. "I don't know, he's gone. Nothing on the camera, walked here maybe. I mean it man, that was an all-timer." He laughed again and returned to the desk. "An absolute all-timer."

* * *

As a young man James recognized and acknowledged he lived an easy life—no irreversible future-killing choices made in the teenage years, no outstanding warrants for his arrest—but sleep was sometimes elusive even under optimal conditions, which this wasn't. That night he lay in bed, facing the door, and ran through the day's events. Fear (no, not fear, but the feeling that some deep, powerful foundation had been irrevocably shaken) had been replaced with annoyance. What type of person went through the world the way this idiot did? How do you survive to however old, when that's your idea of acceptable existence?

Unanswerable. But the other question: people are not born like that, so what makes someone that way? What turns him into... whatever he saw today? Drugs, he guessed, or some imbalance anyway, but this was implacably different. *More things in heaven and earth...* He didn't really believe in the supernatural. Only the limitless human ability to impose meaning on whatever we don't understand. Easier that way. We can recognize ghosts, vampires, and the like as being impossible, but their fictions, "the rules," are easily understood, comforting in that sense. So: explanation, look no further. But the impossible wasn't robbing him of sleep. The man from the gym was.

He got out of bed and walked to the kitchen. 1:25 by the microwave clock. He took a bottled water from the refrigerator and leaned on the counter, looking out the window. A waning gibbous moon, white as birch bark, hung in the sky. Heavy black branches between the window and moon cut across its glowing surface like scars, deep and jagged. He had lived in that house for just over two years, and stood in that kitchen hundreds of times. Rarely in the dark though—funny how much that warped perception.

But so what? And that ultimate variable, so volatile, the mindspace behind our eyes that colors everything we see and do. The world is at the mercy of our conceptions, it seemed, and we along with it. *I could be bounded in a nutshell and count myself a king of infinite space, were it not that I have bad dreams.* That night the kitchen wasn't the least bit homey or inviting. Just another place the same thoughts tracked him. Just another place he wanted to get out of.

* * *

James had met Claire Ventura almost three years earlier, the way most everyone meets. By chance.

He didn't have the motivation or the money to go to college, so it was to the workforce for him. Which was fine, it was a wide-open world and he didn't feel there was any one narrow path to success or happiness, which might be the same thing. The tradeoff was a lot of night shifts and, living in a university town, long bus rides with drunken college students on their way to wherever. There was no more surefire way to appreciate anew the patience, saintly at times, of public bus drivers.

He imagined full-time jobs were all exhausting in their own ways (mentally, physically, other, all of the above), and while the famed vigor of youth granted him a buffer on most days, that was not one of them. Customer service was a monster, no way around it, and the bad days deserved a more satisfying descriptor. Awful, abominable, spirit-annihilating, take your pick. James claimed no exceptional intellect, but even for an average person, dealing with unending foolishness was like stabbing a boulder with a knife in perpetuity. The blade gets dulled, broken even, but the rock isn't fazed any. No fault of the knife, but there will be no awakenings for the stone.

Such was that Monday evening, so unassuming upon its

arrival, that bled into Monday night. The bus' yellow lights lit up the horizon and made their way toward him through the dark. The hiss of the door sounded, and he summoned the courage to drag himself up the three steps and fall into a waiting seat. Any patience that survived his shift had gone from bone-thin to nonexistent—his disgust for the world and all its lousy inhabitants at a zenith. Angry, disaffected, all the rest. But finally he was on a bus back to his peaceful apartment. It felt like seeing the wall of water give way to sunlight after a dive that tests your limits. A dive deep into the endless abyss of human frailty.

The last bus back north left at 2:00 in the morning, and that was his ride. It was always pretty packed, but that day being a Monday was less so than usual. His eyes were drawn to the back rows being commandeered by a group of freshmen guys, maybe a sage sophomore or two leading the charge. It was August, when the freshmen were at their easiest to spot. Impossible to miss really, somehow tourists in their own town. Everything amplified, exaggerated. Full of conquering hero bravado (never mind their station demanded they hadn't actually accomplished anything yet), having made the leap into The World. On their own in every way except the ones that mattered. Always cooler to sit in the back.

They were loud, drunk, and obnoxious. Entitled, fun, and alive. James had been all those things, and would be again, but not that night. It was enough to put on his headphones—*No More Shall We Part*—and let the universe follow its will. Meditation without the silence or focus. Just breathing. He closed his eyes and the world softened, all was softness, and then...

He opened his eyes and that seemed to make the bus stop. The odd feeling triggered by misperception lingered a moment, and then she was next to him. Striking, even in their unremarkable surroundings. Pale skin, dark hair, eyes like lapis lazuli. The back of the bus was still teetering between a light beer commercial and a warzone.

"Can I sit here?" she asked.

The question didn't register initially, but eventually his synapses fired. "Ok." He nodded, still breaking the sleep spell. He closed his eyes, but the album had ended, so he reconsidered and opened them again. She was carrying a book by Henry Miller. James could fit what he knew about Henry Miller on a postage stamp but, with nothing to lose, he took his shot.

"Henry Miller?" he said, not knowing where he was going with this.

She looked up. "You've read Henry Miller?"

"Sure," he said. "Plenty of times."

That got a smile. "Which of his is your favorite?"

She had *Tropic of Cancer* and he knew *Tropic of Capricorn* was a thing, but he wasn't going to commit to having read either; that would be walking right into a follow-up question. He let out a breath, in trouble now. "I try to avoid comparisons, you know? Something always gets diminished when you start putting things against each other." Was that convincing? "I've always liked his earlier stuff." Can't miss.

She nodded, another smile; smart enough to not believe it, kind enough to not press the issue. Time to steer the conversation into more familiar waters. "I'll tell you what I don't get," he said. "Tropic of Cancer, Capricorn, North, South, latitudes... What's going on there?"

She had the book away now and looked at him good-naturedly. "What's going on where? They're like the equator, but north and south."

"Which is which, we can start there." And what did they have to do with whatever Henry Miller was writing about? But he thought it best to leave that part out.

"Capricorn is... North? North. Capricorn is North," she said, less sure each time.

"I'm not sure I buy that..."

"Claire."

"Claire. I'm not sure I buy that, Claire," he said. He had never met a Claire before, but no time like the present. "Are you pretending to know about this to impress me?" Sometimes the best defense was a good offense.

"Capricorn is North. I'll show you," she said, going for her phone.

"No cheating, come on," He grabbed a piece of paper from his backpack and drew his best circle. The bus bumped along and turned it into more of a wavy oval that never quite connected, but enough to get the point across. "The Earth," he announced proudly.

"No, no, no," she said. "Too wobbly."

"The perfect amount of wobbly," he said. "No more on the wobbly-ness. You just need some countries to get your bearings." More turbulence as the bus dipped and swerved. A few shaky finishing touches and then, "North America!"

She laughed for the first time, an effortless melody. "Not a country!" she said. "Definitely not a country!"

"Many countries," he corrected. The bell rang, signaling their next stop.

"Well, three, but who's counting?"

"Sure," he said, "three, great. The point is..." He had lost the point.

"This is my stop," she said, getting up slowly. "Nice to have met you."

"I feel like we've only scratched the surface of this world

geography stuff," he said. "Entire continents unexplored. Maybe we can pick it back up some time." That wasn't great, but he hoped it would be good enough.

She grabbed the piece of paper with his sad little North America and wrote a phone number. "Capricorn, North." She handed him the paper and walked off the bus without looking back. James lifted his eyes from the numbers to the window and watched her fade into the night.

He waited three days to follow up—"*Cancer*, North, Claire"—and before long their days had taken on a new rhythm. She put her hand in his, after which he could find no comparison.

2

Sleep came, as it always did, and the next morning was bright, with a calm breeze snaking through the trees. A day off besides, and James approached it with enthusiasm, set to meet Claire for a beach date. He walked into the kitchen and saw the slip of paper from the gym yesterday. The room was well-lit now, the sun shone strongly in through the windows, and the note had lost whatever dark aura it held the day before. The whole thing seemed silly looking back, and he left it lying there with a bemused wonder it had ever inspired more than that.

The American South in August and the weather to match. He hauled his bike down off of the hooks it was hanging on, and by the time he was out of the driveway he worked up a healthy sweat. Rose Hill turned into Madison. His fingers rested in a relaxed grip around the handlebars, the air flowing gently over his face. He waited until a straight stretch and closed his eyes, letting the world fall away. Only motion and momentum, always forward. Yesterday's events receded and all was right. He felt the bike ease into a slight incline and slowly opened his eyes. Nothing lurking in the shadows. A welcoming return to normalcy.

The bike path wove its way up a hill and James stopped at its crest, as he always did, to admire the view. The asphalt fell away and sloped downward toward the lake. The water was a warm shade of dark blue; now and again it glinted silver as the sun caught the waves on their brief rise before they fell back and disappeared into the waterline. He squinted and the corners of his mouth drew into an involuntary smile. Claire was somewhere below waiting for him. He lingered there astride the bike, scanning the length of the sands beneath him. In time he picked out her familiar blue and orange striped beach umbrella. Stepping onto the pedals, he coasted down to the beach and locked up his bike at the bottom of the hill. From there it was a short scamper across the scorching sands, towel slung over his left shoulder. He found Claire sitting in the shade on a bright yellow towel, one of her heavy textbooks in front of her.

"Doing some light reading?" James asked as he came up behind her.

Her eyes stayed with the page a moment longer before she looked up. "Hey!" She gestured to an oversized picnic basket. "I brought sandwiches and drinks. And," she added, "watermelon and cupcakes. I kind of got ambitious."

"I'll say," James said. "Heck of a job, Ventura." He kissed her on the forehead and took up his spot beside her. "What are you reading about?"

"Just grad school stuff," she said, setting the book aside. "Beautiful day, isn't it?"

"Off to a great start. Way better than yesterday."

"What happened yesterday?"

James laughed. "Some guy at the gym. Seems kind of

funny now, but just a weird guy, that's all."

"Well, there are no weird guys here," Claire said. "Maybe one." She smiled and poked him in the ribs.

"At least one," James agreed. "I'm ready for a swim. You in?"

"Hard pass. I'll guard the sandwiches."

"You do that," James said and ran toward the water. The sand singed his bare feet and he picked them up clumsily, like a poorly-controlled marionette. He plunged his head under the water and felt it wash over him. The sun still beat down far above, but its heat could no longer reach him. He stayed under awhile, then broke the surface and took a deep breath of air. His dark hair hung over his face and he used both hands to push it back out of his eyes. From there he returned to Claire, still on the towel, guarding her picnic basket just as she had promised.

"Be honest," James said, nodding to a beachgoer off to their left. "Scale of one to ten, how much does this guy remind you of a giraffe?"

Claire turned her head to see a gangly man with a spike of red hair and an orange swimsuit covering his skinny legs. She couldn't help laughing. "That's not a very nice question."

"That's not a very good answer."

"Then... I plead the fifth," Claire said.

"Objection!" James protested.

"You can't object to the fifth!"

"No?"

"'Fraid not."

James pondered his options. "Sustained," he decided. "The motion carries."

They shared a carefree morning, in and out of the shade of the umbrella. Seagulls patrolled the sands like sentries, forever on the lookout for anything that might pass for food, while beyond them three young brothers took turns forcing each others' heads underwater. Finally it was time to leave, and they parted ways in the sunshine, planning on dinner with Claire's parents the following day.

It was afternoon by the time he pulled back into his garage, tired and overheated, but feeling cleansed from the night before—energy well-spent. He unlocked his back door and made his way through the kitchen when he stopped cold. Out of the corner of his eye he saw two pieces of paper lying on the counter. There had been one when he left, the one with the nonsense letters on one side and a nonsense phone number on the other. Now, no question, there were two.

The same color and dimensions, dirty white, maybe twice the size of a playing card. Even from a distance he could identify the writing. No mistaking those serrated lines, full, dark and heavy-handed, as though formed under immense pressure somewhere deep in the earth. Past the earth, maybe. If he didn't think letters could look psychotic before, he certainly believed it now.

His initial reaction was not to read the note, not even to approach it, but to scan the room. Something in him half-expected to see the man poised, ready to strike, everywhere he looked. The search turned up nothing, and still he hesitated. His family's house had been robbed when he was a child and ever since he locked his doors religiously. If he didn't remember locking them before he left, it was only because the act had become as routine as putting on a seat belt, automatic as blinking or breathing. And it had been locked when he returned, so... He still hadn't moved.

The windows were open, Charlottesville in August, but none of the screens disturbed. So what then, shamus? No way this guy was some prodigious cat burglar, phasing in and out of buildings undetected, right? Impossible. If not a break-in then... what? Had he slipped through undetected as James left the house? Impossible. He had someone plant the card? Maybe, but who, and why? Even if he conceded the how—an altogether too generous concession he wasn't willing to make—the why was unrelenting. Unknowable, for now.

He pulled out his phone to call the police, but even so he couldn't act. How does that story go? "I'd like to report a phantom monster man who can walk through walls, and also he writes scary letters that don't form words. Please send the National Guard, cruise missiles maybe, as soon as possible, thank you and goodbye." That probably wasn't going to be one of the number choices on the pre-recorded menu. Frustrated, he tossed the phone onto the kitchen table and went to read the note. A moment's courage.

As he got closer, he saw there wasn't much to read this time, and no numbers. Three words and a picture. The picture won his attention first—a face staring back? Made of wings—dark, mutilated wings. He looked again. No face, no wings, just black ink.

"A Rorschach?" They were the first words he spoke since returning home. His mouth was dry and his voice thin, but the words rang out saliently in the empty kitchen. They seemed to echo off the walls, hang for a moment, and then die, suspended. The sun through the windows was now a punishing, inescapable light. A harsh bulb hanging in some lurid interrogation room where he didn't have any of the answers.

Below the drawing, carved into the paper, like arcing electricity, three words. "Not long now." A frozen person in a sweltering room, searching for some way forward. He picked up the other, original, slip of paper (fair to think of these as deranged business cards by now?) and rolled it around on the back of his fingers, thinking. The hell with it. He called the number.

* * *

High school had been no great test and James carried a 3.3 GPA through to the end. Nothing amazing, no end of the year banquets or fancy sashes at graduation, but enough to stay happily under the radar, away from any microscopes. His talents were English and music, weaker in STEM, but (or because) it wasn't something he could see affecting his life, so whatever. After high school, his friends mostly went off to new colleges, new experiences, while nothing much changed for him. Same house, same parents, increased hours and responsibility at the gym.

He wondered sometimes if skipping college was the right decision or not. No getting that back. The best four years of your life, they say. Eighteen to twenty-two wasn't that for him, but he had no complaints, and while his friends were graduating with mountains of debt and degrees they couldn't use, he had built solid savings and worked his way up the ladder in Comperio University's rec sports department. From there it was a small step to a down payment on a modest house outside of the city, and he was well on his way to, well, wherever it was he was headed, by twenty-four.

No drama, no issues. A job he liked (most days), a house that made him feel content if not affluent (better that way), and (most importantly) a girl worth building a future around. Aside from a white picket fence and a golden retriever, every other piece of that Rockwell-ian dream was in place, coming together like a massive and intricate laser-cut puzzle. But lives have a way of surprising, and his did just that, introducing into this immaculate diorama a new sinister agent of chaos. A flaw in the paint, a stain that no amount of washing would erase. What could he do but face it head-on?

Back in the kitchen, he steeled himself and let the phone ring persistently, the silences between rings stretching out like deserts. Finally the other end picked up; a man's voice. "Hello?"

James hadn't thought about how he was going to begin the conversation in the event someone actually answered. "Hi," he said. "Um, who is this?"

"This is Howard. Who are you trying to reach?"

James was honest. "I'm not sure. A man came into my gym yesterday and left a card with this phone number on it."

The other man was confused. "And he told you to call me?"

"Um, no, not really." This was partly what he had been afraid of. How to explain without sounding crazy? "I guess I was wondering what the number was for. Do you have any insight on that?"

"I haven't the faintest idea. Sounds like someone is winding you up. But I don't know what it has to do with me."

Neither did James. "Ok, I'm sure it's nothing," he said. "Sorry to have bothered you." He took the phone from his ear and hung up. The call lasted a minute and a half, revealing nothing. In a quick motion, he tossed the phone onto the counter. What now? Having no better ideas, he pulled out a chair and sat silently, resting his elbows on the kitchen table. What now?

Monday morning, back to work. He strolled into the office

with a cup of coffee, trying to look more chipper than he felt. "What's the good word?" he asked the assembled employees.

"Morning, James," Carrie responded. Could always count on Carrie. Boundless enthusiasm, like a puppy. Straight out of high school, still figuring things out. Sometimes painfully, but always eagerly.

"Anything interesting happen yesterday?" he asked. An open question, but he was wondering if (hoping?) his visitor might have reappeared.

"A woman passed out in hot yoga," Carrie offered cheerfully, before realizing that probably wasn't the appropriate tone. She brought it back down. "EMTs were called, the whole nine. It was... not a pretty sight. But she was ok!"

"That's good," he said. "What about the day before, anything to report?"

She looked confused. "You were here Saturday, right?"

"Right. Just wondered if anybody mentioned anything to you, anything with the guests? Brent say anything?"

"Nope, don't think so. Everything all right?" The concerned look of a kind person.

"I'm sure everything's fine," he said. "Thanks, Carrie."

"You're welcome!"

So, nothing there. He went into his office and closed the door. A stack of paperwork waited for him, banal, tedious stuff. But it was a distraction, which was its own reward just then, so he started checking boxes and copying addresses. The drudgery built upon itself until it was a kind of mindless momentum, and when he looked up it was time for lunch. Near enough, anyway. He opened his desk drawer in search of a takeout menu when he found something else instead.

There, under some outdated rental slips he really should

have taken care of weeks ago, was an old surveillance tape. They didn't even use them anymore, everything was saved digitally now, but it gave him an idea. He could go back and watch the video from that afternoon. With the added feeling of distance and the passage of time, he could re-observe his interactions with the stranger. Objectively this time. Free from the immediacy of living it, the meeting might seem as funny to him as it did to Brent at the time. There would still be the problem of the second business card (indeed, that was how he came to think of them) appearing in his locked house, but he hoped he could recast the man in his mind, defang this viper into something he could better handle. He pulled up the corresponding file on his computer and fast-forwarded to the approximate hour. "There's me, there's Brent, passing the time." 3:00, 4:00, and at 4:15. Without a moment's warning (though he wasn't sure what he had been expecting in that regard, thunderclouds?) the visitor appeared. Out of somewhere, James supposed, but as far as the tape was concerned there was nothing and then, undeniably, something. *Or, more precisely,* he thought, *someone.*

The image was just as he had seen it in his mind's eye. He watched the tape play without audio, and it was as he remembered, except one thing he hadn't noticed the first time. As James (the video version) looked down to read his note, the stranger glanced up quickly—too quickly, an unnatural movement—at the camera. His eyes locked on the lens, the same stare that captured James at the desk. This too was unnatural; human, but not *quite* human. It was ostensibly innocent enough, but the effect was upsetting. James realized he would sooner face a three-headed dragon than whatever it was that was giving him this feeling.

The video played back, those two blue stars shining out

from this mystery's face, boring into the camera for... how long was it? More than five seconds, it felt like an ocean, but there was no way he took his eyes off James for that long in real time. Video James looked up from the card and the rest of the scene played as he remembered, the camera again a silent sentinel.

A trick of the brain, he thought, and rewound the footage. This time he watched the video timer counting the seconds; it was everything he could do to avoid that stare, something reptilian about it now, but he forced his eyes to watch the seconds on the feed ticking away. And there it was again; he took his eyes off of James and stared into the camera for ten (ten!) seconds. Every attempt at clarification buried him deeper in obscurity. James had a desperate desire to reach out to someone, but it was more than he could do. Half of him thought this was all too ridiculous and he would come off like a lunatic. The other half refused to bring anyone else into this world he was falling into, a world that he feared now revolved around an invulnerable and uncompromising danger. He hoped he was wrong on that count, but the premonition was strong and unyielding.

The desk camera was just one, of course. He pulled up the video from the parking lot, anything for more data. Cueing up the footage to a couple minutes before 4:15 he found nothing. The video ran until 4:18 and still nothing. He went back and rewatched the ten-minute windows before and after; the man didn't appear on the tape. So that was out. Exasperation, every path finishing in a dead end. Or rather a cul-de-sac, spitting him out right back where he started. Always moving, never progressing. A mobius strip of wasted energy and motivation.

But how could he have forgotten; there was an avenue unexplored. How foolish, to have gone through all this amateur detective work (and with such sterling results) without talking to the only other person he shared the experience with. Brent wasn't the type of guy he would hang out with socially, but as far as coworkers went, they were pretty in sync. He felt he could go to him with this (whatever this was, still working on that part) and get an honest reading. Brent may have been flippant, but he wasn't a jerk.

James pulled up Brent's entry in the employee directory and punched the number into his office phone. Three rings, four... Déjà vu all over again. "The customer you are attempting to reach—*What up, it's your boy Brent!*—is not available. Please leave a message after the tone." Beep. Cul-de-sacs within cul-de-sacs.

"Hey Brent, it's James, give the gym a call if you get a chance." He lowered the receiver but picked it back up. "Actually, not an emergency, but call me as soon as you get this." He left his cell phone number. "As soon as you get this. Thanks." That was all that could be done, so he hung up, and, having no better ideas, studied the four walls of his office. He didn't find anything there he didn't expect.

He stayed at work longer than needed and it was late by the time he left. Well into the evening, but not yet dark. The days stretched on in summer, yawning jungle cats arranging their cells into their longest possible configurations. No more public transportation for him, one of the nicer perks of full-blown adulthood. He guided his car through its paces, a drive so familiar that it no longer demanded, or even suggested, he keep his attention on the road. The sun was low, almost on the horizon, but the sky retained a pastel blue color with soft white clouds drifting carelessly across it. A pretty night, all things considered, but his mind remained restless. If only he could talk with Brent, he felt that might set everything at ease. No good being trapped inside his own thoughts, that much was clear. Just then his phone rang.

Never a good sign, that. Anyone he would be glad to hear from knew well enough not to call but text. The text was as essential to his makeup as his thinning hair or his eyesight that wasn't what it used to be and would only decline from there. Too young to be feeling as old as he was, and when did that start anyway? His first inclination was to let it ring, but then he remembered leaving his number on Brent's voicemail. He quickly rummaged through the jetsam on his passenger seat, left hand at 12:00 on the steering wheel, one eye (mostly) on the road. Two rings went by before he was able to grab hold and flip it over to see who was calling.

Claire. Odd. If anyone knew how much he hated talking on the phone, it was her. She endured too many polemics against people who called when a text would have sufficed, graciously at first and then with a humored but enduring tolerance. So why was she calling him now?

"What's up?"

"Where are you?" she asked, annoyed. Not a casual question. "Driving home from work. Why?"

"Why are you on your way home? Did you forget about dinner?"

No response, but yeah, he definitely forgot about dinner. "Was that today? Um, Mario's, right?" He had been driving fifteen minutes in the wrong direction. "I'm sorry, I've had kind of a lot going on. I can be there in... twenty minutes?"

"You know what, don't worry about it, I've been here half an hour already. Good luck with everything going on. I'll talk to you later." End of call.

"Look, sorry, but—" Too late. He threw the phone back onto the passenger seat. He would find a way to make it up to her, it would be fine, but it still put him in an even worse mood. Some madman threatening him, a coworker who wouldn't call him back, and now a girlfriend overreacting to a simple misunderstanding. Nothing but roses. The left lane was open so he moved into it and pressed down hard on the accelerator; fifteen miles per hour over the speed limit, twenty, the cars to his right falling steadily behind him.

A massive RV sat heavily in his path, one of those behemoths of the highway, crawling. It grew in his windshield and he was soon upon it. Not even going the speed limit now, probably five to ten under. Despite plenty of opportunities to get over, the vehicle remained resolutely in the passing lane. James stomped on the gas pedal again and gestured out the window with his hand. "Get over!" he bristled. "Get over!" The driver ahead inched along leisurely.

Irritated, he fell back. The right lane was open, easier to get around them at this point. He surveyed the traffic in his rearview mirror and glanced over his right shoulder to check his blind spot. The figure he saw on the side of the road then was unmistakable. Tall, thin (how so thin?), and the head nearly bald. James' attention left the traffic in front of him and he tried to get a better look through his back window, but it was in vain. His speed was too great, and the dark figure already receded from view. He turned his eyes back to the traffic in front of him. Could he have imagined it? Unusual enough to see someone walking along this road, and a pedestrian matching that description? No coincidence, couldn't be.

But then, was it possible, the figure was far ahead of him. James saw his outline up toward the horizon, the form that could have been only one person. Traffic wasn't an immediate concern, and James didn't want to lose him again. He hammered on the accelerator, and slowly the gap between them closed. The man was coming into view, he turned and the two made eye contact. The face was like a mask. James could not look away, and all while his SUV roared down the highway.

The vehicle in front of him did not. Violent as lightning, an old Lincoln that had been biding its time in front of him hit the brakes. From the side of the road the shadowy figure jerked his head toward the car that had stopped so suddenly. Cause or effect? James followed his eyes, but by then it was too late to avoid a savage collision. The crashing sound was just as he had heard them in the movies, but with arresting immediacy and severity. He wasn't at all prepared for his first-high speed car accident. Is anyone?

The impact with the vehicle instantly cut his speed to almost zero. The airbag deployed and hit him hard, but he kept his wits long enough to check his rearview mirror before slowly pulling to the side of the road. The traffic behind them had stopped, leaving a wide berth for the sudden braker and the idiot who couldn't watch where he was going. Not his best moment by a long shot.

The Lincoln veered to the right, not a controlled path, and rested with its front bumper against one of the giant oak trees that lined the road. James made it to the shoulder and traffic gradually resumed its journey past them, carloads of gawkers taking in a full view of the wreckage. Stupidly, his first instinct was to chase after the man (how, exactly?). Concussed maybe, but it made no difference. Whomever, whatever, else the stranger was, he was long gone.

James turned his attention back to his vehicle. Not the worst damage in the world, really. His front end was a mess, but car safety had come a long way and it could have been a lot worse considering the speed and suddenness of the stop. Not even any soreness, though that might have been from the shock. Still, he felt fortunate to be in one piece, and the loss of his temper a short time ago looked awfully petty in retrospect. The other car didn't fare nearly as well, a twisting and contorted mess of metal. And what of the other driver? He forced the door open and went to check.

James stumbled, ducking through the door frame and, ah, there was the pain. Like someone worked over his neck with a crescent wrench. From his head all through the shoulders his body cried out, a dull, aching hurt. This would be no passing thing, he could already tell. But his better nature summoned up a sense of obligation to the person he hit. Still no movement from inside of that car.

He approached the driver's side door. Elderly woman, injured badly, maybe irreversibly. A hard sight. She was so small, heavily made-up. Unclear if she was breathing but definitely losing blood, and it didn't look like she had much to spare. The windshield was a bright red spider web. The force from the collision, his fault, must have propelled her violently forward. Physics didn't restrain her until the windshield left it no choice, and then she stopped savagely. "God," he said. The words came slowly, ineffectual. "No." His fault. Their fault.

Cars had pulled off to the side of the road by this time and people made their way to where the force of the Lincoln met its immovable object. He couldn't take his eyes off the old woman, didn't deserve to sanitize the incident and his culpability therein. The rest was a haze; someone called 911, an ambulance showed up, and the police. The woman was still alive but badly hurt. Paramedics took her to the hospital and two officers led James into the back of a squad car. In the panic, no one had bothered to shift her car into park. As they pulled away, he watched its rear wheels spin innocuously in the dirt.

3

"You want to tell me what happened back there, son?"

"I don't know." Not the truth exactly, but all he was willing to say for the moment.

"Well, we'll get it straightened out at the station," the other cop said. James didn't know if that was meant to be a comfort or a threat, but he didn't much care. He nodded from the backseat and they passed the rest of the ride in silence.

Inside the police station they led him into a corner room with two chairs and a desk between them. Not much activity in the place, but he had the feeling of a thousand eyes on him as he made his way back. "Wait here," the first cop said. "We'll be with you shortly," and with that he was alone.

Several minutes passed before a man in a shirt and tie, a detective apparently, came in and introduced himself. Morley was the name, a heavyset man with a wide chest and a gut that tested the limits of his white dress shirt. He may have been an athlete years ago, a strong man at least, but those days were behind him now. He sat in the chair opposite James, white walls all around them and a pallid light between.

"James Chandler?" He nodded. "Can I get you anything before we get started?"

"Is this the kind of thing I should have a lawyer for?" James asked.

Morley looked at him for a moment and shrugged. "That's up to you. Did you do anything illegal?" No right way to answer that question, so he left it alone. "We just need to know what happened."

"I have nothing to hide," (not quite true) "and I didn't do anything wrong," (even less true) he said. "But I would be more comfortable with a lawyer. Until then, I'd rather not put anything on the record."

Detective Morley looked up from his notepad, unimpressed, and chuckled—a weary, condescending laugh. "Understand, kid, this woman is seriously injured, as you know, and you hit her. Those are the most pertinent facts. Furthermore, I don't need a thing from you; we have witnesses who stopped at the scene and filled in the details. I don't know how you expect this to play out—Atticus Finch isn't walking through that door—but you're not charged with anything at this time. The old lady was cruising along and hit the brakes out of nowhere. I don't know why—stroke, heart attack, God knows. But you couldn't stop in time, right? Stop making this any harder than it needs to be."

"Maybe she saw something." The thought was out before he knew he was saying it.

"What?" That got his attention.

"Maybe that's why she hit the brakes."

"Like what?" Morley leaned forward. "Did you see something?"

"No." Full lies now. "I'm sorry. I should probably get checked out for a head injury." That at least was true; it felt good to be back on the side of the angels, if only for a moment. "I'm not feeling well." Two in a row.

The older man's look softened. "Right," he said. "Do you remember how fast you were going? That might be important later." James shook his head. Morley scribbled a few lines on his notepad and looked him in the eye. "Look... we've got statements from four witnesses at the scene. A car traveling at highway speed that slams to a stop... Nothing you could have done, all right? People forget how dangerous freeways are, the forces involved; the illusion of safety that comes with routine."

Right, the forces involved.

"I should get myself checked out at the hospital." That was a truth that felt like a lie. "Am I free to leave?"

"Give me a minute," he said, getting up.

James looked to his left, into a mirror that spanned nearly the length of the wall. A two-way mirror no doubt, and he wondered how he looked to whoever was on the other side. From his vantage point the reflection was plainly tired, not just his body but his mind. In the deepest parts of him, tired nearly to the point of collapse. Forty-eight hours ago life had been a breeze that he navigated with the gentle ease of a feather in the wind. Now, not so much. What was the comparison today? He turned away from the mirror before he could answer that question. He expected he would not like the answer.

Morley returned, handed him his driver's license, and looked him over for a moment. "Go get yourself checked out. I'm not a doctor, but you seem off to me. Maybe you hit your head without realizing it. We're done here for now, get some sleep. But be reachable." James met his eyes. "You may not be out of the woods yet."

He had a feeling the detective was right about that.

James stopped off at the front desk to pick up his personal effects. A kind-faced old man handed him his phone. "Take care of yourself," he said with an understanding smile. James looked at the man without seeing him, didn't respond, and walked through the station doors in a haze. More reacting than living at that point, he checked his phone, some habits die hard, and saw two new texts. Pulling up the messages, he saw they were both from Claire. At 7:20, "I'm sorry if I snapped at you earlier. There's something I wanted to talk to you about." The second one from 9:12, "Is everything ok? Let me know when you get this." What time was it now? Better question, how could it matter? He turned off his phone absent-mindedly and put it in his pocket.

Traffic streamed steadily on the street before him. He watched in a kind of hypnosis. Einstein said that time was not linear, and James was content to take his word for it, but for his purposes it never made sense to think of it any other way. The cars passed by like a river. A consistent, unbroken line, which was all life ever seemed. Everyone had points of demarcation within that line, and he tried to place his in the dark of that summer night.

He was seven when his family moved to Virginia from Ohio, that seemed as good a first transition as any. New town, new school, second grade. No siblings to help ease the landing. A few anxious days at the start no doubt, but he came out of it okay. Better than okay. By the time middle school rolled around, he found his peer group, and those days as the unknown new kid were a distant memory. Distant to the point that it was like they never happened.

The next one was probably a severe bout with pneumonia, age thirteen. A hospital stay and many miserable hours later and he was good as new. Once the agony of illness was past, and especially now that it was long past, it was like it never existed. The experience made him stronger maybe, but he wasn't even convinced of that. It was just over. That's what always happened to the present—it became the past. And the near past became the long ago past, and at some point that past was so long ago it might as well have happened to someone else. Eventually that would happen to this day's events, he promised himself. As though a promise was going to do any good.

Claire was a boundary between the old and the new, that first night on the bus. He thought back to their chance meeting, his clumsy propositions. It made him smile there in the glow of the streetlights, and still the cars. Three years ago, or was it a thousand? Either way, like something he saw in a movie. It felt a long way away, a distance somehow made of more than time and physical space. A distance of energies. She was still just a phone call away, but she belonged to a different world now. The before world, that radiated aliveness, stitched together with lazy days passed in a blissful naivete.

James realized with certainty he would never get back to that world, not since the man in the gym. He slaughtered that world with a casual wave of his hand, and its destruction was immediate and complete. The man ended Claire's world too, though she probably didn't know it yet. James thought of the possible ways forward from here. Come straight with his girlfriend? He supposed he owed her that much, in spite of whatever consequences that would bring. Or try to shield her from it, solve this problem himself, and hope that they could reconnect when the unpleasantness was finished?

They both seemed like lousy options, but they were the only cards on the table.

Whatever path he took was not going to be easy. He comforted himself with the one bit of conviction that was unwavering. This existential angst wasn't doing him any good, so he decided to direct his animus toward the obvious target. Wherever he was, whatever he was, nothing was going to save his phantom from the reckoning he had earned.

The traffic was much thinner now; a car here and there, good spaces between them, rather than an unbroken stream. How long had he been standing there, statue-like? Long enough to look suspicious, he was sure. The trauma of the car crash lingered, and it likely would for a while, but he was reenergized by a newfound purpose: to find and destroy the cause of all his troubles. That would set everything right again, he knew. But even that wasn't getting him any closer to home, or to solving the Claire dilemma. James reasoned he could maybe split the difference of the two paths that lay before him. Bring her in some but stop short of a total reveal. When you come to a fork in the road, take it. Full disclosure would only make him seem unhinged or, worse, she would try to help solve the problem, and in doing so subject herself to whatever peril lay ahead of him. He wouldn't allow that, no matter the consequence. If he lost her as a result of whatever was to come, better she be free and apart than to go down with the sinking ship he may soon become. A cheery thought there. He turned his phone back on and pulled up Claire's number.

Her name still triggered an instant of lightheadedness every time he saw it. No plan of what to say really, but he hoped he would find the right words. She picked up before the end of the second ring. "Hey, is everything all right?" Her voice was on the edge of panic, not easy to hear.

"Hi, Claire." Great start, champ. "I'm ok. How are you?"

"I was worried," she said. "It's not like you to be unreachable. Where are you?"

He looked for a street sign. "I'm at the corner of..." *Just say the police station, dummy.* "I'm at the corner of the police station," he finished. The confidence in his voice that delivered such a nonsense statement sent him to laughing. Laughing too hard maybe. "I mean, the police station. Is what I am at."

"The police station!" Not an unfair reaction. "What happened?"

"There was an accident, Claire. I'm ok. There was a car in front of me, we were going fast, but it stopped suddenly, really suddenly. And the other driver, she's hurt real bad, Claire, and..." His voice broke and she guessed the rest.

"Oh my God," came from the other side, then silence.

"It's going to be ok. Can you pick me up?"

"Of course," she said. "Of course, I'm on my way."

"Thanks." He hung up and sat down on the curb, thankful to have someone he could rely on without question. The bad breaks had come quickly and in number as of late, and he was grateful for the bright spot in his life that remained. Very few cars on the street now, pushing midnight maybe, he wasn't sure and didn't care to look. Time passed and he saw a familiar red car pull to the side of the road. It was all he could do to get up off the sidewalk and into the passenger seat.

He looked at Claire and didn't know whether he was going to cry or pass out, but she reached across to hug him and it was enough to lay his head on her shoulder and take in the sounds of the night for the moment. "I'm glad you're ok," she said after a time. Nowhere near ok, but he already decided he wasn't going to put that on her.

"Thanks," he said. "Seeing you helps. It will be ok." Lying to her or himself at this point? Probably a little of both.

Streetlights passed rhythmically overhead as the car moved along the road. A picturesque night, despite what brought them here. Again his thoughts went to how different his life was just a short time ago. Those lines of demarcation came rapidly now, each driving him further into the depths of wherever this whole thing was headed. How to slow this momentum, reverse its direction even? It wasn't an easy question, but the primary obstacle was clear. Just a matter of how to eliminate it now.

"Stay with me tonight," Claire said. "We can figure everything out in the morning." She took her eyes off the road, looked at him reassuringly, and the walls came crashing down. "There was a man," he said. "From work. We had an altercation, or something, and I think he may be dangerous."

Tell it all, find the strength. "What? When did this start?"

"It seems like a lifetime ago, honestly. But... Saturday."

"Two days ago? Did you tell the police?" This was exactly what he didn't want, to transfer any of the burden to her. Pull back.

"There's nothing to tell them," he shook his head. "He hasn't *done* anything." Back under the cover of half-truths. Even if he had wanted to, he never would have been able to convey the terror the man sparked in him. A simple retelling of the events may have registered as innocuous before tonight but only because it would be an inadequate shadow of what he was feeling.

"Did he have anything to do with the accident?" That was the wrong word for it. The crash was the opposite of an accident; it was his intent.

"No. It's just something I need to take care of." He chose his next words carefully. "I want to be honest with you." Maybe by saying it he wouldn't have to live up to it. Did that make sense? Probably not. "I have a face, he's on the security tape from work, but no name. Nothing else to go by. I don't know where to go from here." Exhaustion stalked him on the periphery and now it threatened to overtake him.

"If it's serious..." She debated whether to finish the thought. "Could my dad help?"

Under normal circumstances it would have been an insulting suggestion, Freudian at least, but it gave him hope. For the first time he saw a possible avenue out. Claire's father had friends of a certain affiliation (it had come up before but never so explicitly). Not a Henry Hill 'made man' situation, he didn't think those really existed anymore outside of big cities, but the man was connected. There was some embarrassment in going to him with an issue like this, but James figured he could keep the questions vague enough that he wouldn't lose face. Just needed an introduction to the right guy is all. Well, that was a problem for the future. For now, hope.

"Maybe. My head's kind of a mess right now," he never did get to the hospital, "but I think that might be a great idea. Thank you. This will all make more sense tomorrow. But thank you. For that and for picking me up. And for everything." James leaned back into the headrest and was asleep before he could hear her response.

The next thing he remembered was waking up alone in her bed. A familiar place, but no Claire. She had left the curtains drawn but sunlight forced its way into the room around the edges of her windows. James tried to gauge the time...

midday? Past early morning for sure, too bright, too warm for that. He rolled over and winced against the pain that shot through him. Physically he felt worse off than last night, but the rest had recharged his spirits some. He pulled the bedroom door open and wandered gingerly into the hallway, toward the quiet sounds of activity coming from the kitchen.

Claire was at the stove as he turned the corner, her back to him. He lingered in the entryway, not wanting to disturb the diorama of domestic bliss before him, not even sure what to say if he did. Yesterday's events washed over him, hitting with a force that he felt on a physical level. He made his way to the kitchen table and pulled out a chair. Claire jumped, startled at the sound, and James smiled in spite of himself.

"Sorry," he said. "Hi."

"How are you?" She gestured to a pan of scrambled eggs. "I'm making breakfast."

"I'm ok." That wasn't true, he couldn't even remember what ok felt like, but he was determined to face it bravely nonetheless. "I will be ok." Too early to tell if that was true or not.

Claire moved a chair next to him and wrapped him in her arms. They were content not to say anything until a pan on the stove started smoking, and she bolted up to rescue it. She surveyed the damage with a disappointed look. "So much for the French toast."

"It's ok," he said. There was that word again, as though he could fashion a salve out of the sheer quantity of them if his will was strong enough. If it didn't work, it wouldn't be from lack of trying.

"That reminds me." She took a piece of paper from the front of the refrigerator and slid it across the table to him. An ugly kind of remembering swept over him but it was gone before he connected its effect to its source. "I called my dad while you were sleeping. I told him there was a guy causing problems at the gym, not something you could go to the police with, and asked if he knew anyone who might be able to help." She took up her place next to him again. "I left a lot of the details out. Seemed easier that way." So she paid that part forward. Did she know he did the same to her? Probably, he figured. She was the sharper half of them. No chance she knew the extent of things though. Everything was spiraling into chaos, but he was determined to bear that burden alone. To protect her from that much at least.

"Oh, right," he said, taking the paper. "Victor Drake." A phone number below that with a Richmond area code, he was pretty sure. Not far from them then. That was reassuring. "What does this guy do exactly?"

Claire brought over a couple plates of toast and eggs. "I don't know. My dad just said he was—what was the word?—resourceful. Do you want anything to drink?"

He realized for the first time how dry his mouth was. "Water, please." Like talking through cotton balls.

She brought a glass. "Are you going to call him?"

James rapped his knuckles on the table. "Yeah," he said. "I guess so. What do you think?"

"We'll get through it." No way of knowing if that was true, but he could tell she believed it. "If you need to borrow my car for a couple days, I can use Jen's." Jen was her younger sister, away at college. "Do you want to talk about yesterday?"

He sighed. "I appreciate the offer, but honestly, I don't." Too much he didn't want to have to avoid telling (but then what was he doing right now?). Or too much he didn't want to face himself. Either way, the answer was the same. "It's going to take some time. There's the insurance to figure out, and my work schedule, and the police said they might need to talk to me again. And I want to get a hold of Mr. Resourceful as soon as I can. Get to work on putting this all behind me. Can you drive me home?" That might have come off as insensitive, but he was eager to take action.

"You're sure?" He nodded. "Ok. Whenever you're ready."

4

Back home, he took the opportunity to breathe. The insurance could wait, and work; the police would take care of themselves. That left Victor Drake. James went online to see what he could find from the name on the Internet. Private Investigator it said, whatever that entailed these days. This was his life now, he realized with a bemused detachment. A shabby website that was apparently designed some fifteen to twenty years ago, but at least he was ostensibly on the right side of the law. Claire didn't say if he would be expecting a call, but James didn't particularly care about that.

He did his best to organize his thoughts. How much to tell this guy? He had little reason to trust the stranger (and little reason not to), but he needed to unload the whole story to someone soon, unburden himself, and he was running out of options. Outside his window, the afternoon teemed with life. Mowers roared across distant lawns, overpowering the birdsongs that echoed through the trees. It didn't seem fair that the world was allowed to carry on as it had before, totally indifferent to the quagmire he found himself sinking in. He recognized the vanity of his thinking, but that recognition did nothing to abate it. And what did fair have to do with it anyway?

Enough inaction. James laid the paper in front of him, appreciating for the first time the soft blue curls that formed the numbers, and typed them into his phone. It rang twice, then a man answered.

"Victor Drake."

"Hi," James started. "I'm calling about a problem."

"Right," the voice on the other end said. "Why else would you call here?" it might as well have added.

"Right. Well I'm a friend of Michael Ventura. I don't know if he mentioned anything to you—"

"Mike, ok, right. You run a gym?" He was putting the pieces together.

"Sort of. My problem is—"

"Let me give you my address," he cut in. "I'm out of town now, but I will be back Friday. Meet me then." His assertiveness came on a bit strong, but James figured that personality served him well in his field. The same kind of mentality he wanted to handle whatever it was he was up against.

"For sure. Morning or afternoon?"

"Make it 6:00 evening," he said, and gave James the address. "See you then."

With this business done, a pair of quick phone calls bought him a couple days at work and started the insurance paperwork on fixing his car. Those two distractions out of the way, his mind went to work on the job of waiting.

As far back as James could remember, he had a habit of

wishing the days away. Turning five was a big accomplishment, and then six, and so on. Some of that was the birthday parties and presents, sure, but even setting them aside, he was impatient for the future, maybe at the cost of the present. "I'm five" became "I'm five and a half" weeks after the wrapping paper had been cleared away, and when he got older he measured in quarters, counting down the months toward the next milestone.

When a family friend turned thirteen—an honest to God teenager—James bragged about it to everyone he knew. "I'm friends with a teenager," he would drop (or force) into any conversation he could. The friend was a celebrity to him. Not even a celebrity so much as a superhero. By the time James crossed that threshold himself, the number lost its mystique and he was looking to the next great leap forward. Then high schoolers were what they aspired to be. Even better, a high schooler with a car. When high school came, college students were the new bar. A blend of freedom, self-determination, and debauchery that couldn't have been more appealing to their adolescent minds.

Hard to say when that impatience died away; twenty-one, he supposed. No bright lines of division after that. None worth eagerly awaiting anyway, barring an impromptu presidential run in a decade or so. Birthdays weren't a bad thing now, he didn't mind aging the way someone further down life's road might, but he was typically content to take the moments as they came without holding out for whatever lay beyond them.

The days waiting to meet Victor Drake brought back that insatiable appetite for what lay over the horizon of tomorrow. One day went by, then two, and three, and finally it was Friday again. He had done all he could on his end, landing a temporary set of wheels and calling into work to sort out his schedule. He even stopped by the gym early one morning, hoping to avoid a crowd while getting ahold of the surveillance footage. A couple of coworkers were hanging out in the lobby and it was awkward; he felt too divorced from that world to pick up where they left off almost a week ago. They all wished him the best, the bosses told him to take as long as he needed, and while he was grateful to have people who cared about him, they came off as wearisome. What he wanted most was to get what he needed and then disappear.

After some polite pleasantries, he made a beeline to his office and copied the relevant files. He hoped the still shot of the man staring into the camera would be enough to get Drake started, but it was hard to say one way or the other. A face isn't a lot to go on, he told himself, but all the same, he had a good feeling about his new champion. A resourceful guy, Claire's dad said, which was high praise from Michael Ventura. Typically a friendly man with a charming disposition, James had seen him angry only once, but it was enough to convince him to stay on his good side forever. Luckily Michael took a liking to him, and this referral was further proof of that. Then there was the added, implicit, pressure that because Drake was a professional associate, Michael put his reputation on the line for James. He had better not mess it up, and he didn't intend to.

Friday afternoon was unending; too hot to do anything outside, too nice to stay inside. And all the time the feral restlessness. There was nothing else that could hold his attention now, so he put his mind through its paces reviewing the order of the situation as it stood. James tried to see the events in his mind, replaying them like highlights (or, at times, a humorless blooper reel). The entrance in the gym, the chime of the bell. Their idiot comments and then that immediate revulsion to the stimulus. Brent disappearing, leaving him alone to deal with whatever this lunatic was. The whole thing was a joke to Brent, and he had abandoned him. It hit James then that Brent never did call him back. No missed calls, no texts, nothing.

He called Brent again, why not, and this time he was greeted by an automated voice. "The mailbox of the customer you are trying to reach—*It's your boy Brent!*—is full. Goodbye." All wrong. Luckily, it was almost 5:00, close enough to set off for Richmond. Drake's office was in an unfamiliar part of town, off the beaten path as it were, but James followed the directions his phone provided and found it without any trouble.

He parked on the street and approached the address Drake had given him, a squat, crumbling, brick building. Not much in the way of promoting his business, just some small white letters stenciled on to the window. "Drake Investigations, 2nd Floor," and the phone number below. A front, James considered; at any rate, most of his business wasn't coming from walk-ups. *Referrals like me, more likely,* he thought. A tiny bell rang out as he pulled open the door, its sound lingering as he made his way up the wooden stairs that lay before him. Old stairs, unpainted, groaned under his weight every third step or so. Finally, he stood before the door to Drake's office. 5:53 by the clock on his phone. Three sharp knocks, then a voice from the other side told him to come in. James steadied himself for whatever was next and opened the door.

The first thing he noticed about the room was the smell of tobacco. The blinds were half-drawn and he stepped into a smoky haze, closing the door behind him. Newspapers were stacked in a corner, and a chess game in progress lay off to the side of a large wooden desk. The top of the desk was sparse, various papers inside and outside of filing folders, and a framed sepia tone photo of the building they were in now. A charming decor, if anachronistic. The office's tenant was behind the desk, a formidable-looking man with wide shoulders and the first hint of stubble covering a jawline of sharp angles. He gestured for James to sit down across from him.

"You're Mike's referral?"

"Yes, James Chandler," he said, extending his hand.

"Victor Drake." He shook his hand quickly. A strong grip, but not overdone. Nothing artificial in the gesture. "Why don't you tell me all about it." More directive than question.

Down on the street traffic passed intermittently and the sounds mingled with conversations. Together they combined into a sort of ambient noise that was easy enough to ignore. The heat was another matter. It had only been a short walk from the car, but James became aware of sweat forming on his forehead, and he wiped it away distractedly. Drake's eyes, tranquil but persistent, hadn't left him.

James wanted to tell him everything. "Where to start?"

"The beginning," Drake said, fishing a pack of cigarettes out of his desk drawer. "Lay the facts out in order and I'll take it from there." He made it sound so simple, and maybe it was. Just start talking.

"A man came into the gym where I work," James began. "This was Saturday." From there the story flowed easily. Drake broke in with clarifying questions from time to time and in doing so helped James better understand the situation himself, so far as that was possible. He had a long way to go toward making sense of the past several days but the telling of it—all of it, finally—was therapeutic. He lost track of the hour, but by the time he concluded his story the room was getting darker on account of the dying sun.

"...and that brought me here," he concluded.

Drake nodded, reviewing the calculus in his head. He got up without speaking and clicked on an overhead lamp, bathing the office in a warm glow. He had long since discarded his first cigarette into a nearby ashtray and now he reached for another.

"What is it you're asking me to do?" he said at last. Still no indication that the story, the facts, had fazed him at all.

"Find this guy, if that's what he is."

Drake's cigarette rested casually between his fingers. "What else would he be?"

"I don't know," James said. He couldn't bring himself to voice the answers that sprung to mind. Monster, supernatural, paranormal... Demon. "Find out what he wants, or not, just... get him out of my life." It was all he wanted anymore.

Drake nodded. "How?"

"I don't know." James' confidence in him took a hit for the first time. "You're the P.I., or detective, or whatever. You have to—"

"What I mean," he broke in calmly, "is where is your line?"

"What?"

Drake tried again. "You want him gone, and that's all?"

"Yes." James thought he made that clear.

"Carte blanche then," he said, and James finally understood his meaning. "Is that right?"

James forced himself to restrain from answering as quickly as he wanted to. It was important he let the weight of the question settle and appreciate the gravity of the answer and its consequences. "Yes," he said after some thought. "Absolutely."

Drake took a drag on his cigarette and shook his head. "I'm not sure it adds up. He, *It* if you like, doesn't sound physically imposing, hasn't made any explicit threats. Why am I supposed to buy this being some imminent danger?"

"Easy to ask when you weren't there." James felt patronized. "That's a question coming from a guy with no firsthand experience, safe behind his desk."

"They all are today, kid. You don't think you're overreacting?"

"Maybe I am, but you don't understand his... presence," James protested. "You don't know what it's like to be next to him, in his gaze, from the start. There's something horribly wrong here, and I'm not going to sit back and let it destroy my life because I'm afraid of overreacting."

"Fair enough. I had to be sure." Drake smiled by way of recognition and James' trust in the man returned, but now carrying grave undertones. "Let's hope it doesn't come to that."

"I don't know how your fee works, or if you have expenses—"

"It's not like that." He waved him off. "Mike's got you covered. And besides, it gives me something to do. All I need from you is reticence." A ten-dollar word from the chess player.

"Of course."

"And leave me that copy of the surveillance video," Drake added, showing him to the door. "I have work to do."

5

"There was a poor fisherman. He fished for lobster, and one day he saw the finest lobster he could ever imagine. But it was trapped beneath the waves, of course."

"Ok."

"He called out to the lobster, 'What are you doing down there?' And the lobster responded, 'It is dark and cold in the ocean, and I have to live with sharks and other horrible creatures. But I have no choice.'"

"It's a talking lobster?"

"Willing suspension of disbelief. So the fisherman said, 'I can bring you to a place where you will have the water all to yourself. I can bring you out of the dark, and what is more you will never be cold again. Just swim into my tank there.' And so the lobster did."

"Pretty dumb for a talking lobster."

"The fisherman took the lobster to his meager home where his family was always hungry, but that night they had a great feast. It was the best meal they ever had, and the fisherman realized if he could find another one of these lobsters, he could sell it for a very high price. So the next day he went back to the same spot, and, what luck, he found a lobster that looked much the same as the first. The fisherman called out to it and offered the same sales pitch as before. The lobster agreed. But before it could swim in, the fisherman had an idea. He asked the lobster, 'Are there more special lobsters like you down there?' 'Several,' the lobster said. 'I know them well.'

"The fisherman told him to gather up his friends, as many as he could, and he would offer them the same paradise. In the meantime he went back to shore and got the biggest lobster trap he could find. When he returned to the spot, he couldn't believe his eyes."

"No lobster."

"Hundreds of lobsters. All to the same standard of the first one, many of them better. He saw a million dollars below the waterline and needed only to get them in the trap. 'Hurry, my friends,' he told them, hardly able to contain his excitement. 'They will join you,' the lobster told him, 'if you will owe me a favor after.' 'Of course, of course,' the fisherman said, 'Just get into the tank.'

"The lobsters swam in, there were more than could even fit in the trap, and the fisherman was delirious with happiness. His life would never be the same again. He started to pull the boat away, when the lobster stopped him. 'I'm calling in the favor,' it said. The fisherman was impatient, but it was what he had agreed to. 'All right, what is it?' 'I have fulfilled my end of the bargain, you would agree?' the lobster said. 'Yes,' the man said, 'what do you need me to do?' He realized then, or had the first thought, that this lobster was not what it seemed."

"Not your average talking lobster."

"Listen. 'What do you need me to do?' the man asked. Then he saw the beast's true form for the first time, and he was afraid. It answered, 'To live out the rest of your days at the bottom of the sea.'"

"And that's the end? The fisherman just does it?"

"It's a deal with the devil, isn't it? Those trend toward the non-refundable."

"Yeah."

"No misdirection, no language tricks. The point is—"

"I get the point."

"'To live out the rest of your days at the bottom of the sea.'"

6

They said goodbye and Drake watched James leave his office, a fawn in the high-beams. It had been some time since his last case that rose above the rote and he was ready to re-engage his higher-order thinking. He wasn't sure what to make of this latest undertaking. Certain elements of the story didn't sit right; the second card, certainly, would need to be accounted for. It was all too much too fast. These things were supposed to build up to him, and only then as a desperate last resort. This had all started, he flipped through his notes, six days ago. It was all wrong. If it actually happened just as James said (though he was miles away from a conclusion on that point), it's a wonder he didn't have whiplash, car accident aside. Drake wasn't planning on killing anyone, but that had been a valuable question nonetheless. A client's reaction showed him where their uncrossable lines were; in this case there didn't seem to be any.

There wasn't any path forward on the suspect without running a check on the visual, so he started with the kid who had come into his office. Armchair psychology was only sometimes useful, but it was fun and automatic, so no point in fighting it. Initial impressions, then. Three Adjectives was a handy game in his business. In a word, scared. Allow him a second and he would add earnest, which was a compelling combination. Maybe the story wasn't the truth exactly (some elements were hard to reconcile), but it was legitimate insofar as James believed what he was saying.

Likable in a general sort of way, if not particularly remarkable. Tabula rasa was two words really, or it would have made for a solid third leg of the triangle. In fact, he figured, who's making the rules around here? Drake forgave the overage. Sorry to say, or not, but he judged James to be the less interesting of the two primaries. Not the one he cared most about anyway. It was the man with the cards who snared his attention.

His next move was to seek out James' social media profiles. Frankly those were usually of less use to him than the quick psychological overview, God bless the triangle, but he wasn't one to leave cages unrattled. A typical public face of a young man in his mid-twenties. Lots of outdoor shots, pictures of sunsets that looked like everyone else's pictures of sunsets, photos with a girl Drake took to be Mike's daughter; nothing out of the ordinary there. He found the gym from the story and the coworkers mentioned. Their profiles too were every bit as vapid as he expected. No activity from Brent in a couple days, which seemed unusual given the several updates per day that preceded it. He filed a mental note and moved on.

Next the surveillance video, which was as James had described it, and at an impressive resolution no less. The private university had to find somewhere to direct all those dollars from their extravagant and ever-climbing tuition. A distinct face for sure. Nothing supernatural about the stranger obviously, but Drake didn't think Brent's reaction was the right one either. This felt more like stumbling upon a snake with unknown patterns on its back. Could be harmless, he supposed, but there was something undeniably unusual here, and his instincts said the smart play was to stay on guard. In his experience, anyone had the potential to be dangerous. A person looking and acting like this guy did, well that upped the Bayesian estimate. The late hour left him with no immediate recourse so he passed the night in a holding pattern; formulated a few potential theories, but really nothing to do beyond that. After he turned off the light on his way out, the room fell into a dark silence.

Early the next morning he put a call into the Richmond police. "Get me Lieutenant Cavillo." The dispatcher transferred him through and his long-time friend picked up, sounding stressed.

"Cavillo."

"Lighten up, Cavillo, you miserable son a—" Drake gave his hello room to breathe. "I have a job for you."

"Drake? Now's really not a good time."

"Nonsense. Two minutes."

There was a pause on the other end before Cavillo let out an aggravated groan. Drake knew he had him. "What is it?"

"I'm going to send you a picture; see if it matches anybody in your database, will you?"

"Database," he grumbled. "That's not how that works, Drake. You need a high-res digital file and—"

"I have a high-res digital file, you goof. Comperio University surveillance camera. Target stares into it, dead on. Even you couldn't miss it."

"Then go through the damn university police," Cavillo said. "This may surprise you, but my job description extends beyond running errands for my disgraced former partner."

"Allegedly disgraced," Drake broke in, though they both knew better. "I'm emailing it now."

"Give me a few days," Cavillo said. "But don't expect much."

"I never do."

Drake hung up and returned his attention to some of the peripheral players. Given where the pieces stood, he decided Brent was the lead to pursue. His disappearance, if that's what it was, could have been explained away by any number of things, but only one way to be sure. A quick phone call to the university gym would be a good place to start.

"Can you tell me if Brent Dawson is working today?" he asked the young woman who answered the phone.

"Brent's not in today, I think he's out of town," she answered.

"Can you check on that for me? I have a heavy bag I need to get back to him and seeing him at the gym would save me a trip."

"Yeah, one sec." She left to check on Brent's schedule and Drake whistled a little tune while he waited. Soon the woman returned and said, "Looks like he's opening up tomorrow actually."

"Perfect," he said. "I'll come by tomorrow morning."

Two possible paths now. If Brent was at work, Drake could ask about his not getting back to James, and (hopefully) narrow down his list of possibilities. If Brent was not at work, that would be a straightforward missing persons case. Could maybe even have James get the police involved at that point, keep everything above board, given he already had legitimate concerns. Or keep the cops out of it and not let them screw up the works. They had a habit of doing that, and he was confident it was something he could handle on his own. But that was a decision for another time. He would know which way to proceed based on what he found tomorrow; no use in trying to synthesize an answer out of incomplete information before then. That night he slept soundly.

Drake's alarm rang out with the rising sun like some futuristic incarnation of a rooster. A quick shower, coffee, and a cigarette. He shaved in the mirror, threw on a respectable business casual look and headed for Charlottesville with the sun peeking the top of its head over the horizon. The gym was a ghost town, which struck him just fine. The few patrons already working out were the diehards and it was hard not to feel self-conscious in their presence. Like walking through a hall of statues, Greek gods and goddesses made flesh. He shrugged off the feeling and, moment of truth, asked the front desk attendant if Brent was in.

"Yeah," she said, "I think he's in the back. Hold on." She stepped away from the desk. "Brent! Somebody out here for you."

The private eye had always done his best to avoid preconceptions. If he didn't go in expecting any one thing in particular, it couldn't cloud his judgment into seeing only what he expected to see. That was the theory anyway. Putting it into practice wasn't always so easy. The truth was, he didn't expect to see Brent that morning, something about the way James told the story, but within a minute Brent was standing there in front of him. College-aged, tall, with long blond hair.

He looked across the desk confusedly, an expression he wore well. "Do I know you?"

"Not yet." Drake extended his hand. "Victor Drake. Your friend James was worried about you; said he hasn't been able to get a hold of you."

The explanation only deepened Brent's confusion. "Ok. Well I was camping the past few days, but I'm here now. And that's what's most important." He flashed his coworker a goofy grin.

A rather simple explanation after all that then. "Did you see James left you a message? He wanted to talk to you about a man who visited the gym when the two of you were working together."

Brent laughed. "You'll have to be more specific, man. We get a lot of dudes in here. Yeah, I saw he called about the gym when I was gone, but I figured I'd see him at work."

"This guy who came in handed James a slip of paper. It had letters and a phone number, do you remember? James said you ducked away into the back room and the man threatened him."

"The walking skeleton guy?" Now they were getting somewhere. "Ok, I remember, yeah. What about him?"

"Well, as I say, he threatened James. What was your perspective on the situation?"

"Who are you again? There was no situation. A weirdo came in, did weirdo things, and then he left. He threatened James?"

"So he says."

Brent turned more serious. "Has this guy done anything else?"

"That's what I'm trying to figure out. Any more insight you can give me?"

He thought about it for a few seconds and shook his head. "He just came in and then he left. I didn't get a dangerous vibe, but it messed James up a little, yeah. He would be on the surveillance video if you want to look at that, but otherwise… Sorry, that's really all I know."

"I appreciate the time." He handed Brent a business card. "You think of anything else, let me know. Now go call James. He's worried about you."

Exiting the gym, Drake laughed a little to himself. Talk about mountains out of molehills. Brent had not disappeared, he was not the victim of some grisly murder scene as James probably feared. But pieces were presenting themselves, if not quite coming together yet. There was Cavillo and the line out on the suspect's face, and now the benefit of a second set of eyes on the original encounter. Brent was James' opposite in that regard; whereas James was severely rattled, broken maybe, just by being in the same room as this person, Brent maintained a lazy sort of California cool. Why would they have such dramatically different reactions? Hard to say. But time would tell, he was sure.

If James was telling the truth, and Drake believed he was, he was running out of possible avenues to direct his search. The only player left on the board was the girlfriend. He didn't think she was connected, but he also didn't think he had anything to lose by digging into her background a bit. Probably could have called Mike with a couple questions, but hardly an unbiased source there. Instead he went back to his most reliable tools: a laptop and a wi-fi connection.

Drake found what he could on her. Bright girl, and pretty, a physics graduate student at Comperio University. Again a pristine public profile, nothing much to separate her from ten thousand other young women her age. Except the grad school thing, he supposed—Experimental High Energy Physics—nothing unremarkable about that. It was a long shot but the only one he had in front of him. He decided to check into some of her coworkers, or classmates, or whatever they were called at that level. No reason not to start at the top.

Dr. Andrew Beaumont was the head of the department but too far removed from Claire from what he could tell. Below him, her field, was the thread worth pulling at. Two senior faculty there—Dr. Kate Taylor and Dr. Robert Wong. Drake didn't know Isaac Newton from Isaac Hayes, but that wasn't going to stop him from jumping in with both feet. In fact, he thought he could use that to his advantage, avoid putting them on edge by playing the curious novice way out of his element. All he would have to do was act natural.

He pulled up Dr. Taylor's contact information and started to dial the number when he paused three digits in. It was a beautiful day and he could do with a respite from his overly-familiar office walls. Charlottesville was a nice drive, long enough to clear his head but short enough to not be a waste of time. Why not pay the good doctor an unexpected visit? Surprise and honesty were symbiotic, and he had learned it was far harder to blow off a physical presence than a voice on the telephone.

Drake made good time under the afternoon sun and was on campus in under an hour. A busy place with bright-eyed undergrads all over. The building with the physics professors' offices was a short walk away, so he made his way out of the car, cigarette and lighter in hand. He stopped to light up when he had the feeling of being watched. He looked up to see dozens of eyes on him, less judgmental than disbelieving. These were all non-smoking areas now, he remembered (wasn't everywhere these days?). Feeling like a monkey in the zoo he returned the vices to his pocket and waved an apology to the students. Already nailing the 'out of his element' part of the assignment. He angled his way along the sidewalk that split the sprawling emerald lawns and swung open the building's glass doors. They were heavier than he expected, and based on the staff directory, he was going to have to climb three flights of stairs to get to the offices he was looking for. Surely there would have been an elevator somewhere nearby, but he skipped the hunt and started his summit the old-fashioned way. No rest for the wicked. Dr. Taylor's office was 3116, and two left turns later he was outside her door. The door was slightly ajar, so he tapped his knuckles softly and leaned his head into the crack.

"Dr. Taylor?"

A middle-aged woman with graying hair and unfashionable tortoiseshell glasses spun around in her computer chair and greeted him with a surprised expression. "Yes?"

"Good afternoon, Doctor. It's my understanding you work with Claire Ventura?"

"Ventura... Oh sure, not closely, but she is studying in the department. Is there something I can help you with?"

Drake didn't have a specific line of questioning in mind, so he kept the prompts general to see where she would take them. "I'm working on an article about Miss Ventura for an online profile. Sort of a 'Young Women Succeeding in the Sciences' kind of thing. My editor asked me to get some quotes from her supervisors here at the university."

"Oh, how nice." She smiled like a proud grandmother. "I don't know how much help I can be there. Like I said, we do not work closely together."

Sometimes these things went easily and sometimes they were exercises in patience and perseverance. This was beginning to look like the latter. "Well, what do you know about her? We may not even end up using it, but I don't have any quotes yet and I have to start somewhere."

"Let me see. She's a very sweet girl, thoughtful. Loves

science." She smiled again. "We all do here."

Nothing in that. Not for the case and not even for the fake article. Keep digging. "Experimental High Energy Physics, right? Any particular projects of interest she has worked on?"

"Always interesting projects going on around here," she said. "But I'm not her supervisor. You know who would be more helpful is Dr. Fox. Those two have been working on some longitudinal study for a while. I forget the details but knowing Dr. Fox, it would probably be interesting content for your readers. He's the one who really tries to put this experimental stuff into action. Mostly content to focus on the theory side myself."

Not exactly what he wanted to get out of coming here, but at least he wasn't facing a hard ending. A slight detour, Drake told himself. Can't get too far into an investigation without hitting a few. "That sounds great. Thank you, doctor." She gave Drake Dr. Fox's phone number and he left his with her. "Just in case you think of something, here's where you can reach me." He headed for the door. "If you think of anything, anything at all, don't hesitate to give me a call." The door closed softly behind him and he left the woman to her derivatives and integrals.

7

The viability of Sal's Boxing Gym downtown mirrored the rise and fall of pugilism itself with exacting precision. Decades ago the spot was a proving ground for many rising through the east coast ranks, and a handful of fighters who passed through its halls fought for world title belts. Those days were gone, but Salvatore Rondenelli kept the gym's doors open anyhow. Not through any hope of a revival of interest in the sweet science. Only through the momentum of the years and the certainty, somewhere deep down, that if he ever shuttered the operation, Sal wouldn't last far beyond it. No, Sal would go first.

Inside, all four walls were lined with fight posters, posed portraits, and shots of in-ring action. The greats and the near-greats alike were celebrated. Jack Johnson and Joe Louis, Arturro Gatti and Marco Antonio Barrera, hung alongside local boxers who never rose as high as they dreamed. A pair of training gloves made out to Sal and signed by Roberto Duran were enshrined in a glass case behind the desk. These days the clientele was largely older men fighting an uphill battle to stay in shape. A few kids with ambition and talent, some of the MMA overflow. That's where the money and interest was now, with the octagon. Not that that bothered Sal any. He had his regulars, his proteges, his weekend warriors. After all these years, he had his gym.

Victor Drake knew it well. Once in a great while he could almost convince himself he was one of the talented, ambitious upstarts, but mostly he knew time's effects and which category he fit in best now. He stepped out of the broad daylight and into the dingy gym, greeting its owner on his way in.

"How are you, Sal?" Sal looked up from his newspaper and grunted a hello. "That's good to hear, Sal, real good. Wrap my hands, would you?"

"Give me a minute, working on this crossword," Sal said, not stirring from his place behind the paper.

"You know, this place may not have all the amenities of these modern workout centers you see popping up all over, but the service can't be beat," Drake said to no one in particular.

The old man didn't move. "Five-letter word for nuisance," he said.

"The personal touch is what it is," Drake continued to himself. "Can't get that everywhere."

"Never mind, I got it," Sal said, laying down his paper and pencil. "Drake." He shot him a smile and pulled some handwraps from under the desk.

"*I could've had class, I could've been a contender,*" Drake said, slipping into his best Brando impression as he leaned his elbows on the desk.

"Instead of a bum," Sal finished for him, "which is what you are now. All wrapped. Personal touch. Sixteen-ounce gloves?"

"As you say." Drake looked over to the ring, two hulking twenty-somethings warming up in headgear. They were good. Fast hands, pop behind the punches. He watched them for a time until Sal interrupted his thinking.

"Here you go, champ," he said, sliding his gloves across the desk. "Try to leave some stuffing in the bag for the next guy."

Drake kept his eyes on the boxers. "Maybe I'll do some sparring today instead."

"With those guys?" Sal laughed out loud. "Was the sign outside advertising assisted suicide? You'll be hearing from those guys. The one in red especially. The one in black has an Olympics qualifier in three months."

"That one in black, three times he's followed that left jab with a right cross. Step outside of that and I've got an unprotected counterpunch to his head. Only takes one of those."

"That sounds great until one of them lands a shot on you, dummy. You ever felt a punch from a fighter that size? They've got you by fifty pounds. Unless you plan to make up for it with your twenty extra years."

Drake continued to watch them without responding. "You know, Sal..." He turned around and looked at the man's worn, wrinkled face, a few tufts of hair hanging stubbornly to an otherwise bald head, and ears sticking out like little satellite dishes. "Every time I come in here, you look more like Yoda."

Sal squinted. "What's a Yoda?"

Drake's turn to laugh. "A wise counselor." He held his hands up to be laced into the gloves. "Fifty pounds at least. And twenty-five years."

Drake made his way to one of the available heavy bags

and started working punches in. The fists weren't lightning anymore, but they struck the canvas with the sound of thunder and rocked the bag along its support chain. All cases started strange in that they were new, but having seen—how many now?—lots of them, enough of them, each one usually reminded him of another eventually. Sometimes of several in a series as more pieces were added and aligned. This latest problem he was working through wasn't like that; or, if it was, he couldn't see his way to the similarities yet. That maze had not yielded itself and offered up a way through to the exit, or even to a middle by which he could orient himself. Not yet.

Drake built ladders of solid, deliberate strikes. He climbed to ten and then fifteen, and as he did so he worked the pieces in his mind, the possible ways they could interlock. And, from those possibilities, which were the likely and which were the fanciful. There was always the chance that James was a random target, a victim of happenstance or convenience. Random things happened randomly to random people every minute of every day. But that explanation was unsatisfying and, he had to admit, it frustrated him. It confounded his intellect and it wore at his spirit. He channeled these feelings into his motions and the heavy bag swung back and forth, steady as a pendulum.

Maybe he had been going about it all wrong. Back in his office he had tried to carve away the possible explanations until only the sculpture of the truth remained by following up on the principals one at a time. The man from the gym, then James, then Brent, finally Claire. Three cold trails, one possible lead, though nothing there that even hinted at a solution. He searched his mind for other connections, threads he had not yet pulled at, that could reveal the larger picture. Who else?

He stopped punching then (he had long since lost track

of the ladders) and let the bag trace its path unimpeded. There was another connection, one he overlooked, maybe because it was too close. It was likely nothing, but one could never tell which pebble would trigger the landslide he needed. He ran the back of his arm across his forehead, the sweat stinging his eyes. It wasn't going to be pleasant, and he wasn't ready to call him a suspect, but he was going to have to see if Michael Ventura was hiding anything.

Drake walked over to where Sal was still poring over his crossword. The proprietor looked up with a grin on his face. "You were going hard out there. Outlasted those young bucks by fifteen minutes, Drake."

"If I didn't know any better Sal, I'd say I recognized a hint of pride in your tone," he said as he laid his gloves on the table to be unlaced.

"Don't let it go to your head." Sal spit into a nearby wastebasket. "I still say they would've kicked your ass."

Shortly after Drake got back to his office, his phone rang. Cavillo. "What have you got for me?"

"Remember when I told you not to expect much?" Cavillo asked.

"I surely do." He could go one of two ways with that opening.

"Yeah, nothing, Drake. The computer triggered a couple near matches, but they definitely weren't your guy."

"I suppose that would have been too easy, huh? How wide is the net on this thing?"

"We're pulling nationwide," Cavillo told him. "But if he hasn't been arrested before, he's not going to show up."

"Understood. Well, worth a shot."

"It always is," he commiserated. "Creepy-looking bastard,

isn't he? But law-abiding, apparently. Good luck with your investigation, pal. Let me know how it turns out."

Drake thanked him for the effort and hung up. Less than ten minutes later the phone rang again; he wasn't used to being so popular. James this time.

"You can rest easy about your friend, Brent," Drake told him. Nice to be delivering some good news after being on the receiving end of Cavillo's bad news.

"Brent, yeah, he called." The words came quickly, rushed.

Drake tried to calm him by slowing the speed back down to a casual clip. "Not quite the gratitude I expected, but—"

"Listen," James interrupted, "it's happened again."

He dropped his laissez faire disposition. "What happened?"

"He was here, the guy, he—I went out and I came back, and the doors were locked, I know they were—"

Rambling now, so Drake cut him off. "All right, take it easy. How do you know? He leave another card?"

"Not a card—"

He interrupted again. "You know what? Give me your address." Only so much he could do over the phone. "I'm on my way over." He jotted down the address James gave him and left his office for the second road trip of the day. A quick glance at the clock showed lunch had already passed him by, and he hadn't even managed breakfast. No time to stop for food en route and the only thing in his office was a banana that was soft and spotted. Oh well, any port in a storm. "You're with me," he told it and headed down the stairs to his car.

Traffic was heavy and it took Drake well over an hour to

reach James' house. When he got there he found the door locked, so he knocked and waited for an answer. "It's Drake, open up."

The door opened slowly and James was standing on the other side. "Thanks for coming." He was shaken but resolute.

"All right, no cards? I'm taking that as a win. What have we got?"

"I'll show you." James led him inside. There, on the kitchen table, lay four smashed picture frames. The glass was scattered around them but the pictures were intact. The common theme was obvious. "I left them as I found them," he said. "You can find fingerprints if I haven't touched them, right?" he asked.

Drake studied the pictures. "Maybe." Two of a group and two of a couple. James and Claire in all four of them. "You did the right thing. Notice anything else disturbed?"

James shook his head. "I searched the whole house. There's no one here, nothing out of place. And the door was still locked when I came back."

Same as the first time. "Neighbors see anything?"

"I haven't asked. But they didn't when the other break-in happened. And if he came in the back door, no one would've seen him. If he cares enough to bypass locks, I'm sure he can get in without being noticed."

The logic was solid. "Especially when you're as identifiable as that guy," Drake agreed. "You tell Claire yet?"

"No, and I'm not going to. That's why I went to you. To take care of this without getting her involved." The last several days had worn him thin.

"And all I have to do is everything." Drake gave him a wry smile. "Works better in idea than practice, don't you think?"

James could see he was right. "What do you need from me? I'll do whatever it takes."

"I don't have enough information to answer that question yet," Drake told him. "You must have formulated a theory by now; let's hear it. But no ghost stories."

James ran his eyes over the photos, hesitant to answer. "Something connected to Claire? Some jealous stalker?"

Drake was slow in answering. "Jives with this latest piece of evidence. What about the rest? Does your solution fit?"

James had to admit that it didn't. "Well, no, but what then? Coincidence that the pictures he finds and destroys are all of Claire? Without touching any of the others in the house?"

"Probably not. Do you trust her?"

"Absolutely." No hesitation in that answer.

"So she would tell you if any suspicious men entered her life, maybe a stalker like you said? You weren't exactly forthcoming about him to her."

"I know," James admitted. "But that was only to protect her. And I did tell her something was going on—the main details."

"Mostly."

"If nothing else, she wouldn't withhold the information after she knew this person was after me."

That logic was solid too. "Well, as far as I can see, you've debunked your own theory, James. In record time."

"It wasn't much of a theory," he said. "But I trust her. She's not involved in this."

Or doesn't know she's involved, Drake thought but didn't bother saying. "If this isn't a random stranger, and I'd wager it isn't, then we're running out of possible connections. How are you and Mike?"

"Her dad? We get along really well. Too well sometimes,

Claire says. That's her joke."

"Does he scare you?"

James' answer was automatic. "I think he scares everyone." He laughed, but there was no humor in it. "There was this one time, with a hammer—" he stopped. "I shouldn't say. But maybe you know the story."

"Not that one, but stories like it, sure. Mike is a friend of mine, but I know what he's capable of. This wouldn't even test the boundaries."

James was slow to the next part but decided that he wanted to know the answer more than he didn't want to ask the question. He closed his eyes and took the plunge. "There were rumors, but... has he killed people?"

Drake waved that off. "No, not murder. Once you've acquired a reputation for ruthlessness, you no longer have the same need for violence. But you have to earn that stature first, and he surely did."

"No." James couldn't see it. "There are times he talks to me like I'm part of the family. And he's the one who told me to get you to look into the guy. You think Michael has something to do with it?"

"Not really. But—and you'll notice a refrain here, James—I don't know yet."

"What about the fingerprints?" he said. "He would've been the last one to touch the pictures."

"We have his face, and that led us nowhere. I don't know where you think the prints are going to get us. But I'm not going to leave evidence behind either." Drake went out to his car and returned with a small bag of equipment. The pull was quick work and when he was satisfied with the results, Drake packed up his things. "I'll get back to you on these. I have a friend in Richmond who can test for a match."

"Thank you," James said. "We may finally have him."

Drake was less optimistic. "Just remember, he couldn't match the face, so I think it's a long shot. But it is a shot."

"Should I report this to the police?"

"That's up to you James, but if you do, I'm out. Me or the cops; you don't get both. You all right here?"

"I'm ok," James said. "Just need to find some excuse to stay with Claire for a few days."

Drake patted him on the shoulder. "I'm sure you'll think of something," he said. "I'll be in touch." He walked out into the gathering dusk and left James standing alone in his kitchen with the broken glass.

8

James watched Drake's headlights back out of the driveway and closed the door in the silence he had left. A quick check to make sure the doors were locked, for all the good that had done him. It was late, but never too late to call Claire; he didn't want to spend the night in his own house. She didn't pick up, and he set his phone aside dejectedly. Should he be worried about her, given this latest turn in the road? Not likely, he told himself. There was no reason the man should know where Claire lived, even if he wanted to harm her. But then how did he know about the gym or James' address?

It would have been easy enough to drive to her apartment, but he wasn't sure that was the right move. For one, it would scare her; no way to brush off an unexpected late-night visit saying he couldn't go back to his house. He had already gone to such lengths to keep her away from whatever trouble he was in, no reason to change that now. If the man was after Claire, maybe he was waiting out there in the dark to trail James now, flush him like a rabbit and follow where he led. It was a leap, but a risk that felt real. Better to tough it out tonight alone and meet up with her tomorrow in the safety and cover of daylight.

The locked doors didn't feel like much protection anymore so he left all the lights on before retiring to his bedroom. The mysterious stalker never showed up when James was at home—not yet anyway—so he hoped that would afford him some insurance. Maybe this person was more interested in psychological warfare than actually inflicting physical harm. Would that be better or worse than the reverse? Somewhere a confrontation and, from that, a solution, but that was for another time. James crossed the kitchen and passed through the living room, both as illuminated as possible, and closed his bedroom door. The bedroom he lit up too, but he soon found that kept him awake. Not willing to sacrifice a good night's sleep, he switched off all the lights, crawled under the covers, and closed his eyes...

Next he was on an operating table. The doctor had pretty eyes; she slipped a mask over his mouth and told him to count backward from ten. "When you wake up it will all be over," she promised. "See you on the other side." She turned away from him.

James wanted to do a good job for the doctor with the pretty eyes. He put all his energy into counting as well as he could. "Ten... nine... eight..." Nothing yet. "Seven... six... five..." Still no change. "Four... three... two..." Drowsy now, but still very much conscious. "One..." The "zero" that followed it was barely a whisper and his eyelids closed of their own accord. *But I'm not out,* he realized, *I'm not under. Something has gone wrong.* A miscalculation, not enough gas. He tried to open his eyes, to yell out, but nothing happened. He concentrated everything on the eyelids this time, full attention and energy to lifting them, but they were unresponsive to his will.

The eyes no longer served him, but his ears were alert. He heard the sound of metal on metal (a blade?) and the doctors conversing in terms he didn't understand. "Ready for first incision," a male voice said.

James tried to call out. He tried to shout—"Don't do it, you idiots, I'm not under!"—but his body was still, deceptively calm. The female doctor called for a scalpel and James tried again to summon command over his body. No hope for full sentences; a shorter protest, one word. *Stop!* His mind screamed but to no physical effect. The doctor leaned over him, he could not see her but he could feel her, and made a long swooping cut across his forehead.

"Look what wonders man has made," someone said and the room laughed politely. No pain, but he felt the resulting trail of blood find its way through the opening and work down his face. Full-body awareness, full-body paralysis. The doctor wiped the blood away and James tried to calm his racing mind for another attempt to break the biological spell. He pictured his lips moving, the exacting calisthenics of the action. One word, a single syllable. *Stop. Stop. Stop.*

"Stop!" His eyes shot open and he sat upright. No operating room, no pretty doctor. Just the dark and curtains swaying gently in the delicate night breeze. First nightmare in a long while, James realized. Surprising it held off as long as it did given recent events.

The bedroom was dark as expected, but now he noticed a sliver of light shining through underneath the door—that was unexpected. James looked again, had to assure himself he wasn't seeing things or still caught in the stupor of half-sleep. But no, he realized, the light was no mistake. Why it was on, he had no idea.

He slipped quietly from the bed; or tried to slip quietly, but the springs groaned even with the careful shifting of his weight. A shadow darted across the light, but it moved so quickly he thought it perhaps a hallucination driven by confusion and fear. Desperately, he scanned the room for something he could use as a weapon but found nothing. He flexed his fingers, and his ears felt the rapid beating of his heart.

Both feet on the floor now, he reached his hand out toward the door. He didn't want to investigate what was beyond the door, but waiting helplessly in his room seemed even worse. As he touched the doorknob, a curious thing happened. The light from the hall died, and the blackness it left in its wake was deeper, more absolute than normal.

James couldn't explain it, and part of him still wanted to open the door, but the return to darkness convinced him against it. Maybe whatever was outside waited for him in the dark, or maybe it was already gone, but he no longer had the stomach to find out. Instead he abandoned the silent strategy, dragging his bed and pushing it hard against the door so it couldn't open inward. Part of him felt foolish, but the larger part didn't care. He laid back down, eyes on the door, until finally his parasympathetic nervous system kicked in and allowed his eyes to close.

He passed the rest of the night alternating in and out of sleep, never sustaining either. The sunrise was long in coming.

9

Impossible not to feel sympathy for the kid whose happy little life had been so dramatically altered, seemingly through no fault of his own. Or was that last part an unearned assumption? Drake had a good feeling about him, and in a shadowy world tearing at the seams with unknowns, his instincts were his most finely-honed and valued assets. They had always served him well in the past and he reminded himself again to trust them. If James could be ruled out as a cause, everything was pointing to the girlfriend. But in what way? James trusted her, but he was naive and starry-eyed; Drake wasn't going to take his word for it. Dr. Taylor spoke on her behalf too; had to account for that. He still had to get a hold of the other professor, Fox was it? And Michael Ventura—what was his role, if any? Somehow it was all connected.

There was the matter of the fingerprints too. He didn't expect they would be of much value, not after the face came back without a match. The prints looked fresh enough though, and that was encouraging. James seemed enchanted by the idea that this would be the break they needed, but how clumsy would this person have to be to get caught by leaving prints after everything that led up to that moment? If what James said was true, Drake was tracking someone with abilities bordering on superhuman. He smiled at the thought, its absurdity. The kid was obviously exaggerating to some extent, like the fish that got away growing larger with every telling.

Not that he had been intentionally deceptive, Drake thought, just that he had built the events up too much in his mind. What may have started as a fair-sized snowball was now an avalanche, and James' time spent brooding on it only added to its weight and speed. Certain elements that he had heard, or even seen, were strange, no denying it. But there was an answer somewhere out there, and he would find it. Whatever the explanation was, he couldn't see it ending with anything other than a man at the center. No ghost stories.

It was almost midnight by the time he got back to his office. He considered reaching out to Cavillo, letting him know he was calling in a favor, but there was no point in doing it just then. Let the poor boy get some sleep. The thought made Drake realize how tired he was. He ensured the place was locked up, couldn't abide any smashed picture frames of his own, and turned out the lights before making his way home.

The next morning came early, and he met it begrudgingly. He put another call into Cavillo and told him what he needed. "What do you think the chances of finding anything with this one are?"

"Honestly," said Cavillo, "better than the face scan. Can't

promise when I'll get around to it, but we have a lot more prints on file than faces, not just people who have been arrested. People get printed for lots of reasons, and there's a record of all of it. Plus it's easier for the computer to match. Faster, more conclusive. Only a local pull, but maybe you'll get lucky."

"First time for everything," Drake said, and he agreed to run the prints up to Cavillo shortly. With that job out of his hands, he had two choices: follow-up with Dr. Fox for more information on Claire or schedule a meeting with her father. The latest development at James' house suggested a connection to Claire, but whatever that connection was, it could just as easily extend to Mike. The professor would be the easier route, which meant that he should probably talk to Michael first. How to approach that conversation? Play it casually, just that he happened to be asking questions? No, no sense in even trying that strategy. Mike wasn't stupid. He would have to come at it head on; to flinch would only cost him any chance he had at uncovering the truth.

That was the problem with mixing friends and business. When that line of division disappeared, or even blurred, one side couldn't stay strong without sacrificing the other. More often than not, both took a hit from which they could never quite recover. Drake now faced the question of which he valued more: the friendship, that he was suddenly second-guessing, or seeing the job through. It was not an easy question to answer, but if Mike was involved in this madness somehow, he would have already made that decision for him. Meanwhile, honor wasn't going anywhere.

"You're getting ahead of yourself," he said aloud. Call the man, talk to him, then decide what to do. Attempting to trace those steps in reverse would be idiotic.

The Venturas' house was in an exclusive subdivision outside Charlottesville, and as he parked his ancient sedan, Drake felt very much like the element those people were looking to exclude. *How much does a place like this even cost?* he wondered. More money than he would ever see, most of it probably old southern money. How much of it was honest? He couldn't answer that either, but he knew nobody cared about the answer anymore. Had they ever?

Early evening was settling on the giant house and the lights from within radiated out into the coming darkness. He rang the doorbell and set off a chain reaction of dogs barking and footsteps behind the door.

"Come on in!" a familiar voice yelled over the din.

Stepping into the entryway, Drake saw Michael at work chopping vegetables in the kitchen with a knife far bigger than the job called for. He left his shoes near the front door and made his way through the living room.

"Victor, by god, Drake!" Michael came from the kitchen, pulled Drake's arm in for a strong handshake, and patted him on the back with the other hand. His frame was softer around the edges than Drake remembered, but his slate gray eyes retained their feral intensity. "What's it been, five years? No, more than five. Gotta be ten. Jesus, at least ten. Never mind. How the hell are you?"

"Doing fine," Drake said.

"I saw you coming up the road. Driving a real bucket of bolts these days, huh?"

"Well, you know, Point A to Point B," Drake said with a smile.

"If you say so," Michael conceded. "Better you than me though. The boss must be rolling in his grave."

"Probably," Drake agreed. "Never cared for my style, did he?"

"He used to say a bad year in a good car was better than a good year in a bad car. You remember the way he'd go on about that Pontiac?"

"The Pontiac years." Drake chuckled. "He could have gone to work in marketing for GM."

"Not nearly as much money in that. Ah, but enough about the old days. You still working out of that hole in the wall on the bad side of town?"

"That's right."

Michael shook his head. "Past time to move up in the world, isn't it? We're not so young anymore. Oh well, have a seat." He pointed to a sprawling couch. "What can I get you to drink? Beer, liquor? Just picked up a six-pack of a new IPA I've been hearing about."

"Whiskey, neat. Thanks."

"Whiskey, let me see what we've got," Michael said, returning to the kitchen. "Johnnie Walker, Jack... Oh, some Glenlivet."

"Give me the cheap stuff," Drake told him. "Wouldn't want me to forget my station."

Michael laughed from the other room. "You got it, pal."

Drake took in his impressive surroundings as Michael prepared the drinks in the next room. He heard footsteps descending from behind him and turned to see Michael's wife coming down the stairs. Rebecca had aged too since he last saw her, but she had aged well. She wore pink leggings and a tight black tank top, her blonde hair tied in a tight ponytail. He stood up to say hello and she bounded up to him enthusiastically.

"Victor Drake!" She wrapped her arms around him. "Michael said you were coming over but I wouldn't believe it until I saw it for myself."

"Nice to see you again, Rebecca," he said. "You're looking well."

She smiled at him. "You need to come around more often, Victor Drake."

"Well," he said, "I'll see what I can do."

She kissed him on the cheek. "Michael, you tell Victor to come around more often."

"You heard the lady," Michael said, coming into the room with a pair of drinks. "Our door is always open to the great Victor Drake."

Rebecca rolled her eyes and disappeared down a hallway. She came back with a water bottle in one hand and a yoga mat under the other arm. "I'm off to yoga, honey," she said. "Might go out with the girls after, don't wait up."

"Have a good time, sweetheart," Michael told her.

"Bye, Victor," she said, stretching the words out into a singsong tune.

Drake lifted his hand from his lap as she walked out the door. "So long." Seemed awfully late to be going to a yoga class, but he let that go. She looked the part anyway.

Michael let out a long sigh, and Drake made a point not to read too much into that either way. There was a brief silence before Michael broke it.

"So. To what do I owe the pleasure of this visit?"

Drake chose the words carefully. "It's about that man you have me investigating."

"Ah, right, of course. How's that going?"

Good question. "Still a lot of unknowns."

"So what's the guy's story?" Michael asked.

"I don't know."

"Ok, well what does he want with James then? What brought the whole thing on?"

"I don't know."

Michael was still smiling but the smile took on a forced look. "No tricks. I know you too well for that. Light on the talking, but always observing, the brain always working. You've got ideas or you wouldn't be here, so let's have it."

"Sure, I've got ideas." Drake sipped his drink. "Theory One: your daughter is involved, maybe the cause of everything." Neither man was smiling now.

"Impossible." His tone left no room for argument. "She's a college student, studies math and science—"

"Experimental High Energy Physics."

"Right. You don't think I know my daughter? Who she is, the things she does?" His eyes had gone cold, that famous temper threatening to reveal itself.

"I didn't say that."

"You inferred it."

"Implied."

"What?"

"Theory Two," Drake continued, "her involvement is tangential. Indirect to the point that she's not even aware of it." He let the implication fill the space between them.

Michael fell silent then, but leaned forward and held eye contact. "You know who you're talking to?"

"I certainly do."

"And you think I'm stupid enough to send a guy after my daughter's boyfriend, whom I think a lot of by the way, to... do what, exactly? And then, after setting the first half of that brilliant plan into action, I call on the best private eye I know to investigate the case. Leading, as it would, back to me as the guilty party."

Drake set his glass down and shrugged. "Well, when you put it that way..." He smiled to break the tension that had been building in the room. "You can see why I'm stuck."

Michael sat back. That response relaxed him some but his suspicions were not entirely alleviated. "No, actually, I don't. This guy has shown up at James' house... two times, three? That you know of. He'll be back. So stake him out. Didn't you used to be good at this? A guy that looked like you anyway."

Drake reached for his pocket to withdraw a cigarette but thought better of it. Couldn't smoke in a house like this, with its shining walls and immaculate draperies. "Hot night," he observed. "Continue this outside, get some air?"

The night was still as they stepped out into the darkness. Michael reached inside to turn on a porchlight and they stood in its yellow glow. Time for that cigarette. "Sure, Mike," Drake said, pulling out his lighter. "That notion had occurred to me. Then what?"

"Then you get information out of him. If he doesn't talk, doesn't leave, shoot his kneecaps out. He's trespassing in James' house at that point, and you're defending him. The kid doesn't have it in him, I know, but you do." He turned his head and spit into the bushes. "You used to anyway."

"Stand Your Ground." Drake shook his head. "Not in Virginia. Not if he's not posing a threat."

"Isn't he?" Michael was tired of nuances.

"He might be," Drake conceded. "He might not be. Won't know till the moment comes, if it does."

"If you want to deal with him, and you should, you deal with him," Michael said. He spoke as though he were explaining some obvious truth to a dim child. "You didn't get to where you are now by pussyfooting around, paralyzed by overthinking."

Drake thought about that. Michael was right, but probably not in the way he meant it. "And where am I now, Mike?"

"Hell, I don't know, maybe you're broken and miserable. I didn't get where I am by being lost in helpless daydreaming. How about that?"

The subtext between them was working its way closer to the surface. Drake unearthed it. "And where are you now, Mike?"

"What's that supposed to mean?" The temper was back.

"No theatrics," he said, putting out the cigarette. "Just a question. Nice seeing you again. This was useful. I'll be in touch." Drake got into his car and pulled away, watching the lights of the Venturas' house slowly recede in his rearview mirror.

The sky was dark as he exited the subdivision. Dark beyond what usually followed sunset, a black sky further shaded by heavy clouds. No stars found their way through and as the road rose to merge with the freeway, fat raindrops smacked against Drake's windshield. It was just as well, he thought, turning on the wiper blades. Something Michael had said back at the house troubled him, though he couldn't yet nail down what. A steady rain now, unrelenting and driving. The cars in front of him crept cautiously along the slickening roads and Drake filed into his place in the somber parade.

A vehicle sped past in the far-left lane, way too fast for conditions. The driver cut hard into the adjacent lane and passed a string of cars on the right. An entry-level sports car, he noted. There was a time he would have extrapolated a voluminous backstory from a little detail like that. Financially comfortable, but not quite wealthy. Male, the odds said, young enough that he sought transportation-as-identity. Or old enough for the same. A reverse bell curve, losing that sense of self. *You're too old, or young, to be in that quagmire,* Drake told himself. But something his old friend said landed hard and untraceable, like an unseen right hook.

He shook his head. The rain was stronger now, violent even. Large drops washed over his windshield and he slowed down instinctively. On the passenger seat his phone rang, but no time for it now. Water ran down the windows in great streams and visibility became nearly non-existent. Through the deluge he made out the skeleton of an off-ramp and pulled his car off the highway. From there it was a short shot into a gas station parking lot, the building's lights a distant, fuzzy blush scarcely seen through the pounding rain. Content to sit out the storm, Drake turned the car off and stared out the windshield. Just the darkness now—and water. Inside the car was the entire world—beyond that, water forever.

The connection was immediate and unmistakable. The *USS Phoenix,* some twenty years earlier. No, more than twenty by now, at least thirty, he realized. He was a military man, or had been anyway; technically a veteran now, though that had never felt like an essential part of his identity. More a logical path, as logical as anything else seemed at the time. Decent student, not great, no overriding passions toward which to direct his energies. No illusions of grandeur either, of saving the world, or even bettering it, in joining up with the fighting arm of the great United States. It had been more a feeling of Why Not?

The recruiters promised him the world, as they do: he was eligible for officer-training programs, could retire early with a guaranteed future income and time enough to spend however he wished after he saw his commitment through. And the knowledge that he had served his country, protected its people even, though he never felt much connection between his daily duties and the safety of blue-eyed schoolchildren in Omaha. Even after exorcising the sentimentalism, he couldn't deny that the opportunity was an adventure unlike any other, the kind of thing that carries powerful weight with a directionless eighteen-year-old. And it was a whole lot better than working at a gas station or warehouse for the next four or forty years. Hell, Why Not?

And so it was that Victor Drake joined the Navy. Blindly, he knew, but not blinded. It was peacetime, to the extent that ever existed on a worldwide level, and any theoretical danger tied to the decision was a non-factor. Various skirmishes spread across the Middle East—when didn't they?—but nothing that would put the United States Navy in any peril. Even if his country intervened in some struggle between foreign combatants, what would the sailors do, he wondered? Sit out on a battleship, near as he could guess. At most maybe they would fire some shipboard artillery impersonally. He was a young man, didn't know what he was talking about, but at least he knew enough to know he didn't know. That alone made him feel sagely about the future as he transitioned into his new life.

The ASVAB went well, almost suspiciously so, as he kept waiting for an incline in difficulty that never came. Drake's reward was options; available placements were wide and varied. He didn't know enough to have any particular strong opinions, but there was something irresistibly intriguing about submarines. The appointment came with prestige and again that allure of adventure. Like Captain Nemo, he would spend his days and nights jetting deep under the surface of an endless ocean, forever unseen by the waking world. Submarining was cloaked in mystery, a roguish charm to the whole operation. Who knew what they did all the time down there (mostly listened presumably?), but who cared? It was change, undeniable change. At any given time that can be more than sufficient; it can be the most attractive thing in the ever-widening universe.

Initially, the life was as dramatic a pivot as anyone could hope for. The fresh recruits were broken down, built back up, then finally made new and shining. Indoctrinated all the way, sometimes with noble intentions and other times with an ugly and powerful cynicism. From there, the *Phoenix*. She held 110 sailors, a diverse cast made up of nervous rookies, hardened veterans, and most everything in between. The romanticism of a life on (or under) the water united them, and while Drake never felt much of the pamphlet-filling sales pitch about brotherhood, the crew unavoidably became a sort of surrogate family after spending so much time in each other's spheres.

The *USS Phoenix* was nearly 400 feet long, but that sounded a lot more spacious than it felt sharing it with over a hundred had-been strangers. From bow to stern the quarters were cramped without much space to think, let alone maneuver. Claustrophobia wasn't a factor, it would have been an absolute deal-breaker, but he realized that he had never fully appreciated space. Just physical space. The absence of *something*.

An S6G nuclear reactor powered the submarine. The boat was home to some of the military's top engineering minds, brilliant men and women who commanded instruments of such complexity that Victor Drake could never dream of understanding them. Their walls of dials and switches were as dense as any space shuttle's and as inscrutable as heart surgery. Rather than concern himself with the particulars that lay beyond the reach of his purview, he concentrated all efforts on doing his job to the best of his ability. If everyone else did the same (and it was a central ethos of the Navy that they did), Drake figured they would all be just fine. In that regard, he was right.

Training in San Diego provided the first glimpse into a larger world. Those hours passed rapidly into days that built themselves into weeks, and in a flash it was time for the next phase of the journey. A son of the Midwest, Drake grew up around a number of smallish lakes in Minnesota; the expansive Pacific was limitless in comparison. He formed a habit of standing on the shore and staring in quiet awe at the water's horizon, a deep blue sprawl toward infinity. The human mind couldn't comprehend that much water, no chance, but he liked to try. Lake Superior bordered Minnesota to the east and he remembered hearing that its water could flood all of North and South America to a depth of one foot. The Pacific's volume was nearly 60,000 times that.

Some of humanity's greatest leaps happened in the 20th century, a veritable yesterday in the history of its development. The Wright Brothers slipped the surly bonds in 1908, and by 1961 the Russians had a man in space. Eight years later, Armstrong and Aldrin were on the moon. Advances since then had been mostly technological, conquests of the mind, but surely gravity would not be the final casualty of genius. What would mankind achieve next to push beyond the limits it had once accepted as being part and parcel of the species? What was even left?

Witnessing flight for the first time must have been a marvel past expression, and space travel a fantastical dream of science-fiction made routine. To find any achievement comparable, one would have to go back to the first people to take to the water. Untold thousands of years before Christ, in rudimentary, even childlike, vessels at first. A level of bravery modern man could never fully relate to—nothing in the world left that unknown anymore. But they went out, forward into lakes and seas, the wide oceans, to find what was past the end of seeing.

After a very long time, 9,000 years, maybe 10,000 (again, an amount past comprehension), Europeans arrived in the Americas, and enough words have been spent on what happened next. Their ships were wood and tar and their sails could be torn and eaten at by the wind. Navigation was by hand, tracing arcs under increasingly-foreign stars. Regardless of age and experience it took courage, which is easily lionized, but also a kind of dissatisfied wanderlust. This second impulse had neither inherent virtue nor inherent malice; like all tools, it was exactly as good or bad as the person who employed it. But without it, without the restless searching, progress was impossible. Mankind stumbled forward, often gracelessly or violently, but always forward. And once in a great while, an alchemist struck world-changing gold.

These were Drake's thoughts as he prepared for his maiden voyage off the coast of California's soft, sandy beaches. San Diego was as beautiful as he had always pictured it, and now it was time to say a temporary goodbye. He squeezed through the narrow entrance on the topside (no such thing as an obese submariner) and prepared for departure. No windows or portholes to see the *Phoenix* slip beneath the water, but he felt the transition and then, completely submerged. Was this mix of excitement and trepidation the way virgin seafarers of the distant past felt as they watched the last sight of shore disappear over the horizon?

He took in the mechanical masterpiece that surrounded him, the only thing between him and the ocean's crushing depths. Submarines were an unfathomable expense, upwards of two billion dollars to build and typically decommissioned after a couple decades without ever having fired a shot. The United States had fourteen ballistic missile submarines, each with enough firepower to qualify as the fifth most powerful nation on the planet. The show of strength was absurd, Drake thought. Worse than absurd, insulting, to the countless more practical ways that money could have been spent. But oh well, nothing to be done for that. He kept his attention and efforts in his world where they might do some good and concentrated on the tasks in front of him.

The day to day was uninteresting, dangerously so at times. Stakes were high, any one of a dozen mistakes at any given moment could doom the whole crew before lunchtime. Repetition gave way to mundanity, and dull instruments invited peril. Even the most complex and vital of the *Phoenix's* instruments couldn't touch the human brain, and this was the instrument often most vulnerable to lapses in execution. They stayed out for months at a time, and deployments that started in a sense of hyper-awareness slowly ground down to unthinking monotony. No natural light, or even a view of the water, just days and nights woven together in unbreaking eight-hour chains.

That life was long past and would not come around again. He was glad to have done it, content to have left it, satisfied to not return to it. Memories danced across his mind from time to time, in that four-year window he had visited parts of the world that most could only dream of, but episodic events didn't have the same staying power as the general feeling of it. How it felt to be under hundreds of feet of water as the consecutive days piled up into the triple digits. From what they could see from the interior, the crew might as well have been on dry land, or in the air, or on the surface of Mars. But they were wrapped in the arms of the sea, and somehow, with a sense beyond seeing, he could always feel that. The steady hum of the engines, the occasional sounds of marine life reverberating through the sub's steel hull. Something uniquely oceanic about that environment, and, surrounded in rain as he was inside his car, the sensations came rushing back.

What was it Michael had said? *You didn't get to where you are now...* Finally, there it was; that had been the line. Ventura didn't have the talent for subtlety, he couldn't have known what he was doing when he did it, but the trick was effective all the same. With those throwaway words, a taunt bordering on the cliché, he threw Drake down a rabbit hole into the past. So much of his constitution was based on the idea, the misunderstanding maybe, that events flowed logically from one to the next. A preceded B, and usually, even if the connections weren't immediately apparent, caused B, which then caused C, and so on. No event without a predecessor, no effect without a cause.

These things often made sense only in retrospect, with the benefit of history to shoulder the heavy weight of contextualization, but one way or another, they always made sense. Even failure, heartbreak, tragedy, all these were accounted for, part of the deal that no one agreed to but by which they all had to live. Everyone had times of rising and falling. Zoom out far enough and some lifetimes were an upward climb into happiness and purpose while others plummeted like airplanes whose engines had seized in mid-flight. Nothing about this was comforting, really, or even so much as optimistic, but it was order. The wilder, more frightening allowance was that the order itself was an illusion—not a reflection of the fundamental nature of things but rather an artificial overlay imposed by men and women too afraid to deal with the consequences of the alternative.

Either a man's circumstance was the resultant sum of a lifetime's worth of the thousand individual decisions he made from minute to minute, or that was a pleasant lie people used to take credit for their triumphs and accept blame for their losses. Weighing the two possibilities in the dying rain (the storm was either weakening or moving on, a distinction without a difference), Drake couldn't align himself with either. The endless string of unconnected days that led him from a nondescript town in flyover country to life as a submariner to what it felt like he had always been, an operator on the edges. Certainly some of that progression had been his doing, but all of it? No, that seemed too simple. His choices could not account for 100% of how he got to where he was, whatever Michael Ventura meant by that.

To even estimate how much of his circumstances he, or anyone, was responsible for would have been a pure guess without a foundation to stand on. More importantly, what made up the rest? Emerson said the only person you were destined to become is the person you decided to be. That didn't hold with current events. Had James Chandler decided to have his life thrown into chaos by a seemingly-random visitor he couldn't place? Of course not. Or was that itself an assumption too far? Maybe James brought the man into his life, Drake thought—haphazardly, accidentally even. Time would reveal the answer; it always did.

His phone was where he had left it in the passenger seat, showing the missed call. Local area code but not a number he recognized. He had always felt reticent about returning calls from unknown numbers. If someone wanted to get a hold of him badly enough, they could call back or leave a message. But maybe this was connected to the case; he considered the possibility and reached across the car to return the call. Before he could get to the phone it lit up with another incoming call. Another unfamiliar 434 number, this one different from the one the rain caused him to miss. He took a moment to commit the digits to memory and answered the phone.

"Victor Dr—" He couldn't get his opening out before a frantic voice on the other end interrupted him.

"Victor Drake!" A woman, hysterical. "Victor!"

"Slow down," he ordered her. "Dammit, slow down and talk."

"He's dying! Hurry, you have to come here!"

Panic was the easy reaction but one of them had to remain clear-headed and he didn't have any confidence in the other party to hold up. "Who the hell is this?"

"Rebecca! Ventura! Victor, it's Michael, and—" Michael's voice in the background cut her off. "Ok, ok," she said, and after some shuffling Michael's voice took over.

"Drake, how far are you from here?" The words came as though through gritted teeth.

"Distance is such a relative thing," he started to say, then thought better of it. "What's going on, Mike?"

"He came here. I don't know how or why. He showed up, Drake—"

"Who?" Drake was sure he already had the answer but needed to confirm it.

"I don't know his name," Michael said through the pain, "the guy. Listen, he attacked, couldn't get to my gun..." Rebecca still wailed in the background.

"You're shot?"

"No, he didn't have a weapon. Didn't need one," he added, unable to mask the embarrassment in his voice.

"Bad?"

"Pretty bad. I'll be fine, but the leg's gotta be broken. My god, the strength. What the hell have you dragged me into?"

In the car Drake threw up his hands. He knew Michael couldn't see the gesture but it made him feel better all the same. "Then we need to get you to a hospital."

"No hospitals," Michael said. "I've got a guy we can go to, a personal friend."

Of course he did. "Whichever," Drake conceded. "But let's get our stories straight first. I'm on my way."

The old sedan sped into a 180-degree pivot and shot out of the parking lot with an evident sense of purpose. US-29 was dark and slick, and traffic moved warily across it. These factors did nothing to mitigate Drake's urgency and he rushed back to Michael and Rebecca's place. As he pulled into the driveway the Venturas' fluorescent windows glowed onto the lonely street like a lighthouse at the edge of the universe.

10

Claire slept late, but she was still first out of bed and moved deliberately so as to not wake James. The last few days had worn on him, it was obvious, and through him, her. She made a point not to look at the clock, content to meet the new day on its own terms. Searching the cupboards for coffee or tea, she found nothing and settled for a glass of water at the kitchen table. The previous night's storm had passed, and young sunlight washed over the room. For the moment she felt peace. The wind found its way through the screen of an open window and she smiled as she watched it send the leaves outside dancing. Out of every trial, survival, she thought. Stronger on the other side.

Time passed without any sounds of life from the bedroom so she decided to take her phone out to the porch and see what her parents were up to. A call to her father went to his voicemail—unusual—so she tried her mother.

"Hello, Claire dear."

Something short of her normal bubbly tone, Claire

noticed, but she didn't assign much meaning to it and pressed on. "Hey Mom, just checking in. What's up for today?"

"Oh…" Rebecca was long in answering. From curious to curiouser. "No, nothing today. We're just going to lie low."

"Everything all right?" The air around Claire felt colder now, an unseasonable chill passing over her.

"Yes, yes," she laughed unnaturally—a minor deviation but unmissable to her daughter. "We're just about to run actually, but thanks for calling. Have a good day, love you!"

Claire sat motionless in the porch chair, the verdant grass spreading out before her. Life pressing toward chaos in all directions. She resolved to meet it directly. Leaving the idyllic scene of the porch behind her, she walked back inside and knocked on the bedroom door, opening it a crack.

"James, wake up, we both overslept. Something's up with my parents. I'm going to take a run over there. Do you want to come?"

James turned over, his eyes still mostly closed against the intrusive light. "Hmm?" he said. "What's going on with your parents?"

"I don't know," she admitted. "My mom was weird on the phone just now. Just a feeling I have."

James sat up and tossed the covers aside. "Ok," he said, rubbing his eyes. "Give me a second." He checked his phone and gave it a surprised look. "Two missed calls," he said. "Both from Victor Drake, the private eye. Voicemails and text messages too."

"What do they say?"

James read the texts aloud. "'Call me when you get this.' Then an hour later, 'As soon as you get this. Important.'"

"It's a cell phone," she said, a little annoyed that she needed to point that out. "You can talk to him from the car."

"Sure." James balanced the phone between his ear and shoulder and returned the missed calls while he got dressed.

Drake answered partway through the first ring. "James, where are you?" So much for pleasantries.

"Leaving my house, on our way to Claire's parents. She thinks something's wrong."

"Smart girl. Give her the phone."

James paused, sending his eyes to Claire who was waiting impatiently by the door. "Ok," he said, handing her the phone. "He wants to talk to you."

Claire took the phone as a suspicious look crossed her face. "Hello?"

"Claire, Victor Drake. We haven't met, but I'm a friend of your father's."

"Of course," she said, gesturing with her head toward the car. "I gave your name to James. We're on our way to their house now."

"Skip it," Drake said. "They're not there." Claire stopped halfway down the stairs and James ran into her back, sending her down one more step than she had intended. "Claire, your dad's been hurt, but he's going to be fine." She took a quick breath and he repeated, "He's going to be fine."

Claire did a commendable job of keeping her composure. "What happened?"

"I'm going to give you my address," Drake said, side-stepping the question. "Bring James, he knows where it is. The three of us need to talk."

* * *

Drake heard footsteps racing up the old wood steps and a second set of feet struggling to keep up with them. His hunch as to the order of their owners soon proved correct; Claire threw open the door to his office without knocking while James was still navigating the last stair.

"What's going on with my parents?"

Drake got up from behind his desk to greet her. "Claire, good to meet you. Have a seat." James came in and shut the door behind him. "You too, James," he said, returning to his chair.

Claire's eyes were trained on the man on the other side of the desk. "My parents," she repeated.

"To the point then." Drake pushed a stack of papers aside. "Miss Ventura, your father was assaulted." Addressing James, he added, "Going off his description, I can safely say it was the same man who visited you at the gym."

"And my house." James grabbed Claire's hand, harder than he meant to, he realized.

"Right." Returning his attention to Claire, he continued, "Well as I said on the phone, he's fine. Broken leg. We've both survived worse."

"Where are they now?" Claire tried to will her voice to calmness and was mostly successful.

"Better you don't know."

"I need to know."

"Drake, please," James broke in.

"They're safe, the dogs too. Better for them—and you— that you don't know. I have a working theory on how he tracked them down, though not the why. Anyway, the fewer people that know..." He let the two of them complete the thought. He looked across the table; the girl's eyes were the color of the Pacific as seen in the dreams of a sailor, and they were filled with tears. James looking more stoic but perceptibly distressed. The appropriate reactions; nice to know he could count on that much at least.

"Questions," Drake prompted.

No one rushed to fill the dead air that followed. After a time Claire asked, "When can I see them?"

"When we've eliminated the threat." She didn't like that answer so he added, "But they're in phone contact. You can talk as much as you like." That helped, maybe. James shook his head, disbelief at the whole situation. Claire mostly stared at the ground. Onward. "James, the night you had the break-in, the smashed photos..."

That broke Claire from her spell. "What?" She was fully alert again, eyes on James now. "What break-in?"

James opened his mouth to speak but Drake cut him off. "Guess he didn't tell you about that. Didn't want to worry her, that about cover the explanation, kid?" James nodded. "And if I gave him time, he would apologize, but that will have to wait." Claire had not let it go, and probably wouldn't for a while, but he kept it moving before she could object. "James, you had the idea of pulling prints off the frames, remember?"

He nodded again. "Worth a shot, right?"

"I didn't think so at the time," Drake confessed, "but apparently so."

"So?" Claire this time. "So what did you find? Who was it?"

"Two different questions," Drake noted. "Two very different questions." He put out his cigarette, watching to see how they reacted to his stalling. Impatience came first. He waited for annoyance and then continued. "The prints were great." On the far end of his desk was a bottle of water and he reached for it now and took a drink. "But they're not going to help us."

"I don't understand," James said.

Drake capped the bottle, slowly, and returned it to its

previous place. "They're your prints, James."

Claire let go of his hand and turned to face him. "What does that mean? You broke the photos? Or staged the break-in?" James sat bewildered; no actor that good. She turned to Drake now. "What the hell is going on?"

"I'll admit, that's where my mind jumped at first. But no. Relax, James; because that explanation doesn't make any sense, does it? That's fitting facts to narratives, Claire. We're after the reverse."

"So what does it mean?" James asked. "You said things would get clearer with time." There was a pleading tone in his voice now.

"Taking the long view, it will," Drake said, maybe trying to convince himself as much as his younger charges. "Take a long enough view and it all works out, the way Earth looks peaceful from space. I realize that's not much comfort in times of suffering, but there it is. The difference between happy and sad endings depends only on where the story stops. Your job, our job, is to keep the story going till we get there." He paused then, hoping that would add to the weight of the idea and allow it to sink deep into their minds, down to the foundations.

After a time he continued, "The only explanation, as far as I can see, is that your prints are there from the last time you moved the frames, whenever that was."

"Sure," James didn't follow his thinking through to the end but he would get there. "Wouldn't have been that long ago."

"That's the easy part. The question we're left with then is, why no other prints?"

"The man wore gloves?" Claire suggested.

"James' prints were too clear for that. While not leaving prints, gloves would have surely muddled the prints that had been there previously."

"Unless..." James' turn to venture a theory. "He wore gloves and only touched the corners of the picture, where no prints would be."

Drake laughed out loud and then stopped himself. "A violent, obsessive maniac breaks into your house to gently handle some photographs before smashing them to detritus. Narratives from facts, James."

"So what is it?" Claire had tired of the Socratic method.

"We're up to four pieces of evidence that don't sit well with me. We can start with the phantom break-in, the first one. We could maybe explain that away on its own, but the list grows from there. Two is when you saw him on the road from your car, James, moving in ways we know to be impossible. Three, he can interact with physical objects without leaving a trace. And four, Claire, your dad had the misfortune of witnessing firsthand: an incredible, apparently superhuman, strength." He laid his hands open on the table.

"Is that all?" James said, a smile threatening the edge of his lips.

This time Drake let himself laugh. "For now, kid."

The tears were still in Claire's eyes and her voice broke when she spoke. "I'm glad this is funny to you two. We're going to sit around and tell bad jokes while there's some monster out there that wants to kill everyone I love? This is where the greatest P.I. in the world has gotten us?"

"It's a small world, but not nearly that small," Drake said. He turned serious. "If you'd like, I can bring you, or both of you, to the safehouse with your parents. Your dad's lifestyle, I'm sure you know, allows a degree of freedom and he can't do anything but heal up for the time being anyway. I don't know if the two of you are able to miss work or school for that long, but it might not be a bad idea. And it would allow me to go on the offensive without the burden of worrying about your safety." Poor wording, that last line. "That's not what I mean. You know what I mean."

"I have some vacation time built up," James said. He looked to Claire for her thoughts.

"I can't," she said. "I would love to, believe me, but there's no way."

James seemed unwilling to press the issue so Drake took it upon himself. "Why not?"

"There's too much work to be done at the university," she said. "They're all counting on me. I can't just disappear now."

"Consider—" Drake began, but she didn't let him finish.

"I can't." Decisive.

"Then I'm not going either," James said.

For a second, Drake thought of approaching the argument from another angle but recognized the futility and acquiesced. "In the end, we must be who we are."

The space outside the office windows was descending into dusk interspersed with streetlights that radiated like giant fireflies. Above them, like distant echoes, pale stars. The air was hot and still. These three associates, thrown together by some combination of time, destiny, and blind chance, sat without speaking.

11

It was a testament to the craziness of the past couple days that Drake didn't follow up the missed call from the unknown number, the one that came before Rebecca's, until after James and Claire left his office. Too late to return the call now, but he searched the number to see what he could find online. For the first time in a long time he felt like he caught a break when the number returned one clear-cut result: Dr. Andrew Beaumont, Comperio University Physics Department. This was the second time he came across that name. Dr. Taylor's colleague. They hadn't spoken, but Dr. Beaumont must have gotten his number from Dr. Taylor. Though that in itself didn't explain why he would have called last night, or at all.

The sun would be up before long and Drake still hadn't slept. He decided to leave the lead, if that's what it was, until tomorrow and turned off the office lights. The monster, as Claire put it, was still out there but remained as unreachable as ever. Sleep was the next best thing by a wide margin, his sore body and heavy eyes told him, so he didn't fight it. Instead, he leaned back in his padded chair and closed his eyes. Had there been a round timer running, Victor Drake would have been knocked out in the first.

Traffic and the sounds of the street below served as his alarm the next morning. He didn't know how long he slept, but he knew it wasn't enough. What he needed was a week on some secluded ranch in Montana, somewhere he could split his time between fly-fishing and ignoring any world beyond the canopy of cedars. What he had was a half-finished pack of cigarettes and the number of a physics professor.

"Well, let's see what's on the doctor's mind," Drake said to himself. His voice surprised him, thin and dry. The nearby bottle of water was warm, but he drank it quickly. It helped little, but he forced himself forward. Finding the number in his phone's history, he made the call.

"Dr. Beaumont." The voice was curt but professional.

Drake's mind froze. Had he given Dr. Taylor a name when he left his number? He typically didn't extend a lie any further than he needed to. Nothing to do with morality, just less to keep track of that way. He had a couple forgettable pseudonyms he cycled through when the situation called for it, but what had he told Claire's professor? Anything? No, he decided, there hadn't been any need. His mind was sluggish and that frustrated him. He tried to give it a charge, like jump-starting a dead battery.

"Hello?" Dr. Beaumont again.

"Good morning," Drake began in an artificially chipper voice. "This is Stan Savapath, I saw a missed call from you on my phone last night?"

"Are you the magazine writer?" The doctor didn't

reciprocate Drake's tone. "You spoke to Kate, Dr. Taylor?"

"That's right, sir. Online editor actually, but we would love to be in print someday. Gotta start somewhere, I always say."

"Well, Stan, you didn't leave any information with my colleague, not even your name. You can understand my concern when strangers show up asking personal questions about our students. As it happens, I'm at my computer now; what is the name of your website?"

Too early, at least it felt too early, to be fielding these kinds of questions. But Drake tapped into some hidden mental reserve and answered without hesitation. "*Our Scientific World.*" A dull title, nothing that would stick in the doctor's memory.

He heard movement on the other end and Dr. Beaumont said, "Well I don't see any search results for a magazine by that name. Are you sure you have the title right?" he added with a hint of condescension.

Drake played oblivious. "Oh yes, sir, no question about it. We're pretty new, see, and I doubt we'll ping anything on a search yet. But you've gotta start somewhere, I always say!"

"Yes, so I've heard." Beaumont was slow in letting go of his suspicions. "And how did you hear about Claire Ventura, to do an article on her?"

"Her boyfriend recommended her," Drake said. He jotted notes as he talked to keep his story straight; that last lie came with the benefit of not having to remember extra details. "I imagine you've met him by now." James would cover for his story if it came to that.

"Yes, yes, the boyfriend. Well, no, we haven't met, but we have... Excuse me for a moment." Drake rubbed his eyes and tried again to force himself awake. He was returning to life, but slower than he would have liked. Dr. Beaumont returned, presumably with a file of his own. "Steve... Upshaw, yes?"

Was that a test? Didn't sound like one. He took a chance. "That's right," Drake said and held his breath waiting for a response.

Nothing initially, but at last the doctor said, "All right," and seemed satisfied. More friendly now, he continued, "Well, what can I help you with? A quote for your story, a feelgood anecdote?"

"That would be most helpful," Drake said. Helpful to Stan Savapath, editor for the fledgling digital magazine *Our Scientific World,* but it didn't do a whole hell of a lot for Victor Drake. He looked over the notes from his initial visit to the university. One more string to pull at. "You know professor, Dr. Taylor recommended I speak with a Dr. Fox for the article. He works closest with Claire? I've got his number here actually, but thanks so much for your time. Give my best to Claire and Steve."

"That won't be necessary." So much for the softer, kinder Dr. Beaumont. "What is it you need?"

To talk to Dr. Fox, Drake thought, but instead he said, "You know, I really want this thing to pop. I think getting as close as I can is going to give my readers that inside look, if you know what I mean. Maybe Dr. Fox could give us a little background on one of their projects."

"Dr. Fox is a busy man. Part of my job is to manage my team's time and I cannot allow—"

"Well perhaps he would be willing to talk on his own time." Maybe it was the lack of sleep, or the unrelenting heat, or the frustration of the case coming to a head, but Drake was losing patience. The cheerful mark routine hardly seemed worth keeping up. "Surely you wouldn't have a problem with that?"

"What was your name again?" the doctor asked, and Drake felt he overplayed his hand. Of course, he could contact Dr. Fox regardless of what the man on the other end of this call said. Their conversation had already turned up enough oddities that needed answering. Getting those answers would be easier without a paranoid Dr. Beaumont looking over his shoulder.

He forced the sunny demeanor back into his delivery. "That's Stan Savapath. But I'm sorry, Doctor, here you are offering your valuable time and insight and I'm acting like a big jerk. I sure would be grateful for whatever you can give me. I'm such a science nerd and I forget about the pressures and stress you all are under, doing such incredible work. I was way out of line and I do hope you'll forgive me."

Maybe that worked and maybe it didn't, but Dr. Beaumont was content to finish the conversation on friendlier terms and answered all of Drake's asinine questions about Claire's life as a physics graduate student. When he figured he had enough for the cover story to seem believable, he politely ended the conversation and promised to send along a link to the article when it was finished.

"I look forward to reading it," Dr. Beaumont said and with that they hung up.

Drake looked down at his notepad, a complete mess. He smiled; in some respects people never improve. But the scrawls made sense to him and that was what mattered. He backed away from the paper, trying to view it as though from a helicopter—to get the entirety of the picture in one shot. The physics angle had seemed like such a dead end at the time, the follow-up hardly worth his time in light of everything else that had been going on. But now, this changed things.

Start with the fact that Beaumont called at all. That meant

two things. One, Taylor told him about Drake's visit and thought it necessary to pass along his phone number. Nothing particularly unexpected there, especially since it was easy to imagine Beaumont pressing the issue and the amicable Taylor going along to get along. But why did Beaumont feel the need to call the number himself, and why so suspicious when they finally spoke? Never mind that he was right to be distrusting; the point was that as far as he knew, he didn't have any reason to be distrusting. The cover story was totally plausible, Drake knew. At the very least it was good enough. A profile on a successful university student with an interesting story. What could be more commonplace?

Unless that's not what Claire was. She would have to account for this Steve Upshaw too. And what was so verboten about talking to Dr. Fox? Taylor didn't seem to have a problem with it, suggested it even, but Beaumont's reaction, well that was the kind of thing that raised alarms. A call—no, better, a visit—with Dr. Fox would be Drake's next step into the overgrown forest this mystery had become. Somewhere out there, amidst the tanglewood and overgrowth was the trail that would lead him home. He couldn't sit back and wait for rescue; the only way to find the path was to seek it out. Shower, breakfast, Fox.

Drake hoped a cold shower would shock him out of the dragging malaise he woke up in, and it was mostly effective. Sleepy, hungover, or broken-hearted, the body couldn't deny cold water. Feeling refreshed if not yet well-rested, he scavenged a sandwich from his mini-fridge and sat down at the computer to see what he could find on his next lead. Dr. Fox's profile on the university's website was far less robust than Drs. Taylor and Beaumont. Drake couldn't find it without a direct search, and when he did, all it provided was an office number, an impressive educational history, and a couple articles he published.

Partially Entangled Quantum Circuits of Three-Qutrit Systems with Maximally Controlled Dense Coding. Optical Elements, Entangled States, and Quantum Discord Decoherence. System Coherence and Quantum Circuits Slice States at Finite Temperatures. "Going to need a study break just getting through these titles," Drake said to himself. He looked at the abstracts but they might as well have been in an alien language. Something about time, certainly, quantum mechanics, string theory... It was worse than Greek to him.

Drake grabbed his car keys, careful to avoid the mirror that hung in the entryway. He knew what he would find there, he had seen his face in this state before, and wasn't anxious to reintroduce himself. "Mind over matter," he told himself, but he realized the mind was dragging every bit as much as his physical matter. "The hell with it." He slammed the door and raced down the stairs, trying to trigger some buried adrenaline from a fight-or-flight response. It didn't work, but he steeled himself and went on anyway.

Dr. Fox's office was in the same building as Dr. Taylor's. The world was an open place on that first visit, home to any one of a thousand possible paths forward. It narrowed since then, and if he couldn't get something out of Fox, he would be more desperate still. What was left? Use the kids as bait and wait for the monster to show up? That had been Michael Ventura's brilliant idea and look where it got him. With that thought in mind, Drake eyed the stairs but opted for the elevator instead. Dr. Fox was on the top floor, number eight; Taylor had been on the third. Did that convey more or less prestige in academia, Drake wondered as the elevator made its climb toward the top. Around the sixth floor, he decided he was too tired to care about the answer and waited for the doors to slide open at the end of the ride.

The eighth floor was barren compared to the livelier floors below, and he was grateful because that meant less chance of running into Taylor or Beaumont, though the latter at least would be unable to recognize him by sight. He wove through the deserted passageways and found Room 8118 at the end of a long hall, soft light and quiet mumbling coming from beyond the door. On the bulletin board, a cartoon of a lecturer standing in front of a board of labyrinthine equations. *"Along with Antimatter and Dark Matter, we've recently discovered the existence of Doesn't Matter, which appears to have no effect on the universe whatsoever."*

The boxer's footwork kicked in and Drake sidled up to the door lithely as a leopard. He didn't make a sound and leaned his ear against the door to see what he could pick up before announcing his presence. Not much, unfortunately. There was only one voice, which could have been one party monopolizing the conversation, but Drake stayed long enough that he was confident there was no one else in the room. This was a one-sided talk, the kind most people had silently within their own heads. He lingered another half-minute but it was obvious he wasn't going to be able to pick up the particulars of what was being said. He knocked and called out, "Dr. Fox?" That cut off the conversation, if one could call it that, and Drake heard the man turning in his chair.

"Yes, please come in."

Drake pushed the door slowly and was greeted by a large elderly man in a checkered short sleeve shirt and red suspenders. He wore a bushy white beard and hair that followed a style of its own. A sort of Santa Claus-Einstein hybrid, Drake thought with amusement. "What can I do for you?"

"Stan Savapath, *Our World of Science*," Drake said, extending his hand. "I was hoping to ask some questions about one of your students we're doing a story on."

Dr. Fox's eyes flashed alertness and he rose quickly from his chair to shut the door behind Drake. "You're here about Claire," he said, looking him over. "But wasn't it *Our Scientific World?*"

Dammit, is that what he had said? Fatigue had bred carelessness, but he rebounded. "We're still debating that, actually. I prefer *Our Scientific World* myself, punchier, but it's not my decision to make."

"I see."

Drake kept things moving in hopes the mistake would appear less conspicuous as it receded into the past. "Claire Ventura, that's right. I understand you've worked on some projects with her."

Dr. Fox looked to the door and dropped his voice. "You're not from a magazine, are you?"

Drake hadn't known what to expect from the doctor but that wasn't it. "Well, no." He wasn't sure how to handle that question and defensively fell back on the lie. "We're a website, but we'd love to go to print someday!"

"That's not what my colleague believes," Fox said, shaking his head. "You spoke to Dr. Beaumont, yes? He thinks you're a spy of some sort. For whom, he does not know."

Drake laughed out loud. "Why would a spy want

information on a graduate student?" he asked incredulously. The physicist's shrewd stare told Drake the man was unmoved by the whole production. He didn't think Drake was writing an innocuous science article any more than he thought he was the lead dancer in the Russian ballet. No point in even carrying on with the facade, which was good because Drake had grown tired of it. "Why would a spy want information on a graduate student?" he repeated, serious this time.

"Depends on whom he was spying for," Dr. Fox answered. When Drake didn't respond to that, he added, "Well?"

Drake ran through the options in his head, feeling like a computer that had gone from state of the art to obsolete in the past several days. "Ok, no *Our Scientific World,* but I'm not a spy," Drake said. "And frankly, the suggestion is ridiculous." He smiled. "Way above my pay grade."

Fox studied him for a moment and decided he was telling the truth. "What is it you want then, Mr.... ? I trust it's not Stan Savapath."

Drake looked over the man across from him and it was his turn to trust his judgment. "Victor Drake, private investigator."

The doctor nodded. "For whom?"

"I have reason to believe Claire and her boyfriend are in serious danger." Concern washed over the doctor's face. "Not that the university is connected," Drake assured him, "but we've reached the point in the case where I'm desperate for information."

"Data, data, data... You cannot make bricks without clay." Dr. Fox smiled at him genuinely, the kind of smile that extends to the eyes and can't be faked. "Are you a fan of Sherlock Holmes, investigator?"

"Well," Drake said, "aren't we all?"

There had been no sounds from outside the door, but Fox got up and opened it to look into the hallway. Finding it empty, he closed the door and returned to his chair. "Not here, Mr. Drake." He reached into his pocket for a pen and jotted an address on a nearby notepad. "Can you meet me tonight, say 9:00? I'm sure I don't need to say this, but make sure you're not followed."

It was tempting to chalk that last part up to paranoia, but the professor spoke with a gravity that belied such eccentricity. "Certainly."

"Then we will say goodbye until then." Dr. Fox stood up and gestured to the door with his arm, patting Drake on the back as he stood. "With any luck we can clarify some things for each other."

"Certainly," Drake said again, but amended that to add, "I hope."

12

James convinced Claire that if she couldn't go to the safehouse, she needed to stay at his place until the danger was past. He didn't like the idea of her being alone at all, but he couldn't very well chauffeur her and babysit her through classes. It was as good a compromise as they were going to achieve, meaning it left them both equally unhappy.

"You're overreacting," she told him as they were getting ready for bed that night. "He's come after you and my father. And I hate that, but it doesn't mean I'm in danger. I've never even seen this person."

James was tired; not sleepy, but the full-body exhaustion that comes from emotions worn down past their limits. "You're the connection," he said, both of them knowing she hardly needed him to point that out. "He hasn't gone after you yet, but what do you want to do, sit back and wait for that to happen? By which time it's too late to do anything about it?" Pivoting in thought he added, "Is there something you're not telling me? I need you to be honest."

"I've never lied to you," she said.

"That's not the same as being honest."

"You're treating me like a child," she said. "What do you want to do? Keep me under guard, or lock and key, until this gets resolved? Which, I hate to say it but we're both thinking it, might be never?" She took a deep breath and rested her hands on the bathroom sink. Continuing more softly she said, "I can't live my life afraid of what might happen, James."

She was right, of course. "That doesn't make this any easier," James protested, but he knew he lost.

Turning off the bathroom light, she met him in the hallway and wrapped her arms around him. "Then you need to be strong," she said, "for both of us."

Unsure of what to do next, he leaned his head down to kiss her. They went into the dark together.

Claire was gone when James woke up and the house had that museum-like quality he sometimes felt in the morning. Today would be his first day back at work since taking some time off. His shift didn't start until 1:00, so it would probably be dark by the time he got back home. He especially didn't like the thought of Claire alone after the sun had set, but as she said, it was going to take strength to get through this—the strength to let go. They went over every possible precaution, were ready for every paranoia-dreamed situation that would probably never happen anyway. With that done, he could only leave the rest to her and hope for the best. He locked the door behind him and made the drive to work.

His coworkers were welcoming and friendly, but James found it hard to adjust. They had no idea what he was going through; he had neither the desire nor the intention to fill them in, and this created an unseen wall between them. On one side of the wall, the side James wished vainly he was still on, the concerns of running a university gym. Make sure there are enough towels by the pool, don't forget to open up the extra racquetball courts at 4:00, someone reported a leaky faucet in the second-floor women's restroom. These concerns were worse than mundane to him; they were idiotic, the veritable rearranging of deck chairs on the *Titanic.* He couldn't bring himself to care about them while the monster roamed free. The other side of the wall, the isolated side, was James' alone. He shared it with only the dark thoughts and nightmare what-ifs that ran through his head like panicked house flies trapped inside a lightbulb.

He passed the time in this irritated headspace, looking at the clock too often and finding it never progressed as far as he hoped. The door to his office was closed, and while he sat ostensibly alert at his computer, he had mostly resolved to study the pattern in the woodgrain of his desk, eyes and mind zoning in and out in parallel lapses of concentration. The sound of a ringing phone snapped him to attention. Not the professional chime of his work phone but the polyphonic melody he had chosen for his cell phone. The display lit up with an unknown number and he answered it uninterestedly.

"Hello."

A man's voice came through. "Hello, have I got James?"

"This is James."

"James, Detective Morley. We spoke the night of your car accident."

More than a lifetime ago, James thought. How many lifetimes did it take to get back to the existence of perpetual ease he had lived before that day in the gym? Two was selling it short; more like four to six, he figured. "I remember."

"Then you'll remember I said at the time that we weren't

looking at prosecution. Freak accident, the other driver's fault if anything." Indeed, the police's judgment in his favor was one of the only things that had gone his way lately. "Listen, we've had a complication on our end." And... there it was.

"Ok?"

"I'll try to make this as short as I can. Mrs. Haverford, the woman you hit, was a widow, and quite wealthy. Her children, all grown now of course, are making a whole bunch of noise about suing for damages."

James didn't see the connection between any of that and why the detective was contacting him again. But the stronger realization was as to how little time he spent thinking about the poor woman, his victim really, in the wake of the accident. He had never even asked her name, let alone given any thought to the life she had lived, the life he altered forever in his distraction. Excuses could be made: the monster was the one who stopped her car so suddenly, not James. It wasn't clear how he did it, it defied explanation, but James had no doubt that he had, somehow, willed it into happening. Collateral damage be damned. Anyone else behind the wheel of James' car would have suffered the same fate. He was too shocked in the immediate aftermath to summon any compassion, and in the time since then he had moved from one crisis to the next, unable to reflect on what happened on the road that evening.

These rationalizations did little to assuage the guilt that washed over him, powerful and novel. The phone call brought the woman back into sharp focus. She lived as multi-faceted a life as James or anyone he knew, and without the slightest benefit of warning, that life she knew was almost ended. He didn't want to think about what her new life might look like and how the ripple effect of that would affect those closest to her. Were they able to comfort themselves in the unforgiving randomness, in knowing there was nothing they could have done to prevent this, or was that extra torture? Lost in these thoughts, James was aware he hadn't responded in some time. He wondered if that was the appropriate reaction to the call, or if the appropriate reaction even existed.

Morley spoke again. "So there's a son and a daughter and, again, long story short, some big shot lawyer convinces them to make a play for the money. This opportunistic vulture sees this accident, this tragedy, as an opportunity to make a quick buck if he can show you were negligent." Still nothing from James. After a deliberate pause the detective made the implicit explicit: "Which it's easier for both of us if you weren't."

"But I wasn't," James said. "Forget convenience, that's the truth and that's what matters."

"Of course, of course." Morley's sentiment was unconvincing. "The point is, we want to be on the same page for if and when this goes forward. Are you able to meet tomorrow?"

Why did he have to make such a straightforward statement sound so underhanded? Had the detective blamed James as well but was too lazy to fight for a conviction? The idea that Morley, or whoever, looked out for him, saw past the initial appearances of the collision to a measure of wisdom and justice seemed hopelessly naive in retrospect. Better for the department not to have the incident show up on their crime statistics, and better for the prosecutor to not have to risk losing a difficult case, James thought. Was the whole world so cynical and cruel? And, since the answer was so obviously yes, how had he missed it before?

The strong mostly survive, but never mind about the good. Don't ask that question without being able to handle the answer. A month ago it would have been easy for James to place himself favorably on both of those spectrums; not so today. He came to a crossroads and he saw the disparate paths spread before him as clearly as any southeastern sun. If the moment came when he was forced to choose between strong and good, and by all indications, that moment was coming, he would not hesitate. To hell with the good.

"Just let me know what you need," he said.

13

The Blue Valentine was well outside the city, and Drake drove over half an hour into the woods before finding the address Dr. Fox gave him. The bar itself was surrounded by towering pines that blocked out what light the setting sun gave off. He pulled into the small dirt parking lot, gravel crinkling under his tires, and took his keys out of the ignition. Two well-used pickup trucks were off to his left, twenty years old if they were a day, nothing he figured would belong to Dr. Fox. The only other vehicle he could see was a black Triumph motorcycle parked off on its own at the far end of the lot. He made note of the rustic sign, nothing put on about that look, a weathered blue heart with solid block letters carved across its face. A quick scan of the surroundings revealed nothing else of much interest. Drake walked through the door and into the establishment.

He stepped into dim lighting and the sound of country music, George Jones maybe, though he couldn't swear to it, playing from a jukebox standing against the wall. The whole decor was retro, if that's what one could call it, not as a result of keeping up with cycling trends but rather by standing steadfast until the styles looped around again to find themselves back in fashion. Old Budweiser and Miller Lite signs with a shotgun hanging between them behind the bar, which held an array of hard liquors and the basic domestic beers on tap. The bartender was a wiry old man dressed in a black and orange flannel and a scratchy white beard. He glanced up as Drake entered and then returned his attention to the baseball game playing on old CRT television.

The tables and booths were empty, so Drake sidled up to the bar and nodded to the other two old-timers who were drinking there. They didn't pay him any mind and continued their conversation, too low to make any of it out. He arrived early, planned it that way, and didn't count on seeing Dr. Fox come through for a while. The liquor bottles stood lined up like soldiers, and Drake studied them. He silently appreciated the way the running lights played off them, shining like little stars reflected in the mirrors behind them. The bartender still hadn't given him any attention so he raised his hand and asked, "Can I get a whiskey over here?"

The old man turned his head but kept an eye on the TV. "What kind?"

"Make it a White Horse. Double, neat."

Reluctantly turning away from the screen, the bartender pivoted and pulled a bottle out of the line.

"Know your stuff, huh?"

"Nah," Drake said, taking the glass, "just liked the name." He passed a bill across the bar and waved off his change when offered.

The bartender took another look toward the baseball game but decided his new visitor was more interesting. "Haven't seen you in here before," he said casually while grabbing a rag to wipe down the bar.

"First time," Drake agreed. "Nice place."

He nodded. "Well, thank you. Mostly just the regular crowd these days, but I don't mind that too much. Keeps me busy."

"Your place then?"

"Has been for thirty-eight years," the man said. "And I can tell you I take no small amount of pride in that. Ups, downs, whatever changes in the world, The Blue Valentine sees her way through."

"Well, cheers to that." Drake raised his glass. "How's the ballgame going?"

"Ah, hell, the Orioles never did know what they were doing. But I'm dumb enough to keep watching them, so which one of us is the real problem?"

Drake smiled. "Not since Ripken anyway. But he's been gone since, what? Has to be... 2000?"

"Oh, Cal, now he was a ballplayer," he said, returning the smile. "I went up to a game in Camden once, they were playing the Athletics, hell, had to be the early '80s. You remember Oakland had some good teams in those days." Drake didn't remember, not really, but was content to go along for the ride. "Now Baltimore was still a year away at that point, but even then we knew Cal was special. Well, it was early in the game, third inning maybe, and we're down. The A's, they jumped out to a quick lead as I recall. But Cal comes up and he's got a man on base. Pitcher zooms one down the middle, and CRACK! Boy, you should've heard the sound of that bat on the ball! I mean he just hammered it up into the air. It was a night game, and once that thing lifted off, you just lost sight of it. Like that." He snapped his fingers. "Off to the stars."

"He would have been a kid then, just starting out."

"Sure he was. Didn't matter; he was poetry that night. I swear he had a hit every time he came up to the plate. The Orioles pulled ahead then, but Cal wasn't done. Next time he comes up to bat, same pitcher, and WHACK! he hits another one out. Right up into that night sky and out of the stadium, crowd going wild. Knew I was watching something special then." He called down to the two men on the other side of the bar. "You guys remember that O's game we went to? When Cal hit two homeruns?"

The men nodded and voiced their agreement. "Oh sure, Danny. That Cal was something else, wasn't he?"

"Wasn't he a ballplayer?" Danny smiled and returned his attention to Drake. "We used to go to a lot of the games, me and Terry and Fred down there. Not lately though."

Drake sipped his drink. "Ticket prices, parking, traffic on the way back. I don't blame you. A shame some things can't stay the way they were."

"Well, that's the nature of it, isn't it?" Danny said and leaned his back against the wall behind him. "What brings you in, anyway? Like I say, mostly just the regular crowd these days."

"A friend recommended it to me," Drake said. "I'm expecting him shortly actually. Do you know Dr. Fox?"

"A doctor?" Danny was confused. "If anybody that comes in here is a doctor, I sure don't know about it."

"Not a medical doctor, a PhD. He works at Comperio University." No recognition. "Bigger guy, white beard, kind of looks like Santa Claus?"

The light came on. "Howie, you mean. Haven't seen much of him lately. But sure, he would come in once in a while, watch the ballgames in the summer. He recommended it, huh?"

"Said it would be a good place to meet." Drake checked

his watch. "Should be here any minute I think." Finishing his drink, he set it aside. "I'm going to get some air but it was nice talking to you, and I'll be back shortly. Go O's," he added and raised a fist as he made his way toward the door.

"Didn't get your name," the bartender called after him on his way out, but Drake pretended not to hear him and pushed his way into the cooling night.

He checked the time again. After 9:00 now and no sign of the professor. Dr. Fox's number was in his phone, but instead of calling he took out a cigarette and lit it. Maybe he should have felt more urgency than he did, with the monster on the loose, a cryptic physics professor MIA, and several people in varying degrees of danger. Had the monster gone for Fox, gone after him for what he might know? Competent as the professor seemed in his office, Drake didn't like his odds against the man stalking James.

He asked James and Claire to send periodic texts confirming their safety, so he wasn't worried about them for the time being. No one knew where Michael and Rebecca were, which made them just as safe in his mind. He still blamed himself for what happened to Mike, though he hadn't admitted that to anyone. The first time he visited, to see what he could find out about Claire or her father's connection to the events, he made no attempt to travel covertly. If the monster knew all of James' movements, he surely could have tracked him to Drake's office and followed Drake to get to Claire's parents. It wasn't the only possible explanation, but it was the one Occam would have favored.

Which led to another question: how long before Drake himself was added to the man's list, he wondered. Or was he already on it? All these considerations, these thousand possible ways everything could go against him, but in the cool of the dark, breathing out a trail of gray smoke, he felt immune. His needle had been pushed into the red over the last few days, but then a curious thing happened. After the dial moved through Caution and past Extreme Danger, it settled in an area of calm. Maybe it was emotional surrender, or the feeling that things couldn't keep getting worse forever, but he wasn't afraid of the future. Or for the future. What would be, would be, and rather than punch himself ragged trying to fight that, he assented. He would do what he could, everything he could, and then he would succeed or fail. The end result, which he could not control, became less important than how he got there, which he could. At least that's what he was telling himself when a silver hatchback came along kicking up dust and pulled into the parking lot of The Blue Valentine.

Drake and Fox settled into a back booth, as far from the bar as they could, not that the other patrons' actions suggested they were interested in anything other than the baseball game and their own conversation. Drake had another double White Horse in front of him and his companion nursed a pint of beer.

"Where would you like to start?" Drake asked.

"You said Claire is in danger. Serious danger, wasn't it?"

"I did."

"Start with that. How did you get tied into this and what have you learned?"

Drake took a slow drink to let the question hang in the air. When he was finished he said, "Who is Steve Upshaw?"

"Steve, who cares about Steve? You said the young lady is in danger; that's the priority. We start there."

Drake looked away from Fox, slowly, and made a production of picking the drink back up. He met his eyes and raised his glass. "I've got all night."

"Now look here," Fox rested his palms on the table, "you show up at my office, give me a fake name, start asking personal questions about my student, and expect to dictate terms to me? You're dreaming, sir."

"Don't tell me my business and I won't tell you yours," Drake snapped. "We're done lying to each other; we have to be for Claire's sake." He leaned forward. "You want to protect the girl you'd better wrap that brilliant brain of yours around three simple truths. Claire's in trouble, I'm the best chance of getting her out of it, and the longer you hold on to your pride, or whatever it is you think this posturing is accomplishing, the worse it is for her. Do you understand that or do you need a few more diplomas on your wall?"

"You know we typically call them degrees at the post-secondary level," Dr. Fox said kindly.

The remark abated Drake's anger. "Well, there you go." He threw a hand up. "Stepped out of my element and made a damn fool of myself. Not for the first time. You stop trying to play the tough guy and I won't try to accelerate any particles. I promise you, that's going to be best for everyone."

Dr. Fox looked around to see if their rising voices had attracted any unwanted attention, but they were as invisible as ever. "I won't betray her confidence."

"Who is Steve Upshaw?"

Fox looked down into his beer and let out a breath. "That's what I don't understand, Mr. Drake. Well," he laughed softly, "one of the things. We're done lying, right?"

"On my word."

"And you said her boyfriend hired you?"

"Yes."

"But Steve is her boyfriend."

Drake swirled the drink in his glass but had otherwise lost

his interest in it. "That's what Dr. Beaumont said, too. Have you met Steve?"

"No," Dr. Fox said. "But why would I have? I didn't find anything strange about that."

"Nor should you have," Drake agreed. "But I have met her boyfriend, spent time with both of them and her parents." He hesitated before continuing with the last part but felt it was important that both he and the doctor share full-truths. "His name is James Chandler. So why are you all talking about Steve Upshaw?"

"I don't know any James Chandler, but she provided the name herself. There can be no mistake there." They sat in silence and mulled the problem over. "You haven't asked her about it?"

"No. I haven't seen her or James since Dr. Beaumont called me, which led me to your office, which led me here. If the time comes to ask that question, I'll do it in person."

"Well," Dr. Fox said, "I won't tell you your business."

"Sometimes a little subtlety goes a long way, Doc," Drake said, but he had to admit it was a valid point. "Two possibilities then," he posited. "Either she's got a guy on the side, and who am I to judge, or James Chandler and Steve Upshaw are one and the same."

"She's too kind-hearted for that," Dr. Fox said. "The first one, I mean. That's not her. You think this James could have given you a fake name?"

Drake shook his head. "Her parents know him by that name, and his job does too. If that's his con, he's been awfully thorough. And then there's the fact that it doesn't make any sense, does it?"

"Not that I can see. But it's not my business, is it?" Fox had finished his beer.

"Yeah, yeah, take it easy, Doc."

Fox smiled. "Can I get you another drink?"

"Damn right you're paying after that crack. Double, top shelf," Drake said and downed what was left in the glass in one go.

He watched Fox leave the table and turned over the possibilities in his head. He didn't much like either of the explanations he suggested. Unless there was no Steve Upshaw and Claire invented the name for reasons that weren't clear. That fit more with her character—independent, creative, forward-thinking. But it didn't help him answer the question of motive. Not yet anyway.

Fox returned with two drinks. "Cheapest stuff they had," he said, sliding Drake's glass across the table. "Hoped you wouldn't notice the difference."

"Well, I will now... and ice. You couldn't have messed this up more if you tried."

"The night is young," Fox said and toasted. "I answered your questions. Are you ready to answer mine?"

On the television, the baseball game ended in an Orioles loss. Fred and Terry got up from their stools and said their goodbyes to Danny at the bar. "Getting ready to close it up, boys," Danny called out across the room. The two men in the corner booth ignored him and he was content to let them carry on as he packed up the place for the night.

The whiskey was cold in Drake's throat and it followed gravity downward to cool his stomach. He thought of the calm he had felt outside the Blue Valentine and tried to summon its return.

"Shoot."

"What danger is Claire in?" Dr. Fox asked.

"There's a man, at least we think he's a man." Drake laughed at himself. "We've taken to calling him the monster. You have monsters in science, right? You remember

Frankenstein, Doc? They brought him to life with lightning."

"I've read it, yes. That's science-fiction, you understand. We don't sew body parts together and bring them to life, with lightning or otherwise."

Drake nodded and felt the room tilt around him. "Not yet." He laughed again.

"Tell me about the monster."

"The monster. Wait. There is a man, and I know he's a man, but you can call him a monster if you want." He gestured with his drink hand. "I won't stop you. There is a man called Michael Ventura, and in the past he did some bad things." He forced himself to slow down. "Suffice to say, Doctor, some very bad things. And he married a stunner and they had a daughter. And they named her..." Drake pointed at Fox like an overly enthusiastic conductor.

"Claire."

"And they named her Claire," he confirmed. "And she grew older, as children do, and somewhere along the line she met James Chandler. And the two of them," he clapped his hands together. "Ok?"

"You said James was her boyfriend, yes."

"Fast forward to about a week ago. Mike, Michael, whatever, calls me up and says he has a job for me. Now we've hardly spoken in years—no Christmas cards, Doc—but Mike, for all his faults, he remembers the old days. And by god, he remembers Victor Drake. So when his little girl comes to him looking for help, he comes to..." He pointed at himself.

"Victor Drake."

"The one and only. And the price is right and it's what I do, so why not? So James comes to me and tells me the story of this monster who showed up at his work, threatened him, and then at his house with more of the same."

"And now this man, monster if you like, has expanded his target to Claire. Is that the long and short of it?"

"That's certainly the short of it." Drake finished his third drink and set it on the table gracelessly. "The long of it involves superhuman abilities, a seriously injured old woman, a crippled father, and... and a collision course with the unknown." He lifted his head and looked at the professor with eyes like graves. "We're leading to something, Doc. I don't know what." Dr. Fox stayed quiet until Drake spoke again. Finally he said, "What do you make of it?"

The professor's face was reposed in deep thought, just as Drake imagined it must be when he was poring over some especially difficult equation. He had the pieces but could not quite connect them. When he finally spoke, his tone was shaken. "When did you say this monster showed up?"

"About a week ago. Pay attention."

Dr. Fox pressed him. "Surely you have the exact date?"

He should have known that. Maybe he did when he walked into the bar earlier that evening, but he didn't now. "It's in my papers," Drake said. "In my notes at the office, sure."

At the bar, Danny turned out most of the lights and he now came over and rapped his knuckles on their table. "Appreciate you gentlemen coming out tonight, but I've gotta get home to bed. We open at 3:00 tomorrow if you want to come back."

"To Cal Ripken." Drake made his way toward the door with the professor in pursuit.

"I need the date, Drake." That face that had alternated between congenial, annoyed, and perplexed was now scared. "The date the monster came to the gym."

The bar had been dark enough, but outside was solid black except for a couple far-off streetlights hanging over the road. Drake waved his hand as they left, Danny locking the door behind them. "You're a man of science; drop the monster stuff. It—he—is a man."

He fumbled in his pocket for his keys but stopped when an unknown figure stepped into his peripheral vision. "No," it said in a voice like sandpaper.

The alcohol slowed Drake's reflexes and it felt like a tremendous labor to turn his head in the direction of the voice. His senses were blunted, and he reacted to what he found there with a passive sort of placidity. It was James' visitor all right; there was no questioning the veracity of his description now. Drake stood in the cool of the night air and regarded those sunken eyes for a moment, profoundly unsure what he saw in them. And a moment was all he had, because before he could open his mouth to speak, the figure before him changed.

Too dark to see the finer details of the transformation process, he heard a chilling guttural sound and what stood in its place an instant later was enough to break his insistence on using the word man. From now on, no question, it was a monster. At 6'4" Drake had to crane his neck upwards to take in the full scope of the beast, well north of seven feet tall with hands that looked like they could palm boulders. On the end of each of them, claws sharp as concertina wire. It was thin but unmistakably powerful and its eyes shone black, making the darkness around them seem washed out in comparison.

No time to dwell on particulars. Drake's first instinct, as it always was when his life was at stake, was to reach inside his coat for his gun. But his usually-dexterous hands were sluggish and clumsy, and he couldn't grab it cleanly. The creature took one elongated step toward him and swung its left arm, batting its adversary aside as though he were weightless. Drake flew backward into the front passenger side door of his car, landing sideways and denting the panel with a dull thud. Trying to press himself up on his elbow, he found his body insubordinate to his command. Instead he could only lay his head in the dirt, helpless to stop whatever was going to happen next.

The lights in the bar were all turned off now, but Drake counted on Danny still being inside. That was the best place for him. Even if he came out with the shotgun firing, it might not have been enough. No reason for an innocent old man to get caught up in the carnage. But that didn't mean he couldn't help them from where he was at. "911!" Drake yelled. The chances of a police vehicle in proximity weren't great but it felt like the only shot he had. "Danny, 911!"

The monster turned its head at Drake's shouting but regarded him uninterestedly, like a bone a dog has grown tired of. Instead it pivoted to Dr. Fox, who watched the scene in frozen wonder. He stepped backward now, slowly, until he felt the wall of the bar against his back and there was no more room to retreat. The monster approached him carefully, studying him quizzically. "It can't..." he started but couldn't finish. A second attempt: "It can't be."

His voice broke the spell the monster had been under and it pounced, a bolt from the blue. An arm's length away now, it towered over the professor and stared down at him, unspeaking. Eyes still trained on Dr. Fox, it tilted its head, confused as to what it saw when it looked at him. His mouth was open and trembling in an attempt to speak, but no words came out.

The beast reached out a massive hand (or was it better to think of it as a paw?) and put its fingers on either side of the doctor's throat. Not squeezing yet, no pressure, but enough that Fox wasn't going anywhere before it wanted him to.

Laying in the dirt, Drake had been angling his working arm toward the Glock and was finally able to free it from its holster. He pointed it at the monster and yelled to get its attention. "Hey!" His chest cried out in pain at the word; broken rib maybe. Rather than speak again he raised the gun, unsure if that would mean anything or if a bullet would even do anything, but thankful to have the option nonetheless.

The monster locked its attention on Drake and the eye contact made him wince. A color past blackness, those two eyes, something only found in the deepest reaches of space. Never seen on Earth in such raw, unadulterated form, until now. He kept the gun up, finger on the trigger, but didn't move to fire it. Man, demon, or whatever in-between that this form was or had been, he only ever shot as an absolute last resort. And as dire a tableau as this was, he didn't sense he was there yet.

Again it tilted its head, not understanding, but seemingly trying to. It gave up and faced Dr. Fox again, this time closing its hand and lifting him off the ground, closer to its face. The monster leaned forward, eye to eye now, its sulfuric breath filling his senses. Drake angled his gun upward and pulled the trigger, zipping a warning shot over the creature's head. It didn't react but stayed focused on Fox, neither of them speaking. When that didn't help he fired a second shot, closer this time.

"Don't shoot, don't shoot!" Fox looked at him between gasping breaths. "—ake, stop —ting!" In the distance, police sirens; faint but getting ever louder and ever closer.

Drake could tell from the professor's cadence that he was close to passing out from lack of oxygen. Turning his attention back to the monster, back to those onyx eyes, Dr. Fox said, "It's me."

At this the creature howled out and flexed the muscles in its hand till they stood out like steel cables. Drake fired again, at it this time, but between the awkward angle and his exhausted arm, the shot missed badly. Red and blue flashes were visible intermittently in the night sky and the sirens were strong now. The monster sensed them too and let Fox drop to the ground. Still breathing, Drake thought, but in the darkness he couldn't be sure. He stayed conscious long enough to watch the monster cradle Fox in its expansive arms and disappear into the trees.

14

Detective Morley was already sitting at the campus coffee shop when James arrived. He was dressed in plainclothes and nothing about him suggested law enforcement. Still, James recognized him immediately and joined him at his table.

"This lawyer," Morley said, shaking his head. "You've got something simple, you've got it sewn up, and these pricks come along..."

"You said we needed to get on the same page," James said. "How do we do that?"

"Right to it, I like that. Who else knows about the accident?"

"Lots of people. It was pretty big news."

"Not who knows that it happened," Morley said. "Who knows about it, the details."

"Like what?"

"I rewatched the tape of our interview that first night. You remember anything about that?"

"Not much," James said, an honest answer.

Morley leaned in closer and dropped his voice. "There was a comment that struck me as strange. You said you saw something, or maybe the woman saw something anyway, and that's why she stopped so suddenly. That ringing any bells?"

Of course it was, but Morley would have had him involuntarily committed if he told any part of that truth, let alone the entirety of the story. "Seemed like the only possible explanation," James said. "Why else stop like that?"

"To be honest with you, I like my theory better. Stroke, heart attack, whatever... Something medical, we don't need to prove what. And more importantly, it'll play better. The doctors' full focus was on keeping her alive, and it was no easy success from what I'm told. We may catch a break if the injuries she sustained prevent them from conclusively proving or disproving any specific cause. So we keep it vague; reasonable doubt is all we're looking for."

"Aren't you usually on the other side of these things?"

"You're damn right," Morley said, "and that's why I know the strategy. Understand, they're on a wild goose chase here, and it's not about the lady and it's not about the truth. Like everything else, it's about money. And if you saw these people, kid, they're not hurting for money. It's, I don't know, eight million versus nine million. On the math of it that's the same difference as between zero and a million, but you and I know better. It's just these rich people, the dollars become like oxygen, and the more they get, the more they need. Does that make sense?"

It didn't, but James wasn't interested in pursuing its refinement. "Sure."

"I'm not out to do you any favors, you can get that straight too. But these people are making a mockery of the law, twisting it for their own ends, and using this poor woman's tragedy on top of it. Makes me sick." He had finished what was in his paper cup and turned in his chair to toss it in the garbage can. Returning to James, he said, "Now, back to the first question. Who knows, really knows, about the accident? Meaning you told them more than the basics, maybe even mentioned this weird thing you saw? Which, let me finish, if you did see something and that caused you to take your attention off the road, would open you up to a whole mess of personal liability? Who heard that version?"

There were only two other people who knew the whole story at this point. "I told my girlfriend about it, but only the events. I didn't mention seeing anything." He decided to leave Drake out of the answer, less complicated that way. "But listen, if I said something like that in the immediate aftermath, that doesn't mean anything. I was in shock and I had hit my head and it was my first time sitting in a police interrogation room. It doesn't mean anything."

"Right," Morley said. "Go on."

"In fact, sitting with you here now, going over the details in my mind, I don't recall seeing anything strange at all. I don't know why she came to a dead stop, poor choice of words, in the middle of the freeway. Probably some health thing, like you said. But my attention never left the road. It was a terrible accident and I'll live with it forever, but there wasn't anything I could have done to stop in time."

"And that's how it went down, exactly what I've written in my report." Morley seemed satisfied. "You're solid, James, but I'm not taking any chances here." He reached into his coat and pulled a card from his wallet. "A lawyer friend who owes me a favor," he said, handing James the card. "She'd like you to stop by this afternoon."

James looked over the business card he had been given. "Nia Lionel, Attorney at Law," a phone number and email address below that. "So soon? I can't, I have to—"

"You misunderstand," Morley said. "She'd like you to stop by this afternoon, which means you're going to stop by this afternoon."

"I have other things going on in my life you know," James protested.

Morley was unmoved. "Probably so. But I'm in the mood to tie up loose ends, which benefits the hell out of you, because I'm handing you a literal get out jail free card here," he said. "Make the time. Today, 2:30. In and out, and it won't cost you a dime."

The appointment was an inconvenience when he least wanted one, but considerably less of an inconvenience than charges would be if it came to that. He was juggling enough balls for the time being; facing a court case at the same time would have been throwing a chainsaw into the production.

"Fine," James said, "in and out." He thanked Morley for his time and departed the café.

There were fifteen minutes left on his break so he took the opportunity to call Claire and see how she was getting on.

Busy, it turned out. "Yeah, kind of not a great time to talk," she said. "I'll see you tonight though?"

Not the reaction he had been hoping for. "Ok," he said, "sure. Well, take care."

"Actually, one more thing. Did you get a weird text from Drake about an hour ago?"

The three of them had been in consistent communication when they were apart but James hadn't received anything that recently. "No. What did it say?"

"He asked if I had seen Dr. Fox today."

"Your research guy, or mentor, or whatever he is?"

"Yeah. But two things: I haven't, he was supposed to be in today, and how does he know who Dr. Fox is?"

"I don't know, he's a detective. I guess the question is why does he know who Dr. Fox is?"

"Yeah..." Claire didn't elaborate from there. "Weird. Well, like I say, really busy here, but I'll see you soon!"

James had heard Dr. Fox's name in passing, but he didn't know much about him and even less about what Drake would want with him. And why shouldn't he know? This Drake guy was supposed to be working for him. Claire wasn't any more helpful. If they wanted to stay vague and keep him in the dark, let them. That didn't mean he had to sit back and accept it. Stonewalled by his girlfriend and marginalized by his private eye, James resolved to do some exploring of his own.

But first a visit with the lawyer to put that chapter behind him.

15

Claire was able to find Drake's office by herself on her second visit. She knew he wouldn't have summoned her there if he wasn't seeking answers, but she had some pressing questions of her own after that morning so it seemed worth the tradeoff.

"Have a seat," he said when she came in. He moved gingerly and his face was bruised. "Can I get you anything?"

"I'm good." She sat down. "What happened to you?"

"Dr. Fox didn't come in to work today."

"No."

"Do you know where he is? Any contact from him in the past twenty-four hours?"

"No."

"Claire," he said, "I saw the monster last night. It looked like James' visitor at first, but it changed, transformed right in front of my eyes. And then it took Dr. Fox."

She bolted up out of her chair. "What?"

"I don't know which part you're asking about, so let me

just lay it out. Jump in as needed. Please, sit down." When she did, he continued. "We met for a drink last night, some out of the way place he picked. I thought he might be a lead, but last night changed things."

"What made you think he was a lead?"

"Some inconsistencies I found when asking around. I'll get to that. He and I threw some ideas around, more questions than answers I'm afraid. We were just getting somewhere when it was closing time, so we left the bar. The monster was waiting for us outside."

Claire's face was strained in disbelief. "You said he transformed. How is that possible?"

"I wish I knew," Drake said.

"And how did he know you were there?"

"It. It's not a he, Claire. I don't know what the hell it is, but it's not a man."

She bit her lower lip and looked away. "Ok. But you've all seen it now. James and my parents, you and Dr. Fox. Why?"

"I don't know, but you're the only thing that connects all five of us. This keeps getting more dangerous for you, for all of us."

"So we go to the police. I'm tired of living my life looking over my shoulder. It's all gone too far."

"The police showed up last night, but that's getting ahead of it," Drake said. "When the professor and I left the bar, the monster was there. And it's so much worse than James said, Claire. I don't know if it can change at will or if it's evolving, or devolving maybe, but it absolutely is a monster. Some human qualities I'll grant you, the damn thing can talk, but it's not human. Can't be."

"What did it do?"

Drake pointed to his face. "Well, this was first. I went for my gun, but I'd been drinking and it was no good. The thing swept its arm and sent me flying into my car. Knocked me down for a while, but it's a miracle I got away as easily as I did. Next it went for the doctor."

"No," Claire said. She looked away again.

"It picked him up like he was nothing. Fox has to be over 250 pounds, and it lifted him as casually as a glass of water. And it held him there. I couldn't move; I fired a couple rounds from where I was, but he kept saying not to shoot. The bartender was still in the bar and he called 911. By this time the sirens were coming for us, and on some level the monster must have known it was running out of time. Fox was pleading with it, but he could hardly breathe. He told the creature, 'It's me,' and at that it squeezed his throat then let him fall to the ground."

A tear rolled down Claire's cheek. "It's too terrible, stop."

"He's alive, Claire. At least I'm pretty sure. It was hard to see in the dark. But after Fox fell, the monster picked him up, so gently, like a mother. They were gone by the time the cops showed up."

"What did you tell them?"

"That we were jumped. Never saw the guys who did it or what happened to Dr. Fox after they knocked me out. And that the bastards had made off with $200 out of my wallet."

"And the bartender?"

"Cagey old guy. He heard me yell for 911, made the call, and hid under his bar with a shotgun. Heard the commotion outside and decided it was safest to stay put. Best decision of his life."

"So he didn't see anything."

"No."

"And the police bought your story?"

"Of course."

"But that doesn't explain where Dr. Fox is."

"That's why you're here."

Her eyes widened. "How would I know?"

"Well, I don't think you do. But one of the things I discussed with Dr. Fox was Steve Upshaw." She didn't respond. "That name mean anything to you?"

Claire's answer came quickly. "That's the name of my boyfriend I submitted to the university on my personnel file."

"Who is he?"

She shook her head. "This is between us only? I don't know what the confidentiality rules are. You're a private eye, and I'm not even your client..."

"Do you have a dollar?" Drake asked.

"I think so. Why?"

"Give it to me." She did as he asked. "If you only knew how substantially this increases my profits for the year," Drake said. That garnered no reaction so he repeated, "Substantially," and gave Claire a smile. She didn't return it. "Ok," he said, "not in the mood for jokes then."

He continued, "Now you're my client. You can trust me, but I need you to be honest if I'm going to help you and Fox. And James. I don't care enough about what you do in your personal life to judge you for it. Who is he?"

Claire breathed as the weight came off her. "He doesn't exist. I made him up."

"Why?"

"How much do you know about what I do at the university?"

"Not much," Drake said. "I can't make any sense of that physics stuff."

"Well, it's high level for a grad student. They've invested a lot in me and they like to have a lot of information on file."

"Blackmail? Doesn't sound like any university I've ever heard of."

"No, not that," she said. "Just to know if we have relationships that might compromise us."

"Compromise you? You guys stand around filling chalkboards with Greek letters and operations the rest of us have never heard of, isn't that it? Will Hunting stuff?"

"No," she said. "Well, yes. But at some point we have to apply them. Comperio University; we're some of the best."

"I don't doubt it. Sure seems like overkill to me but ok, as you say. So you made up this Steve Upshaw to... what?"

"To protect James. If something goes wrong, I don't want him to be connected. To me, to any of it."

"They have your parents' names, your sister..."

"All that, yes. That would have been easy for them to verify. Relationships come and go, and I figured they wouldn't take the time to check into all of them. We're supposed to update the file any time something changes. It's creepy."

Drake nodded. "Ok. Well you can see why I didn't want James at this meeting, but we'll consider that part solved. Any idea where Dr. Fox could be?"

"He pretty much keeps to himself," Claire said, "as far as I know anyway. Where did you meet him?"

"The Blue Valentine. He ever mention it?"

"Yeah, I think so."

"Any other places he talked about going?"

"Dr. Fox is," she paused, trying to find the wording, "not antisocial, but un-social. Like he carries at all times this sadness below the surface. People think he's aloof but I'm not sure that's quite right."

"Still waters run deep," Drake said offhandedly. "Any other places?"

"I really don't know, Drake."

"That's fine, kind of helpful in its own way, actually. You know where he lived?"

"Somewhere outside Charlottesville. An apartment I'd guess, but I don't know specifically."

"I imagine the university would have that on file," he hinted. She didn't pick it up so he continued, "Do you think you could find out?"

"I don't have access to that," she said. "We're grad students."

"No staff directories?"

"Again, this project, they're all careful. Most students in the department aren't even aware he exists."

That wasn't good enough. "I need the address, Claire, and you're my best shot. His life is at stake; if you could've seen this thing... You need to do everything you can, as soon as you can."

Deep breath. "I'll find it," she said. "And if I have to break the law to do it and get caught, I expect you to be there bailing me out."

"Helping a Ventura navigate the wrong side of the law," Drake said. "It'll be just like old times."

"James will ask what we met about. What should I tell him?"

Drake responded as though the answer were self-evident. "The truth."

16

Whereas Drake's workspace had been a mess of scattered papers, James found Lionel's office to be the paragon of organization. A formidable library of books stood behind her, mostly dark red and dark blue spines, with gold stripes across the tops and bottoms, all lined up immaculately. He tried to make out some of their titles but to no avail. If these volumes represented Lionel's arsenal of arguments, that was encouraging. If nothing else, they made for a reassuring backdrop.

The woman who sat in front of them was smartly dressed and wore stylish glasses with her dark hair up. She wasted little time in guiding James into the seat across from her.

"You got your story straight with Morley?" she asked.

"Yes," James said. "Sudden stop, totally unexpected. Nothing I could have done."

"Good. You stick to that and we're fine."

"That's it?" It seemed too easy.

"I've reviewed their case, if you want to call it that, and

it's such a reach," Lionel said dismissively. "Scare tactic, nothing substantial behind it. Can't say I blame them for trying though. You're a young kid, no representation as far as they know, why not rattle the sabers a little and see if they can shake out some money?"

"Right," James said.

"Scare tactic," she repeated. "Sign here," she said, passing a pre-drafted letter across the desk to him. "I'll send out our response today, and that will be the end of it. Get them off your back; more importantly, off Morley's back. And then, most importantly, he's off mine. Win-win-win."

James read the letter and, satisfied, signed and dated at the bottom. "I really appreciate it," he said, rising from his chair. "This was such a weight on my mind and—"

"Have a great day, James." Lionel shook his hand and led him to the door. "Time is money, as they say."

With that, James was walking back across the parking lot feeling as though he had just barely arrived. But what did he care if the lawyer wasn't the empathetic, nurturing type? She would free him from the legal and mental trap that threatened to pull him under.

The sun greeted him warmly and he jumped into the air just to appreciate the power of his legs propelling him upward. It was a capricious thing and, as he landed, self-consciousness won out. He looked around the lot with a little embarrassment but found no one watching him, so he jumped again. Returning to the ground, he allowed himself a brief smile. It didn't last, and his mind returned swiftly to the reality of his circumstances.

Nothing from his meeting with Morley made James believe the detective thought him innocent. At best the man was indifferent to James' culpability in the old woman's injuries. Luckily that lazy brand of cynicism was working in

James' favor for now, but that didn't do much to lessen his annoyance. At least he had Claire and Drake, except maybe not even that, now that they were conspiring to meet behind his back. Even before their exchange this morning there were times he felt like an afterthought to Claire. Like her job at the college was her number one priority and he was a distant second. That, tight as their bond was, they were on different trajectories. A slow drip of water; nothing that would compromise the structure of the relationship in the immediate future, but there was a National Park of some renown in Arizona that was testament to the power of subtle force plus time.

He was already on campus anyway, so James ventured over to the Physics Building. It was not somewhere he generally spent time, a couple visits with Claire in the early days, but he hoped he might catch her. If he was honest with himself, he knew she would be annoyed at him showing up unannounced, especially at such a busy time, whatever that meant. But under this ugly cloud he didn't much care about how she'd react. It seemed more important to have a talk in person and not a conversation by proxy through their phones.

Classes were getting out as James arrived at the building. After a brief, futile attempt to fight against the stream of students exiting he conceded defeat and waited for them to pass through the doors before making his way inside. They weren't much younger than him, some of the grad students were probably even older, but he felt apart from them even while surrounded by them, a poor imitation of their brilliance. It was the height of egocentrism, he knew, to think they noticed him at all, but he still imagined them looking down at him as he stood outside waiting for them. These young men and women would go on to put airplanes in flight, patent life-saving inventions, manifest their ambitions in ways he wouldn't even be able to understand. Ten, twenty years on, would he still be filling out guest passes and checking pH levels in the pool? Would that be his lasting contribution to humanity? Claire fit so much better into the first world, he realized with heartbreaking clarity. No wonder her work had resulted in a wall between them.

The students were gone now but still he lingered outside the door. The entrance became a threshold, or maybe a yawning chasm, and he wasn't sure that if he stepped across he would land safely on the other side. Instead, he stood outside the building a while longer; its upper floors loomed above him and he stared up at them as though he had just arrived from some distant past, never before glimpsing such an impressive edifice. The brick was deep red, blood red, and the mirrored windows looked like they had been transported from some fantastical dream. He didn't even know where to look for her, James realized, or what his cover story would be if he had to ask about her. She discussed so little of what it was she actually did here, resolutely dancing around the specifics when he asked until it became easier to avoid focusing on the details.

Did graduate students have their own offices? Some of them taught classes as part of their scholarships, and they would need a place to meet with students, but Claire was strictly research-oriented. He could have asked someone, but his pride was already hurt and he refused to do anything that would further solidify the fact that he didn't belong there. Not that he belonged anywhere anymore, except maybe on the defendant's side of a courtroom soon. This relationship had been the bedrock of his life for what felt like such a long time. He was starting to conceive of it closer to a freshly painted house of wood that had rotted from the inside, and the paint could not mask the deeper problems forever.

There was his job, suspended in some strange state of stasis; he didn't want to lose it, but the thought of keeping it long-term depressed the hell out of him. It felt too late to start over; his age didn't rule out a career change, but he would be entering the workforce with no college education and no specific training. Maybe the managerial experience would transfer to the business world, but that existed in his head as some vague nondescript ecosystem no more attractive than another thirty years at the campus gym. Beyond that, no alternatives that called out to him with arresting passion. The only feeling worse than wanting something and not getting it was not wanting anything at all.

He nearly decided to turn around and return to work, or not, to just go wherever. But that felt like the lazy, even cowardly, way out. Letting out a breath, he crossed over the barrier he built up in his mind and located the directory. A list of names he didn't recognize, no Ventura, but finally toward the end he saw Dr. Fox, Room 8118. That name meant something to him and he hoped Claire would be there, or at least nearby. She said Dr. Fox wasn't in today but even so, maybe he could find someone who knew where she was. James didn't know what he would say if and when he did find her, but he trusted the words would come. A cloud mirrored his movements lately and maybe seeing her would be enough to break its spell. A chance worth taking if nothing else.

The elevator carried him to the top level; when he got out the floor was deserted. Finding Dr. Fox's office, he knocked on the door but got no response. "Excuse me," he said. "Dr.

Fox?" Only silence in return. He turned down another hall. "Claire?" Nothing. Circling the floor he called out, "Hello, anyone?" Again only silence. No sounds even from the other floors or outside—just stillness and that fog-like silence. He felt like the last man on Earth, some unlucky survivor of the total destruction of humanity and maybe all life. It was an unsettling feeling, and he walked over to a window to make sure he could still see people when he looked out. Sure enough, far below him, pedestrians walked past and cars moved down the road in an orderly file.

In that moment he was a part of the world but separated from it too. He watched the people transversing the perfect geometry of the sidewalks or lying in the grass like dead soldiers. They were ants on a farm and went about their lives not knowing or caring about his presence, his very existence. The idea was lonely and it was freeing; while part of him wanted to join them and interact again with the world, he didn't move—just stood watching. James Chandler's Tower of London, except his warden wasn't a paranoid uncle; he had imprisoned himself. Less imprisonment than removal, he thought, and those two things aren't the same at all. Except maybe in consequence.

"Hey!" he yelled, surprising himself with the volume of his voice. "Hey, how is this whole floor empty? I demand," he laughed, "I demand an explanation! My taxes pay your salary!" He laughed again. This impressive structure, all brick and ivy, reaching a gravity-defying eight floors into the air. A product of the intellect and work ethic of people long since dead, architects and laborers, imagination and muscle. But now, in this moment, it was his domain alone.

If he wanted to smash out the windows, put a sledgehammer through the wall, or marry a match to gallons of gasoline, no one was there to stop him. He was tired of being afraid, tired of hurting, and the best solution seemed to redirect that pain, to destroy something beautiful. Destructive impulses pulled at him like wild horses, but he fought against them as best he could. The peace of the 8th floor would be an adequate victim. Nothing was more beautiful than silence, and shouting out seemed to him wholly-justified rebellion.

"Hey!" he yelled out again. "I'm talking to you!" He stomped his foot and, finding that wanting, stomped them both, then jumped up and down for maximum impact. He pounded on the walls, unconvincingly at first, then powerfully, like a silverback separated from its infant. The framed pictures lining the hallways trembled and eventually fell, their connections to the walls broken. They came tumbling down and some broke, but James didn't care. He kicked the walls now, a viciousness borne of something other than anger. He had just begun to tire when the sound of an elevator bell rang down the hallway. The doors opened with a mechanical whir and James heard footsteps approaching. He surveyed the damage around him but made no effort to escape.

Two sets of footsteps it seemed, though the echoes danced around him and made it hard to differentiate where one ended and the next began. He cast his eyes down the hallway and waited for whoever was coming, like a dog who sensed its owner would soon return home, patiently but persistently. They turned the corner synchronized, two large men in dark polo shirts.

"Hold it!" one of them shouted. James regarded the men with a passive kind of curiosity but otherwise didn't react to their presence. Apparently they expected him to run. When he didn't, they exchanged a glance with one another and approached him slowly.

As they got closer, James got a better read on them. Even larger than they appeared at a distance, mid-thirties he guessed, clean-shaven with dark hair and dark eyes. They shared an unusual degree of resemblance. Not twins but maybe a cloning experiment gone almost, but not entirely, right. No distinguishing characteristics in their faces and hair really, only their muscular builds stood out. He racked his brain in search of what adjectives he could use to describe them if it came to that. Generic? Forgettable, unremarkable. *That's convenient,* he thought.

"What's going on up here?" The other one spoke this time. James scanned the halls as though the answer might be there.

Finding nothing, he returned his attention to the men. "Who are you?"

"What are you doing on this floor?"

"Isn't it obvious?" James said. He gestured around him. "How long do we have to keep talking in questions?"

One of the men reached into his pocket but the other stopped him. "We're security," he said. "This is destruction of property."

"No," James said. "To the first part. The second part, um, yeah, you've got me there. You're not DPS, not cops, so..."

"Campus security."

"No uniforms, of course, that's only natural," James nodded. "Well then, open and shut case I'd imagine. Destruction of property, caught in the act even." He kicked the wall again for good measure. "Just let me see some credentials and you can take me in."

Instead, one of the men reached out with his right hand and grabbed James' shoulder, pinning him against the wall. His back hit hard and he lost his breath momentarily as the nerve endings in his left shoulder cried out in distress. Gasping for air that wasn't there, James tried to free himself from the vise that ensnared him. It was no use. Before he could think about his next move, the man raised his left arm to eye level and threw a punch at James' right ear. The fist exploded as if spring-loaded; it whispered past him with violent velocity and found its target in the wall behind him. The brick shattered beneath its force and the man withdrew his hand gingerly.

James recoiled in disbelief, distrusting of what his eyes saw. The man across from him wore a blank expression. Their eyes met but James could read nothing in them. He tried again to shake himself free but it was no use; he kicked at his captor with full force but would have had better luck trying to go through the wall behind him. Tiny pools of tears filled his eyes and he felt a hand seize his throat and its fingers contract. Inside his ears, he felt his heart pounding like a timpani. Steady at first, then swelling to an orchestral climax before the distant sound of a bell pulled away his attacker's attention.

James felt himself slowly lowered to the floor. The soles of his feet touched down first, but the legs above them were not strong enough to support his weight. He collapsed in a heap, like a curtain knocked from its supports. Through bleary eyes he saw the man nod to his companion in the direction of the chime. James was unsure of, and not especially interested in, what caused the sound, but he wanted to kiss it all the same. The mental image made him laugh weakly, from his ridiculous pile on the floor. He closed his eyes then, anything for a moment's respite, and heard people speaking in deep, low voices. There was another sound he couldn't place; a high-speed fan maybe, or a spray of liquid, but it quickly died off. A scent came over him, lemon-like but more acrid and intense, and the voices resumed. *Can't make out the words,* he thought, *but almost.*

"Whoozee?"

"Donno. Nupin arown a pier."

"Tell you do atfour?"

"Donno. E gots mart."

"Kimmup."

"Huh?"

"Kimmup! Now!"

James felt the strong hands shaking him vigorously and flashed back to seeing the gorilla in the suitcase commercial, with his limp body taking the place of the luggage. More stupid laughter. The shaking resumed, harder now, and James' eyes opened of their own accord. He squinted against the new light (when and how did it get so damn bright?) and saw three men looking down at him. The two he had seen before were still there—"Tweedle Dumb and Tweedle Dumber," he tried to address them but his mouth wouldn't cooperate—but they were now joined by an older, dark-haired man in a white coat. "And who might you be?" James tried to say, thinking this very suave and clever, but it came out a slurred mess.

"Get him up," the older man said. He had dark, serious eyes and heavy creases across his face, and he wore a red ring on his right hand. The bruisers lifted him to his feet but found he couldn't support himself.

"No balance," James said. That realization should have scared him, but he was instead overcome with a sense of accomplishment at finding that the words came out clearly this time. "Hold me up, will ya?" He laughed again.

The man in the lab coat nodded at his goons and they each took an arm to keep James standing. James and his new acquaintance studied each other for a moment and the man said, "Again, who are you?" Patient but firm, that question.

"I'm here to see Claire." That banished the delirious lightheadedness.

A note of recognition in the other's face and he asked for the third time, "Not what are you doing here. Who are you?"

"I'm her boyfriend. Who the hell are you?"

James felt the grips on both arms tighten violently. This time his mind flashed not to cartoonish advertisements but to medieval scenes of doomed men being drawn and quartered, screaming as malevolent forces overwhelmed their bodies' structural integrity. He winced audibly but it had no effect on the man across from him.

After what seemed a very long time the new man's face relented and he said, "No need for that." The grips loosened in synchronicity, not to the point of comfort but at least they were no longer actively punishing James' aching arms. "We're very fond of Claire here," he continued. "She does great work." He smiled. "Do you feel well enough to stand?" Another nod and the two men on either side of James released their handle on him.

He set his arms out uncertainly, feeling like a novice surfer whose ambition may have overshot his skill. But this time instead of tumbling down he remained upright. "Thanks," he said, unsure of whom he was thanking or for what exactly. Only then had he steadied himself enough to notice the name tag affixed to the white lab coat.

"You're Dr. Beaumont," he said, a revelation. "Claire talks about you. She says you're some kind of super-genius."

Dr. Beaumont laughed softly and looked away from him. "Well... Do you believe her?"

"She's never given me any reason not to. Is it true?"

"It's certainly true she says that," Beaumont said and put a hand on James' shoulder. "We're all set here, gentlemen," he said to the others. "Thank you as always for your enthusiastic service." The two men departed in the opposite direction from which they had come, bound for somewhere James couldn't tell. "Walk with me... I'm sorry, your name?"

"James."

"Walk with me, James. I don't know if Claire is downstairs, but you certainly won't find her up here."

"Right," James said. It seemed so simple now.

"Are you a student as well?" Dr. Beaumont asked, his hands on James' back, pushing him gently toward the elevator.

"Yeah," James said. "I—wait, no. No. I was, well we all were, but—" The words deserted him. "What was I saying?"

"This way, James. Let's see if we can find Claire."

James stopped moving and turned around. "No," he said. "Or yes, but wait." He looked back to where they had come from, where he had his encounter with the nameless men. He never got their names, but he wouldn't forget their faces which were... No, he didn't know those either, not anymore. They were twins though, or almost. But not quite. Spiky hair, or maybe bald, but they had beards, he thought. Goatees anyway. And there was a question he should be asking, an obvious thing, but...

Dr. Beaumont put a hand on his shoulder and pointed him back in the direction of the elevator. "This way. Can I get you something to eat, or drink? Hot out there today, isn't it?"

James offered no resistance. "Hot out there today," he agreed. "Could be hotter tomorrow."

17

Claire came through with Dr. Fox's address almost immediately. Smart girl, Drake thought, a problem solver, and it made him proud to know her. No missing persons report, not yet, but there would be soon so he wasted no time in heading over to see what he could find. Claire's apartment hunch had been way off as it turned out. She was smart, not infallible. Fox's homestead, like his bar, was set apart from civilization proper. Surrounded by tall pines, it was a modest house but well-built and well-kept.

Drake kept his senses alert as he pulled into the empty driveway but noticed nothing out of the ordinary. When he cut the engine and stepped out of the car, the only sounds left were an implacable buzzing of insects and the occasional birdcall from high in the trees, sounding for all the world like some too-perfect nature soundtrack. Every so often a welcome breeze blew in from the east to do what it could to alleviate the stifling heat. What it could do didn't amount to much.

After walking up the drive Drake circled the premises slowly, casting a deliberate eye over the house. Better to call it a cabin, he thought, its exterior a skeleton of wide, strong logs. One and a half stories by the looks of things with a roof that sloped low over the sides of the place. Peering in the front and back windows, he could see no signs of activity and resigned to leave the cabin be for the moment. The silence (or as close as nature ever came to silence) was like the glass surface of an undisturbed lake. Drake looked around a couple seconds longer and, finding nothing of interest, called out to see if that would have any effect.

"Fox!" he called. "You in there? Or out here?" His words rang out for an instant, then died unanswered. "What the hell did that thing do with you?" he wondered more quietly. The curtains were mostly drawn over the windows and both entrances to the house were locked. He opted for the back door where he wouldn't be seen by anyone passing by on the road. Picking the lock was easy work, but when Drake pushed the door inward it didn't move. Deadbolted apparently, and damn well at that. The front door was equally fortified and none of the ground floor windows opened.

Tiring work sometimes, getting nowhere, and he stopped to wipe the sweat that pooled on his forehead. He spit in the dirt and looked for another way in. The sloping roof looked promising, if a bit higher than he could get to on his own. Not finding much around the property, Drake pulled his car up close to the house and stood atop it. The footing was a little awkward but he persevered, using an overhand grip to boost himself up onto the cabin's roof. Not a bad view from the higher elevation, and although time was against him he paused for a heartbeat to appreciate it.

"*I think that I shall never see a poem as lovely as a tree,*" he said to himself, and it was true the dark evergreens rose beautifully into the cloudless wall of blue. He singled out an especially tall straight one and ran his eyes from its wide base up toward the thinning branches. His eyes stopped before they reached the top—something unnatural in the innate geometry. A pair of binoculars lay on the front seat of his car, so he had to descend to retrieve them then climb back up to his perch to investigate his suspicions.

The object appended to the tree bark, for that's what had caught his eye, seemed impossibly small and well-disguised in a color close enough to make any paint matcher proud. But it bulged slightly against the clean line of the tree, and a more detailed inspection revealed elements of metal and glass entirely out of place in the forest. Whatever it was was pointed directly at the house, which suggested a camera, though Drake didn't see what a physics professor would need with a high tech and elaborately-hidden camera, hell, maybe a whole system of surveillance. Paranoia was a possible explanation, but it was an unsatisfying one. No, Fox seemed sound enough... Some other reason then.

Drake saluted the camera, though he didn't know why, and returned to his search for a point of entry into the cabin. No luck with the windows on the upper floor either. The sun beat down on him and he didn't know how much longer he could count on having a private audience with the doctor's residence. Convinced he had exhausted all his other options, he took out a slapjack and broke one of the windows. He half-expected to trigger a barrage of machine gun fire, or a shrieking alarm at least, but the glass only shattered cleanly, almost silently. He carefully cleared away the jagged edges left behind, pushed aside the thin dark blue curtain and crawled inside.

Must be what climbing into an oven feels like, he thought.

It didn't take a particle physicist to know that heat rises. The combined effects of the sweltering August day and the total lack of ventilation made the room hot enough that it became difficult to breathe. The sweating had been a minor nuisance while outside, but upon entering the cabin he felt as though he had spent the last several hours hiking through some tropical rainforest. Shedding the short-sleeve button-up shirt he had been wearing, Drake stood in a sleeveless white undershirt and worn jeans. He wished he could ditch the pants too but resisted the urge.

Outside, he needed to squint against the harsh sunlight, but the other side of the window required peering into a cave by comparison. Drake waited for his eyes to adjust, thought of throwing open all the curtains, but decided the cover was more valuable than the extra illumination. He knew this would likely be his only shot at searching the cabin. Time was running out, either before someone found Fox (hopefully alive, but maybe otherwise) or he would have to be reported missing. His car left behind outside the Blue Valentine may have already raised questions. Either way, this place would soon be off-limits to freelancers, regardless of their intentions.

Darker than in the full rays of the sun but not dark enough for a flashlight. A fraction of the sunlight powered through the curtains and Drake saw dust particles floating in the light that survived. He had no choice but to take a deep breath of the stuff, searching for fresh air within the oppressive heat. Mostly dead skin presumably, some of it maybe decades old. His mind went to an image of Fox as a corpse—pale, cold, and rigid; immediately identifiable as anything but alive. Nice guy, the professor, but he was soft. The monster could have torn him to ribbons at a moment's inclination. It could have done the same to Drake, to be fair.

But it hadn't.

The sounds of the world were left outside. They refused to follow Drake into the house, ostensibly out of respect or maybe apprehension. Not that he'd blame them. He didn't believe in supernatural ideas like dark energy but the place was creepy, and although he was as present there as anywhere he'd ever been, it felt more like looking at a photo from a history textbook of the unremarkable that no one could be bothered to read.

The carpet under his feet was a heavy green shag. He couldn't imagine it had ever been in fashion, though he had to admit he hadn't paid much attention to interior design trends over the years—always best to recognize your limitations. It had the effect of making his feet feel heavy too, like he was wading through quicksand, and he hesitantly stepped deeper into the maw of the seemingly-empty house.

The upper floor was one open room that felt cavernous despite its modest size. No chairs, beds, or anything that indicated anyone spent time up there; more of a storage space it seemed. Cardboard boxes were piled high, along with newspapers, printer paper, and an assortment of scientific-looking instruments Drake didn't recognize. *Part hoarder, part hermit, part mad scientist,* he thought. A cursory glance revealed physics articles, academic journals, study data, whatever else; he didn't comprehend any of what he was seeing, let alone retain it. He resisted the temptation to go through the boxes, or to see what he could make of the strange devices. Crowded and claustrophobia-inducing as they were, there might have been a system of organization behind the clutter, the specifics of which were perhaps known only to its deviser. With nothing more to gain on that level, he found the railing leading down and slowly descended the stairs.

Not quite as hot on the main floor but still warm and dim with a heaviness to the air that made him feel as though he were moving through molasses. A more conventional scene down there with a standard living room, dining room, kitchen setup, all of which Drake could see from his station at the foot of the staircase. Where the upstairs was a chaotic sprawl of accumulation, Fox had gone the opposite direction downstairs, and the other rooms were exceedingly sparse. Some slight, scattered decorations on the wall, no TV in the living room, no books or papers left lying around, nor anything else to suggest a man lived out his life in that space. *Might be he doesn't spend much time here*, Drake thought.

Something out of place though. Along one wall he saw a flowing blue blanket wrapped clumsily around something good-sized. More than good-sized, he realized, human-sized. His eyes swept over the room one more time before cautiously approaching the pile. No bad smell, which was a good sign, but the heat in the house was unrelenting and his instincts told him to expect the worst. He pushed at the blanket gently with his foot and felt something hard beneath it. A body, little doubt.

Drawing his gun in his right hand, Drake reached out with his left to pull the blanket away. Two schools of thought here: quickly and decisively, like a Band-Aid, or gradually and methodically, revealing the picture a fraction at a time. No sense in putting off the unpleasant; Drake ripped the cover off in one smooth motion. He might as well have pulled back the sheet in a morgue. Fox was underneath, and he was as still as midnight. No signs of distress that Drake could see; more like Sleeping Beauty, hold the beauty. His hand shot to the professor's throat and found a weak but persistent pulse. Fox's chest rose and fell in slow, sedated breaths, and Drake had to remind himself to let out a breath of his own.

The doctor was unconscious and didn't respond to his gentle summons to break back into the land of the living. Drake took the opportunity to step back from the scene and consider his next move.

Priority one was obviously Dr. Fox. The blanket was no longer smothering him but the house remained dangerously hot for someone in his condition. The easy solution was to move him outside and call for an ambulance, but he saw two problems with that. Firstly, he couldn't be sure of Fox's potentially unseen injuries, maybe internal, maybe the spine or neck. Medical degree or not, he knew enough that his first obligation as in loco caregiver was to do no harm. Too risky to move him until he knew how he ended up buried alive in a sweltering, and locked, house.

Secondly, selfishly, a hospital visit would invite the police and all their encumbering questions. Whatever this case was, he felt he was progressing slowly (maybe too slowly), and it called for a delicate, deliberate touch, not whatever bunch of clumsy meddlers they called up from the local precinct. No police, not yet. He had yet to see a bad situation that couldn't be made worse by getting the cops involved. But it wouldn't be up to him for long. Fox was missing, the university knew it, and the room he stood in would be their first stop when the authorities were inevitably contacted. He could tell Claire he found him, but he couldn't say with certainty that her first call wouldn't be to the police too. Lies of omission were easier on the conscience, so he held off on contacting her until he had more to report.

No air conditioning in the house but Drake plugged in a nearby fan to get some air flowing over Dr. Fox. There was a pitcher of cold water in the refrigerator so he filled a glass and brought it over to where he had left the other man lying. He poured some of the water into a rag and placed it on

Fox's forehead.

"Ground control to Dr. Fox," he said. "Can you hear me, Dr. Fox?" That got no reaction so he grabbed ahold of Fox's shoulders and shook him carefully. "Nap time's over, Doc. We're up against the clock here and I need to lean on you some." A flutter of eyelashes, or was that his imagination?

"The hell with it," Drake said and threw the icy water over Fox's face. That startled the professor awake, though not as far as alert. He sat up and looked around the room without comprehending his environment, a puppy trying to navigate stairs for the first time. "There he is! Take it easy Doc, nice and easy." Drake put a hand on his chest. "Slow breaths, all right now."

Finally Fox's gaze settled on Drake and recognition flashed across his eyes. "Mr. Drake? Where the devil am I?" he asked, sitting up.

"You don't recognize this place?" Drake gestured to their surroundings. "It's your house, man. Come to it."

Fox nodded, maybe not believing him yet, but willing to entertain the idea. Drake patted him on the shoulder and went to refill the water glass. "What happened?" Fox asked, trying to get to his feet and then thinking better of it.

Drake returned with the water and handed it to him. "I was hoping you'd be the one with the answers. Are you hurt?"

Dr. Fox took the glass from him and finished half of it in one unbroken drink. He set it aside and wiped the water from his lips, took a deep breath, then returned his attention to Drake. "No," he said, "not hurt. Not at all I don't think."

"Thank God for small favors," Drake said. "The last I saw of you was outside the bar and that creature, or person, or whatever the hell it is, dragged you out. Thought you may have been done for. What do you remember after that?"

"How long have I been out?" Fox asked. "The university, they must be in a panic. I've got to tell Dr. Beaumont and—"

"Take it easy, Doc. Take a minute here, or five." He patted his shoulder, hoped it came off more reassuring than it felt, and infused his voice with a slow, deliberate calm. "Nice place you've got here. Bit rustic for my taste, but..." Drake's eyes monitored the professor's breathing as it took on a more composed rhythm.

Drake got up off the floor and walked around the room, taking in what he could of the scenery and decor, looking for something he could use to raise Fox's spirits and get him back to right.

An old newspaper affixed to the wall bore a front-page story on the Boston marathon. Seven, maybe eight, runners in the foreground clad in red, blue, and a wash of neon aged by light and time. "You a distance runner?" Drake gestured to the photo.

Fox's eyes went to where Drake was standing and some color came back into his round face. "Oh my, no," he laughed and patted his considerable midsection. "I just admire the spirit of the thing—the mental toughness. That was one I traveled to see in person."

Drake nodded but kept his eyes on the wall, seeing through the years. "No," he said at last. "That's you, third from the left." Dr. Fox rose from the floor, a great labor in his condition, and joined him at the wall. "An impressive eye. Thirty years gone by, sir." He gazed wistfully at the man he had been. "Where does the time go?"

"Thirty-three years," Drake pointed out the date in the upper left corner, "but who's counting?"

"I was a fitness freak like you wouldn't believe," Fox said, his spirits brightening. "Like you wouldn't believe."

"What happened? No offense."

Fox laughed again. "Oh, don't worry about that. Not like I haven't noticed." He slowly found his way to an overstuffed armchair, content to leave his answer at that.

Drake was less satisfied. Turning away from the wall he repeated, "What happened? Nothing so pedestrian as a slow decline, career commitments, the research... No, I don't buy that." He turned back to the picture. "Not this guy."

"Quite right, Mr. Drake, quite right." The other man had no response for that so he added, "Life happened."

"Sure," Drake said, still studying the paper. "Well I didn't bring it up to bring you down."

"*Though much is taken, much abides,*" Fox began. "*And though we are not now that strength which in old days moved earth and heaven, that which we are, we are,*" he continued. "*One equal temper of heroic hearts made weak by time and fate, but strong in will, to strive, to seek, to find, and not to yield.*"

Drake had turned his attention back to the doctor. "Byron?"

Fox shook his head. "Tennyson." He added sympathetically, "Close though."

"How about that? A man of science and art," Drake remarked.

"The same thing, Mr. Drake, when done well."

"I've felt that way myself sometimes, a foot in each world," Drake said. "Standing on the shoulders of giants."

"Indeed. Now are we done dancing around what you really want to ask?"

Drake grinned. "I suppose that'll do, sure. Let's step outside. Hot out there too but it will do good to get you some air."

"Yes, air sounds good, and more water. My mouth is a

desert." The two men made their way into the bright sun and found a shady spot underneath one of the tall timbers.

Drake gave Fox his arm to steady him to the ground and prompted him again, "The last thing you remember from that night at the Blue Valentine."

"I'm not sure," Fox said. "Let me sit here a moment and the recollection may come. It's in there somewhere, I'm sure, but I can't yet grasp it."

"Memory can be like that," Drake nodded. "Ghostlike, on the edges. Take your time," he added, although he wanted nothing more than to rush the answers out of him. Fox was right about the urgent need to contact the university, which would of course lead to questions about his disappearance. They'd need some way to spin that, he knew, something believable. To say nothing of the monster that was on the loose, and maybe after James or Claire. He wanted to call and check in on them, but they would want information like anyone else, information he didn't yet want to give them.

"We stepped out of the bar, into the dark," Fox spoke up.

"That's right."

"And he, or it, was there, waiting for us."

"Too convenient to be a coincidence," Drake agreed. "Didn't know at the time if it was after me or you, but maybe we got our answer on that account. It's a start anyway. Then what?"

Fox chose his words carefully. "It picked me up. And you had a gun, you wanted to shoot it. I tried to stop you, but you shot anyway."

"Missed badly for what it's worth. Why didn't you want me to shoot?"

Fox ignored the question and continued his retelling of the night in question. "I guess that scared it anyway because it took off, with me in tow, through the woods. It was so fast, Drake. Swift as an arrow through that heavy forest, never a misstep."

"That matches up pretty well with what I saw from my vantage point on the ground. But I couldn't follow, and that's where we separated. What next?"

"I was knocked out," Fox said. "I must have been."

"By the monster?"

"No, not the monster." He laughed bitterly. "Listen to us, two grown men, with this monster talk. It's not a monster, Mr. Drake."

"I saw it," Drake said. "Monster fits the bill just fine."

"It didn't hurt me. I hit my head on a tree maybe. The speed we passed through those woods, it would have been a miracle if I didn't. Next thing I know, you're throwing a glass of water in my face."

Drake thought that over and decided he was satisfied with the answer. "Ok. So it knew to bring you here, that's something. Why take you in the first place? What's the connection?"

"It was scared," Fox said. "If it stayed any longer, you would have killed it."

"God willing... So why did it come to the bar?"

"I don't know."

"Maybe not, but you must have an idea. Why you? And what's this got to do with James and Claire?"

"We have to get back to the university," Fox said. "I don't have answers and that's the truth, but that's our best hope of getting some."

"Now don't hold out on me," Drake said, looking through him. "Not with my people at stake and that thing running around out there."

"I have a possible explanation," Fox confessed, "but I

refuse to believe it. Not without a lot more evidence behind it."

A beat passed and then Drake grabbed ahold of Dr. Fox's collar and slammed him back into the tree. "Have I got your attention now? I don't take chances. Tell me what you know and then we take you back. Not the reverse."

The initial alarm gave way to resolve in Fox's pale blue eyes. "Impossible," he said. "We can hole up under this tree all day if you want, or you can keep hitting me, but they will come for me. Unless you want to kidnap me? Time is against you."

That was true, and while Drake didn't want Fox to know he had won the point there didn't seem to be much chance of hiding it either. "As you say," he growled, and stormed off in the direction of his car. "Well, let's get going then."

18

Dr. Beaumont led James into some kind of holding tank of a room and he had been waiting there for... hard to say how much time. It was a pleasant room really, cool yellow walls and soft lighting, painted scenes of beaches and open oceans spread evenly across its walls. James felt as if he had been there no more than a couple minutes, but no, that couldn't be right. He checked the time on his phone, almost 5:30. But he had come to see Claire back at... he couldn't say. After lunch anyway, so 1:00? And he looked for her, but he couldn't find her, and he went upstairs, and then he was down here, waiting for her. So where had the rest of the time gone?

There was no more time left to wonder because just then Claire came into the room. "James," she said, "Dr. Beaumont said you were looking for me. Why did you come here?"

James looked at her quizzically. "Because I was looking for you."

"Didn't you get my text? I saw you called but I responded and said we could talk after work. You can't just show up here, James."

"I came to see you because I was worried about you, all that's been going on, and you're going to scold me for it, like a child?" The tone was harsher than he intended but he resisted his instant inclination to back off it. "And the police detective called, my case might not be as clear cut as he said it would be."

"I'm sorry," Claire said, but that too came out too sharp. "It's good to see you and I want to hear all about it, but this isn't the time."

James looked around the room before responding. The pleasant aura vanished, this place now seemed suspiciously inviting, entrapping even, and just where had that extra time gone? He leaned in closer to her and spoke quietly. "Claire, we need to talk, but not here."

"Sure," she said, "I'll meet you at your house. Give me an hour."

James looked her in the eyes. "Now," he said, and took her by the wrist.

Claire's eyes flashed and she recoiled from his grasp like a cat from the bathwater. "What are you doing?" She took a step backward and the space between them felt as wide as an ocean. "I will see you tonight, but you need to leave. Now."

A faint electric buzz from the lights was the only sound in the room and its pastoral facade seemed now a sinister and mocking caricature of all things good. James kept his eyes on her but stepped away too. When he finally spoke he said, "Whatever work you're doing here, whatever this place is, on some level I always suspected it was more important to you than I was. But I was never sure until now." He was out the door before she could respond. Whether her silence was because she couldn't find the right words or because she just didn't care enough to say them, he didn't know.

19

"What's the plan?" Drake asked Fox as his car rolled toward the university. "Or don't I get to know that either?"

"Do you know what your problem is, Mr. Drake?"

"You've narrowed it down to one?" Drake said with mock enthusiasm.

"Your problem, one of them anyway, is you're a hammer. And I might even concede you're a good hammer. Strong, unthinking, mostly effective. Would you agree?"

"To have an opinion on that matter, I'd have to think," Drake said. "So you can see the problem with your question."

Fox ignored him. "And because you're a hammer, you approach every problem as though it were a nail peeking its head up above the line where it should lie flush. So you knock it down in your way; maybe your fists, maybe a gun, and move on to trying to find another nail. Repeat till the grave."

"Fascinating," Drake said dryly. "And original."

"But what happens when a builder needs to make a precise cut across the face of a board? Seven and three-eighths of an inch, no more, no less. I'd go for the circular saw myself, measure twice, cut once, accurate as a surgeon. But not a hammer. No, the hammer is going to sit that job out."

"Damn obsolete is what it is. And I suppose a killer monster on the loose strikes you as a finesse job. A lot of good that approach did you while the beast was crushing your trachea. Or later, when it left you for dead in the middle of the woods. Lucky for you the unthinking hammer was there to bring you back to the world. Terrific work, master carpenter."

"It's not a killer," Fox said. "If anything, it went out of its way to keep me alive."

"Fine," Drake said, "not a killer yet. As far as we know."

"And I suppose I never did thank you. I owe you at least that much." Drake nodded but kept his eyes on the road. Dr. Fox sighed. "See it my way if you can. This lifeform, do you know what it is?"

"Of course not."

"So you call it a monster because that's what it looks like to you."

"Makes sense to me."

"Mr. Drake, what do you know of the Sapir-Whorf hypothesis?"

"Nothing," Drake said, "or zero, whatever the scale is. But I'm sure you're about to change that."

Fox smiled. "By way of brief overview, I will simply say it is the idea that language affects perception. The things we have words for, and the words we choose to use, determine how we see the physical world."

"So I make the sounds 'black dog' and you picture a dark

canine, is that it?"

"Partially. There is no Russian word for blue—they have two, one for dark blue and one for light blue—English is 'blue.'"

"Or 'dark blue' and 'light blue.'"

"Sure, but connected by this idea of 'blue.' So they do an experiment with different shades of blue and ask English speakers to pick out which of several circles is the unique color. These are particularly closely-related shades, you understand. And they do ok. But then the Russians do the same test, and what do they find? They are better at differentiating between the different blues. Because, so the theory goes, their language has shaped their brains to see the differences."

"Like the Inuit and their hundred names for snow."

"Exactly. Fifty words, I think, but the same principle, yes."

"And Wittgenstein said if a lion could talk, we'd never understand him. Well that knowledge seems powerfully useful, Doc. It's a wonder I lived this long without it. Talk about your practical everyday use."

"The point is, you can't throw around words like 'killer' and 'monster' without it affecting how you see this thing. You're going to see it as a monster because you've repeatedly drilled that idea into your own head."

"Or," Drake countered, "I'm going to see it as a monster because it has smoldering black eyes, fangs like steak knives, and inhuman claws out of Lovecraft. Could be that too, you know."

"You don't know it's a monster," Fox insisted. "We need another word, something whose connotation doesn't invite, demand, immediate judgment."

"Beast," Drake offered. "Hellbeast."

"The Individual," Fox said. "You can't argue that's not accurate."

"Monstrosity. Sin Against Nature and God... I'm sure the right answer is just around the corner."

"The Individual, Drake, at least until we know more."

Drake dropped the antagonistic routine. "Someday Doc, maybe very soon, you're going to need a hammer. And you'd better hope there's one around when you do." A vibration next to his leg sent Drake fishing into his pocket to pull out his phone. James calling. "Victor Drake," he said as he lifted it to his ear. In the passenger seat, Fox shifted his attention and watched the conversation with interest.

James recounted his day in one long unbroken stream. Drake didn't interrupt but occasionally nodded and cast a glance at Fox every so often. When James finished, Drake had to choose between the two possible paths that lay in front of him; he chose the honest one. "Listen James, I'm with Dr. Fox right now, he works with Claire— No, no, listen James, too long to explain right now—we're on our way to the university."

Dr. Fox grabbed Drake's right arm, and Drake fought to keep the steering wheel from jerking. "Claire?" he asked. "What's this about, Mr. Drake?"

With the car safely back between the lines, Drake pulled his arm away from Fox. "Not you too now, Doc, just give me a minute, dammit." He redirected his voice. "James, we're on our way to the university. Fox knows about the monst—" he sighed but corrected himself, "the Individual we've been dealing with. Fox knows about it, saw the thing, and he's going to help us. There are answers at the university." He didn't know if that last part was true, strictly speaking, but he hoped it was. On the other end, James pleaded with Drake not to go back to where he had come from, the strange doctor and his stranger associates, whatever had robbed him of the time he missed. Drake brushed him off. "It'll be fine James; I can handle myself. Talk to Claire when she gets home, patch things up. This isn't the end, and maybe not even the beginning of the end, but it may be the end of the beginning." His decision made, he hung up the phone before James could object.

"Churchill," Fox said.

"Or something like it," Drake said with a shrug. "You're not telling me all you know Doc, and I'm going to have to live with that for now, so ok. But I want you to know I know that. And if the moment comes when I have to make a tough call, my loyalty isn't to you."

"Nor mine to you," Fox agreed. "But that's only fair. We'll be at the Physics Building soon."

"Not soon enough," Drake said and pressed harder on the accelerator.

20

Claire pulled her car into James' driveway under a deep purple sky. She turned off the engine and readied herself for the conversation to come. Through the windows she saw the soft blue glow of a television but no other lights. She walked up the steps and knocked on the front door.

"It's open," she heard James say.

True enough, the door was unlocked and she opened it carefully. James was laid out on the couch, distractedly monitoring a baseball game on the screen. He didn't avert his eyes or otherwise acknowledge her as she came into the room.

"What happened to always locking the doors?" She hoped that didn't sound as nagging as she feared it did.

"No point," James said. "What will be, will be."

Claire set her purse on a chair and turned the lamp to its brightest setting, washing the room in warm yellow. "So are we going to talk or is this game more important?" She sat down across from him. "You hate baseball."

"So much standing around..." he said flatly. James muted the TV and finally looked at her. "So now you have time for me? I can never be sure anymore."

"That's not fair."

Looking away, he unmuted the broadcast and forced his stare on the game. The Nationals scattered three hits over the course of the inning but couldn't get a runner across the plate. The two of them sat alone together, each one stubbornly refusing to break the heavy silence. With the third out recorded, the announcer pitched it to a break and a commercial for a local car dealership came on.

They weathered three more ads before James said, "I talked to Drake. He's got your guy—Fox."

A mix of panic and relief shot across Claire's face. "What happened? Where are they?"

"Don't know," James said with apparent uninterest. "Don't much care," he added.

At that Claire stood and stormed up to the TV, shutting it off manually. "Are you done whining yet? I apologized and I don't know what more you want me to say."

"No you didn't," James said. "Apologize, I mean. Do you have any idea what happened to me today? Did you even care to hear?"

"I apologized, James," she insisted.

"You didn't, but it doesn't matter now. Whatever you're into with these doctors, and being gone all the time, and the secrecy, and whatever I saw there today—I'm out. I love you Claire, but I'm out."

Claire spoke softly. "What did you see there today?"

"I don't know," James said and brushed the remote control to the floor. "They took time from me. I can't explain it, but from when I got there to when I left, it was like waking from sleep. Time passed, I could tell, but I hadn't been aware of it. And I have no memory of what happened in between. Nothing Claire, besides this sinister feeling about the whole thing."

She joined him on the couch and took his hand but still said nothing.

"What the hell is going on over there? I've been so understanding, too understanding, with all this cloak and dagger stuff, but I'm asking now. And if you decide I'm not worth answering, I won't be around to ask again."

Claire had to fight to keep her voice from shaking. "I don't know, James; not completely. More than I've let on, of course, and I am sorry for that, but it's not like I had a choice."

"You always have a choice. Between what is right and what is most convenient."

"I suppose," she said, "but I did what I felt was right. This program, our work, could, and I think will, change the world. Irreversibly. It's bigger than any two people, James, so much bigger."

"Specifics," James said.

Claire hesitated but finally said, "I'll take you there. It's the only way to explain."

"Tonight. No more waiting."

"Ok, but I need to know what's going on with Dr. Fox."

"Call Drake if you want," James said, "but they're on their way to the university now. We can probably meet them there."

Claire nodded, aligning the facts in her head. "I will," she said. "It will be better with him there. Maybe not Drake though. Dr. Fox will know what to do."

"And what about Dr. Beaumont?"

"No," she said. "Better he doesn't know." She sighed. "Last chance to turn away and pretend this never happened.

I promise your life will be so much easier that way. If you go forward with this, I can't guarantee your safety. Maybe not even my own."

James got up from the couch. "I'll drive."

21

Cresting a hill, Drake saw the treeline part before him and looked down on the road as it fell away into a shallow valley. He and his passenger had passed the last several minutes in silence, each of them keeping his thoughts alien to the other. A shrill buzzing vibration from Drake's pocket cut into the silence and he grabbed for his phone to see Claire calling.

"Who's that?" Fox asked, but the question went ignored.

"Victor Drake," he answered.

"It's Claire."

He kept his eyes on the road. "Ok. What can I do for you?"

"James said you found Dr. Fox and you're heading for the university." A note of alarm in her voice but mostly keeping it together.

"Right."

"We're meeting you there," she said.

"If you say so," Drake said, and he hung up.

"Mr. Drake, who was that?" More urgency in the

question this time.

"Damn telemarketers," Drake said and shot a sideways grin in Fox's direction.

"Do you think I'm stupid?" Annoyance.

"In some ways, I'm sure you are. I might even say you've demonstrated as much in the short time I've known you. But," he waved his hand, "we've all got our blind spots."

"This isn't one of them," Fox said. "You're in over your head, a guppy in a sea of sharks."

Drake nodded. "Could be. I've considered as much."

"You're going to get yourself hurt, which is fine by me, but this is bigger than you, far bigger. And I can't have you messing it up. It's too important."

The obvious questions weren't always worth asking, but sometimes. "What's too important?"

Fox shut down, his answer cold and dismissive. "You don't get to know that."

"That's fine," Drake said casually. The doctor wouldn't tell him outright but that didn't mean he wouldn't get his answer. "Up here on the left, yeah?"

They pulled into the Physics Building parking lot with night on the edge of falling. The lot was mostly empty and James' SUV sat off on its own in a patch of darkness. Drake kept his distance and stopped the car in a spot near the entrance. He took the keys from the ignition and elbowed his sullen passenger. "In we go."

Fox didn't move. Instead he looked at Drake. "What do you expect to happen next?" he asked sadly.

"No expectations," Drake said. "Never let down that way."

Fox sighed but got out of the car and walked toward a side entrance. "Come with me," he said. "The only entrance without cameras."

Drake swept his eyes over the parking lot one more time, trying to will his vision through the dusk. No sign of movement from the SUV; at this distance he couldn't even be sure if anyone was inside. Should have cut it closer on the way in maybe, seen if James and Claire were in the car, but getting in unnoticed had been the bigger priority. Whether or not he was successful in that he couldn't tell. The two men ducked toward the side entrance; once there, Dr. Fox flashed an ID card at a sensor that beeped and the door made a soft clicking sound as it unlatched.

Fox stepped inside first and held the door ajar behind him. The door opened to a staircase heading down to the basement. No windows down here, Drake noticed, just tube lights that illuminated the walls a pale and sickly yellow. Like a hospital missing its patients. An unsettling thought, but he was determined not to be the first to speak. Fox led and Drake followed, unsure whether he was merely a fish out of water or a fish in the frying pan. Instinct had him leaning toward the latter, but it would hardly be the first time. He hoped it would not be the last.

Even the aged professor seemed foreign in these new surroundings. He had been easy enough to muscle outside, a soft-handed academic whose brilliance in his field wasn't a threat so long as Drake operated outside the limited bounds of those confines. He had been safe early on, but that was before he literally walked right into the one arena in which Fox had the advantage over him. It wasn't a smart play, he knew that, but it felt like the only way forward. Maybe that's what the old fool had wanted all along, despite the appearances of what may have been feigned reluctance.

The walls were brick and bare but for the white paint. They seemed to twist, turn, and stretch on into forever, longer than what appeared possible given the view from the buildings outside. This visual trick combined with the unbroken silence to produce a hypnotic effect and Drake found himself unable to gauge how far the two of them had walked since entering the basement. He resolved to keep a running count of his footsteps from that moment forward, but without knowing how far they had already gone it would be an incomplete measurement at best. Still no words from Dr. Fox.

Finally the eerie silence got the better of Drake and, though he had endeavored not to, he was the one who broke it. "Some kind of laboratory down here?" He was sure the question didn't sound as nonchalant as he meant it to.

Fox looked over as if noticing him for the first time. At first he didn't respond but then smiled and said, "Something like that. Not long now."

Where is Claire? Drake wondered. He should have brought her with him, some kind of insurance; maybe that had been the wrong play too, losing her and James in the parking lot. Not a soul knew he had gone down into this underworld, down with this eccentric physicist into this strange place. Had he told Dr. Fox that Claire was going to meet them here? He didn't think so; he had kept that card close to his chest, saving it for when its reveal would have the biggest impact. But now, in the unending and labyrinthine halls of the underground, he couldn't be sure of whether or not he'd dropped that on the professor during their car ride.

No, he decided, or else Fox would have had questions about that when they reached the parking lot alone. Yes, he was pretty sure that was right. But it bothered him that he had to wrestle with such a simple question. That was not the incisive mind he had known for so long. *Gasses,* he thought vaguely, but the concept was gone before he could wrangle it into something of substance, let alone direct it from there.

"Listen, Doc," Drake started to say but Fox looked back and shot him a glance that cut him short.

Fox raised his left hand in a bid for silence. "Not here. My workstation is just ahead."

A second workspace then, to go along with the first one Drake visited on his original fact-finding mission to the university. Well that was natural for a man of his stature. Was that natural? He decided that was natural. True to his word, Fox stopped shortly thereafter and ran his keycard along the slit next to a heavy metal door. The door swung open automatically, slowly, almost regally, and Drake followed Fox into the dark room.

What had been blackness receded as powerful overhead lights leaped silently into action. The floorplan was sprawling and open with high ceilings that looked down on the two men far below. The walls were lined with computers and between them a multitude of mysterious instruments of bright and glittering steel. Drake looked over some of the flashing digital displays to see what he could glean from them but came up empty. Intensive record-keeping of some kind, and math, all full of codes he could make no sense of.

"A little out of my element here, Doc," he said, knowing they both recognized it as a massive understatement. "You want to clue me in?"

"We need to draw The Individual out of hiding," Dr. Fox said. "It's a theory, but a blood sample... maybe even hair..." His eyes took on a far off look for a moment but he snapped back to attention and continued. "Do you think you can get that?"

"Maybe," Drake said. "What's the theory?"

"How many days until August 27th?" Fox said to himself. "Twelve? Twelve."

Drake ran the math in his head and was satisfied it

checked out. He didn't see why that date should matter but filed away the information just the same. The professor was hunched over a computer, tapping away rapidly at the keys. The hard sell hadn't worked, but Drake was where he wanted to be, and he could feel himself getting closer to the truth, if ever so incrementally. Patience was a fleeting thing even in the best of times, but he took a deep breath and forced himself to play it as coolly as his nerves would allow.

Spotting a padded office chair, he spun it away from the desk and wheeled over to where he could put his feet up. "I'll get you your sample," he said. "I don't know how, but I'll get it." Fox ignored him. "What's it for?" That went unanswered too, so he picked up a pen from the desk and twirled it in his left hand, waiting for whatever was so important on that damn computer screen.

Footsteps from outside the door. Not loud, but there. From his perch in front of the computer, Fox paid them no mind, probably hadn't even noticed them, but Drake moved his hand in the direction of his gun and watched the door intently. The steps came closer before stopping immediately outside the room's entrance. Silence followed and Drake wondered whether his ears had deceived him. But then came a sharp knocking, and a voice called out from the hall, vaguely familiar but not something he could place.

"Dr. Fox? Are you in?"

Fox's head shot up from his screen, his senses sharply alert in the new direction. He gave Drake a panicked look and motioned for him to hide behind the desk. Drake didn't move; his eyes were calm and stayed fixed on the door.

"Down!" Fox whispered and looked again toward the entrance.

"We're in here," Drake announced to the unknown voice. "Come on in."

A brief hesitation from the other side before the door opened. Three people he had never seen before walked into the room. The one in front was an older man in a white lab coat, academic type by the looks of him, his face a convergence of sharp angles. Behind him, two men who seemed anything but—both big, burly, and not especially sharp-looking. *The brains and the muscle respectively,* he thought.

"Dr. Fox, what's going on in here?" the lead one demanded. Fox looked from Drake to the newly-arrived interlopers.

"Dr. Beaumont," he answered weakly, "something's gone wrong."

The comment didn't seem to faze Dr. Beaumont, who instead looked over Drake, taking the size of him. "Who is this?" he said. "Why are you here?"

Drake got up and walked over to where Beaumont and his two goliaths stood. "Victor Drake, private eye," he said, extending his hand. His offer went unreciprocated, so instead he gave Dr. Beaumont a good-natured pat on the arm, which the other two men didn't seem to appreciate. "Howie thinks some of the work you're doing here—"

"Howie," Beaumont cut him off. "Dr. Fox."

"Sure," Drake said. "Well he thinks some of the work you're doing here might be connected to a case I caught."

Dr. Beaumont only stared at him, then walked over to Dr. Fox and his computer. "Dr. Fox," he repeated, "what is going on here?" The two brutes sidled up behind him. "I won't ask a third time."

"It's as he says, Dr. Beaumont. Something's gone wrong, terribly wrong, and there may be time to fix it, but... there may not." He looked down and rubbed the sides of his head. "This man doesn't know anything about what we're working on," he was quick to add.

"Not the first thing," Drake confirmed from behind them. "Howie has been pretty tight-lipped about your whole operation here. Just the sort of thing that makes me want to dig in deeper and see what's so secretive and worth protecting. Unless you want to go ahead and fill me in, of course," he said, and reached out for another pat on the arm.

His hand never got there. The two men flanking Dr. Beaumont moved in perfect synchronization, impossibly fast for their size, and before he knew what was happening, they wrenched Drake's arms behind his back and pinned him facedown on the cold steel floor. He struggled against their grip but it was a pointless exercise. Like being crushed by a hydraulic press.

"Take it easy!" Dr. Fox called to them but to no effect.

Dr. Beaumont waved that away and crouched down so he was closer to Drake's eye level. "Is the fish smart enough to know when the hook is irretrievably deep in its gullet?"

Drake tried to answer but the takedown must have knocked the wind out of him because he couldn't produce words. He closed his mouth and gave Beaumont the best nod he could manage. "And the fish is done thrashing around in the boat?" Drake nodded again. "Julius, get him up," Dr. Beaumont said, tapping one of the men on the shoulder. They stood Drake up but kept his arms behind him. "Alexander, search him." A quick pat down revealed Drake's gun and the man grabbed it, emptied it, and set it on the table.

"Private eye," Dr. Beaumont said dismissively.

The breath had returned to Drake's lungs, so he decided to test his voice. "What next?" he asked. Not much power there but it was something.

Dr. Beaumont turned his back to them and said

something to Dr. Fox, something low and out of the range of Drake's hearing. Dr. Fox shook his head. "Nothing," he seemed to be saying. More from Beaumont then, admonishment apparently, and finally he looked back over his shoulder at Drake.

"You are trespassing, Mr. Drake," he said. "You can leave immediately and never return or I can call the police."

That was a bluff, and a lousy one besides. "Sure," Drake said. "I imagine they'll want to hear all about this. We have nothing to hide, men like you and me. Send in the clowns."

A tense silence hung in the air and the mood of the room hinged on what happened next. Drake watched Dr. Beaumont with resolute eyes and was surprised when the doctor's mouth broke into a Cheshire smile. The smile gave way to a laugh, quiet at first, then full and unrestrained. His two men exchanged uneasy glances behind him. "Send in the clowns," Dr. Beaumont said after a deep breath. "Isn't that the truth?" He gestured to the two giants. "It sounds like Dr. Fox and I have work to do. Show our guest out."

Each of the men seized one of Drake's arms and shoved him toward the door. "Not so fast," he said and tried to wrench free. "What the hell's going on here, Fox?" Over his shoulder, Dr. Fox aimed his eyes at the floor to avoid taking in the scene unfolding. "I saved your life, dammit!" Drake added to no avail.

Finding himself physically outmatched by Dr. Beaumont's men as they neared the exit, he had no choice but to play his final card, the one he had been saving until no other option remained. "That's fine you don't want to tell me what this place is, what you're doing here," Drake said. "Just fine." Behind him Beaumont and Fox were huddled together and hardly seemed to take notice of his parting words. He added, louder, "The girl will tell me."

At this last comment one of the bruisers slugged him hard in the gut and Drake felt his legs go weak under him. Only the strong grips on either side of him kept him from collapsing to the ground in a sad little puddle. For the second time in a handful of minutes, he found himself struggling to breathe, this time with the added pleasure of trying to get his feet under him. He could only hope the remark had been enough.

For a moment it seemed like it had not, that the comment would amount to no more than words wasted in the ether, like so many others. Then Dr. Beaumont's voice sliced through the air like a scalpel. "Stop." Alexander and Julius froze at the command, the two of them propping up Drake's shoulders like crutches. "Get him up," Beaumont told them and they lifted their paws up higher in unison. Drake's legs kicked underneath as though he were running in place until they finally found solid ground. With that job done, he planted them and worked to steady himself.

"All right boys," he told the men on either side of him. "Think I've got it from here." They stayed in place until Dr. Beaumont nodded at them. Then they released their holds on Drake carelessly and left him to gather himself with all the grace of a baby giraffe. He could still feel the impact of the blows he'd taken and his arms were raw and sore where they had grabbed him, but he was determined not to let anyone else in on the fact. "Is this what passes for muscle these days?" he asked Dr. Beaumont. "Back when I was coming up..."

"What girl?" Dr. Beaumont asked before Drake could finish the thought. Though not a young man, he moved faster than Drake expected and in one smooth motion the two men were face to face. Impatience was in the doctor's eyes, and annoyance. Annoyance that he had been momentarily usurped as ruler of this little kingdom he built, whatever it was. The loss of control didn't suit him. "You don't know what you're talking about," he sneered.

"If you believe that, go ahead and throw me to these wolves. Nothing to lose." Dr. Beaumont had to think that over, and without a direct mandate his entourage could only stand by. "Look at me," Drake said. "I mean what I said. You know it's true."

"He knows Claire," Dr. Fox confirmed. "But that's all he knows. You can let him walk, Dr. Beaumont," he said with pleading eyes. "Honestly."

"To hell with that," Drake said. In truth he didn't have any reason to believe Claire would tell him anything, but as long as the suggestion was lodged inside Dr. Beaumont's head it was doing its job. "She's got me in it now, and the fact is maybe I'd rather not be involved, but it's too late for that. And it's gone out of control, and from what Fox says, you haven't got the slightest idea how to handle it. Except maybe I do. So we hang together or hang separately."

"You may be right," Dr. Beaumont said. "At the least, it's going to take some thinking over." Then to Dr. Fox, "The two of you came alone?" Dr. Fox nodded. "My apologies," he said, redirecting his words to Drake. "My hope is this won't take long."

He turned away and before Drake could react he felt a crushing blow to the back of his head. Not the first punch he'd taken, not even the first from the blindside, but he couldn't remember one that ever landed harder. His left leg splayed forward in an attempt to recapture his balance but it was no use. Drake saw the floor coming at him fast but not fast enough. He was out before body met ground.

22

Only Claire knew the main entrance wasn't the one that warranted watching as she and James sat waiting in the parking lot. She decided not to volunteer that information to James. Maybe she still held on to the notion that she could safeguard him from whatever was going on inside, or maybe it was simply easier that way. For his part, James kept focused on the main doors, neither of them saying much, their shared impatience growing stronger with each passing minute. Finally, two figures moved carefully toward the hidden entrance in the dark. Claire tensed up when she saw them, trying to watch without seeming to be, doing her best not to let on that anything changed. Dr. Fox and Victor Drake, they could be no one else, slipped through the door and the night reasserted its unbroken calm.

She coughed involuntarily. A quiet sound, but in the noiseless stillness of the car it was like a cannon shot. "They should have been here by now," James said. "Don't you think?"

"Probably," Claire agreed. The silence re-embraced them and held on for minutes, James watching the main door, Claire trying to decide her next move. She wanted to follow them in, with or without James, but couldn't force herself to take the initial action. As though if she waited long enough, the situation would resolve itself. It was a stupid thought, nearly impossible, but she clung to it like a life ring in the midst of a desolate ocean.

"So what do we do?" James said finally. "I'm going to call him again."

"No point," Claire said flatly. She was right but he didn't know that, couldn't know that, so she indulged him when he made another call to Drake's number and came up empty again.

"Why did he want to meet us here anyway? Maybe he's already inside. You can get in, can't you?"

She wasn't sure how to answer that last part, but she knew what would happen if she told the truth. "Not this late," she said.

"Oh, come on," James said, turning in his seat to face her. "How many times have you been here at all hours of the night? You don't expect me to believe that."

"Changed a couple weeks ago," she said. It was a weak lie, even weaker than the first, and she knew it wouldn't mollify him. But she felt she had to at least try to avoid that which was quickly becoming unavoidable.

"Then you won't mind if we try," James said. She couldn't meet his eyes. "Claire, please," he added, softer.

She nodded. "Just me."

"No way," James said. "You said we were past this, the secrets and the lies. It's all or nothing now."

"Just me," she repeated. She wanted to tell him she was sorry it had to be this way, and she truly was, but didn't see what good that would do.

"You walk away, we're done," James said, trepidation in his voice. "That's not a threat or an ultimatum, or any kind of head game, but I can't go on like this. I won't." She looked at him sadly, her mind made up. "Claire, don't do this," he said.

"I'm sorry," she said. "It has to be this way."

She opened the passenger door and James could only watch her go. She disappeared into the night, James' words sounding ever fainter in her head as she walked toward whatever destiny awaited. Claire followed to the door Dr. Fox led Drake through, pulling an ID card from her pocket, and with a soft click of the door she was inside. Eerie how different familiar surroundings could feel once the context of being there got turned all upside-down. Past upside-down, more like inside-out, or looking at the negative of a well-loved photograph. She hadn't been sure of where they were headed while she was waiting in the car but now that she was inside the building, those halls, those lights, it was clear. Her steps were graceful but purposeful, a dancer with a destination.

Part of her thought of turning back, saying something to James if he was still out there. Not a full explanation, that was impossible, just something that might offer some measure of recompense. But it would do no good, and once she decided that, she resolved to put the idea out of her mind entirely. Better to direct her undivided attention to what lay in front of her, what chance remained to save her father's friend Victor Drake from a path he never should have gone down.

The basement was as quiet and still as death. Claire knew the way well and navigated the winding halls with ease. She paused outside the entrance of the lab, listening. Were those low voices coming from the other side of the door? Nothing she could make out, just confirmation bias maybe. No activity outside the room so she lingered a moment longer, leaning an ear against the door. Definitely voices. Dr. Beaumont's was the louder of the two; the second she couldn't say for sure, too quiet, but probably Dr. Fox's. Either Drake was listening respectfully or unaccounted for. The former was hard to picture, which left the odds favoring the latter.

The room was only a step away, but Claire couldn't take that step without being ready for what would follow. Once inside the room, the men would want an explanation for her presence there, and how could she possibly account for that? There was the truth of course, but she didn't like where that might lead. Meanwhile, time was against her and maybe even more so against Drake.

As it turned out, that wasn't a decision she had to make. While she stood in the hall running the possible plays in her head, the door swung open wide and Dr. Beaumont walked out hurriedly with Dr. Fox trailing behind him. They almost bowled Claire over in their haste, all three of them surprised to be meeting this way.

The doctors especially took a moment to get over the shock. Claire was somewhere she wasn't supposed to be and any attempt at a cover story would have been transparent as the wind. A move of instinct, she went on the offensive before either of the others (Beaumont, really) could dictate terms.

"Where is Victor Drake?"

Dr. Fox averted his eyes but Dr. Beaumont held her gaze. "Who?" he asked. Too calm, insincere.

"Dr. Fox," she said, "where is he?" Nothing from him, so she moved on to Dr. Beaumont. "I saw him come in." She found her voice breaking. "He didn't leave."

A beat. "He was trespassing," Dr. Beaumont said matter-of-factly. Claire waited for him to elaborate but it never came.

"Where is he? Dr. Fox, where is he?"

"The work is too important," Dr. Beaumont answered. "He won't be harmed, but we can't let him interfere."

"I want to see him," Claire said, "talk to him. I've given my life to Horizon."

"You've given four years." Dr. Beaumont's reply was sharp and curt. "*I* have given my life, decades, to the research, and Dr. Fox as well. You're astonishingly lucky to be included. Do not forget that, Miss Ventura." He eyed her coldly. "And we're lucky to have you," he added by way of perfunctory compensation.

"Then I'm out," she said, turning toward the exit. "It's cost me too much. Whatever happened to my parents, and James, the innocent people getting hurt. The people I love. Nothing is worth this."

Dr. Beaumont seized her arm and prevented her from moving. "You know that isn't true. Anyway, it's too late now." Claire tried to pull her arm free but his grip was unrelenting.

"Let me go," she said. The fingers slowly unclenched and Dr. Beaumont's countenance softened.

"Of course," he said, "forgive me. But we can't have people just showing up, asking questions. No one is going to hurt your friend. We just need to convince him to stay out of the way."

He was right. She hated that he was, maybe even hated him, but that didn't make the man any less right. "Where is he?" She felt the heat rising to her face. Hopefully they were as tired of hearing that question as she was of asking it.

Now Dr. Fox stepped in. "You will see him tomorrow. I promise. But Claire," he implored her with kind eyes, "please go home."

"Twelve days," Dr. Beaumont said. "We're so close now."

"I want to see him tonight."

Dr. Beaumont shook his head with finality. "Out of the question. You know better than to push this."

"Tomorrow," she said to Dr. Fox. "You promise I'll see him tomorrow. And he won't be hurt."

"Tomorrow," Dr. Beaumont answered. "We promise. Goodnight, Miss Ventura."

It would have to do. She looked them both over, really seeing them for the first time, then turned to leave. As she walked out, Claire wondered whether she had done the right thing. But that was unproductive thinking. The decision had already been made; all she could do now was ensure whatever happened next would justify it, retroactively if needed. She couldn't reverse a choice, right or otherwise, but where things went from there, the future, that was still in her control. Partially anyway.

The outside air was cooler than she expected and Claire shivered as she stepped into the night. No sign of James' SUV; she hadn't thought about how she was going to get home now that she chased her ride away. Call a cab, she supposed, and finally put an end to this miserable day. But as she reached into her pocket for her phone, a university bus crested the hill. It wouldn't get her exactly where she needed to go, but close enough.

Awfully late for the bus to be running though; she reasoned it must have been the last run of the night. The door hissed open and the driver gave her a friendly smile she did her best to return. Claire climbed aboard and closed her eyes.

A night of deepest sleep. Deep but harried, a plummet into the land of fevered dreams. She didn't dream of the physics department or the professors, not even of James or her family. The visions were more ethereal than that, unseen sand always passing through her fingers. Sprinting after something she could never quite catch, growing more tired all the time but never able to stop the futile chase. In another she was surrounded by wild beasts, frightening and otherworldly. Held hostage in a hall of mirrors. No abrupt awakenings to a dark room; only the long, steady descent.

When Claire finally opened her eyes it was to the sound of her phone ringing. An unknown number and, with her mind still stuck in the lethargic haze of dream, she opted to answer it rather than try to deduce who might be calling first. "Hello?" she said, her voice arid and unresponsive.

"Claire, Victor Drake. Where are you?"

"What time is it?" she thought aloud before answering him. "I'm at home." Slowly the pieces of last night came together in something approximating recollection. "Wait, where are you? Are you ok?"

"Yeah," he said. "Fine. When can you meet?"

"Today. Wait, what day is it? I'm sorry, I'm just waking up and I feel..."

"Off," Drake said. "Me too, but it's lifting. Anyway, Friday. I'll be at my office in an hour. See you then."

He hung up before she could confirm or say goodbye, so Claire set the phone down and lay in bed studying her ceiling. She knew she should call James, but acknowledging the impulse fell short of leading to the action. They would work it out, she thought, or hoped, but she wanted to let last night sink in fully before saying or doing anything irreversible. There was wanting to talk, needing to talk, and then there was being able to talk. For now the gap between them was too far to bridge.

An hour later, she sat across from Drake, hoping he felt better than he looked. On the edge of disheveled even under the best circumstances, his eyes looked worn now, the age lines on his face more pronounced. Claire felt bad for him but didn't think saying so would improve the situation. Both were content to skip the pleasantries and get straight to the events of the night before.

"Where were you?" Claire asked.

"I talked to the doctors," Drake said, not quite answering the question. "And I think you should quit."

Claire sat silently, thinking, and Drake gave her the time. "I can't," she said finally. "They didn't hurt you?"

Drake reached into his pocket for a cigarette. "I'll be fine. I suppose you've got questions and I'll try to stay ahead of them. Dr. Fox knows more than he's letting on about... whatever the hell is going on. He's got himself wrapped up in something, in over his head maybe, and it's all connected. James, the monster, you, that damn building. All connected." He took a drag off the cigarette and looked out the window, gathering his thoughts. "But I failed last night, Claire. I thought I could get it out of Fox, get something at least. Said he had a theory. That's as far as we got."

"I saw the two of you go in together," Claire said. "By the time I got to the lab, it was just Dr. Beaumont and Dr. Fox. We argued but they said I would see you tomorrow. That's all I could get out of them. I guess I failed too."

"You did what you could. Anything more to report?"

"No. Well..." She thought of how to word the next part. "James wanted to come too. I told him he couldn't and he didn't take it well. When I got back to the parking lot he was gone. We haven't talked since."

"Understandable," Drake said, "on both ends. I'll reach out."

"What about my parents?"

"What about them? They're still hiding out; it's for the best. Your mom is taking it a lot better than your dad is. I don't know how much longer he'll go for it."

"Not long," Claire agreed.

"No. In the meantime, you want to tell me what Dr. Beaumont was so eager to keep secret?"

Claire frowned and looked away. "Not yet," she said. "Soon. That's the best I can do."

Drake could tell the point wasn't worth arguing, not then anyway. Still, his disappointment was evident. "Then I guess we're done here."

The two of them stared at one another, each recognizing the impasse. "What will you do now?"

"I've got another angle I'm working," Drake said. "And let me talk to James, better you give him some time."

That capitulation came almost too easily, suspiciously so, but she accepted it. "Ok, and you're sure you're all right?" Drake nodded. "Ok," she said again. "Stay in touch."

Drake set his cigarette in the ashtray on his desk and got up to walk her out. "As you say," he said and closed the door behind her. As Claire navigated down the old stairs, a fragment of some long-forgotten song flashed across her mind: *And when the day is gone / Stars shine on / Far away from here.* It disappeared as quickly as it had come.

23

Three minutes, maybe five, since Claire left; Drake figured that was enough time for her to get down to the street and into her car. He sat back in his chair and kicked hard at his desk, sending reverberations down through the floor. Truth be told, he had pretty much forgotten about Mike and Rebecca. Left to their own devices he didn't trust either of them to make the rational, practical decision. It had been all he could do to get them out there in the first place. Mike, the classic hothead, tried to solve all his problems with aggression. When that failed, his solution was usually to get even more aggressive. Strategy and tactics, those were further down his list, if they were on there at all.

Rebecca was slightly more pragmatic, but just as childish in her own way. How long could she stay away from the action and attention of her social circles? Hell, she might break before her husband. Either way, there wasn't a voice of reason he could count on, probably not even half of one between the two of them. But what was reason at this point anyway? They couldn't waste away in some remote cabin because something might be out there to hurt them. Except there was no might be on the first part; something was most definitely out there, still. Whether it would return for them, Drake had no idea. He didn't even know why it had gone after them in the first place. Some detective he was. And yet he was confident the pieces would fit together if he could just wrestle them into their proper places.

Maybe a call to Mike, get an update on the situation. Would he follow some sound advice, for old time's sake? Probably not. Then there was Rebecca. She would answer but that might be more trouble than it was worth. Rebecca wasn't one he could trust. Michael wasn't either, but he was a simpler machine, a more known and predictable quantity. Drake tried to imagine their movements, using what he knew about each of them separately, what he knew about the two of them together. They had already returned to the house, he decided. The fact that he had told them not to clinched it. They were too arrogant and myopic to let anyone, or anything, else dictate the terms of their lives to them. That he was sure of.

Rather than give them any forewarning by way of a phone call, he decided it better to show up unannounced. Get a more natural reaction that way, see what was really what. Which meant another drive. A PI's work was never done, he thought, at least not if he was any good. The trek back to the Venturas' took on a meditative quality, the way his long drives sometimes did. Not calming exactly, but he felt the impatience and apprehension that had been building recede. They were still there, but their effects were dulled, like he was watching someone else struggle with them. A tepid empathy rather than any kind of recognition of their power and urgency.

His previous visit was at night. The neighborhood seen in the full light of an unblemished summer sky was even more striking. Rows of immaculate houses and their expansive lawns expertly laid out without so much as the hint of a break in the uniformity. Like something from a commercial, he thought. And though the aesthetic was not what he would have chosen (too samey, no personality), Drake couldn't deny the artistry of it all. On some level he even admired it, though that wasn't something he would ever let on.

No cars in front of the Ventura estate but that didn't necessarily mean anything. Satisfied with his subterfuge up to that point, Drake pulled right up to the house and rang the bell. The sound of rummaging from inside, some movement, and then stillness. He stepped back, made a production of looking around with a whistle and swinging his arms back and forth like he had seen on an old Mickey Mouse sketch. The stillness from inside persisted so Drake looked up to the security camera above the door and gave it an exaggerated shrug, arms extended, palms to the sky. "Come on, Mike," he said. "The quicker we talk, the quicker I'm out of your hair." *Out of your life with any luck,* he thought.

That didn't work so he leaned against the frame of the entryway and considered his next move. The camera's mechanical eye was still trained on him, so he took out his phone and held it up. "Calling your wife now," he said. That ought to get a reaction one way or another. The phone rang but went unanswered. "Strange," Drake addressed the camera again, "she's always taken my calls before." The fuse lit, he waited for an explosion that never came. A dearth of sound from the other side of the door. He looked at the house again, not casually or carelessly this time, but intently.

The lines on his face set in a deep frown. Nothing out of the ordinary there, he decided. One more try.

"Mike, they've got Claire." Nothing. "For God's sake, she's your daughter, open the damn door!" Leaning his ear against the door, Drake drew hard on his senses, trying to salvage something from the data, but there was nothing to be gained. Inside the house, it had gone quiet as a tomb. There was no trigger past Claire, she had been the big guns, so Drake stepped off the porch in the hopes that a zoomed-out view might reveal something he had missed before. "Pan out and it all becomes clear," he said, but reality refused to yield to the force of his optimism.

The camera's eye was still there, unblinking, so Drake bid goodbye to it. "The hell with you," he said, turning away. Except that wasn't enough so he offered it a finger too. Juvenile as it was, the gesture did him some good and he felt he salvaged some recompense of his dignity as he climbed back into his car. The vehicle crawled out of sight of the camera and continued on until Drake was sure he couldn't be seen from the house at all. From there he parked again and made his way back toward the Venturas'. Give them a chance to let their guard down, he thought; it was worth a shot.

A fine art, moving surreptitiously. Slinking almost, an inherently conspicuous motion that must not look conspicuous. Drake was well-practiced and maneuvered himself into a position from which he could see the house but was reasonably certain no one in the house could see him. He studied it for a time from a distance but found the exercise wanting, lacking in the details. From what he could see the front of the house looked as pristine as it ever had. The front of the house.

That left the sides and, a chill climbed the ladder of his

neck, the back of the house. While the front was in full view of the street, the back opened up to a private lawn and beyond that a small stretch of woods. Drake started to his left, circling the building slowly, carefully scanning for anything the slightest bit amiss. That chill in his spine lingered, but the side checked out fine and he continued to the back of the house. Rounding the corner, he saw the back door hanging askew—only slightly, and that might have meant nothing at all, but his instincts told him otherwise.

As he got closer, Drake could see the door wasn't connected at all but rather off its hinges and leaning nearly vertically against the house. He shot a glance around the surrounding area and found it as peaceful as could be, tranquil even. Whoever removed (then replaced) the door vacated the immediate premises—whether to the inside of the house or the outside, he wasn't sure. *Only one way to determine that,* he thought.

Stepping purposefully through the full grass, Drake approached the door with respectful caution. His gun was on his hip but he hadn't felt the need to draw it just yet. The door was heavier than it looked, a thick oak job, but he lifted it from its resting spot and set it off to the side, leaving the bare entryway looking like an open wound. Dark inside, darker than seemed possible, like all the shades had been long-drawn. Drake stepped through the doorway and was reminded of Dorothy stepping from monochromatic gray into the technicolor world of Oz, but this time in reverse. The house felt stuffy, the air as heavy as a battleship.

He replaced the door behind him as best he could and made his way inside. Even so, the natural light from the outside felt a distant memory after a few steps into the dim heart of the unfamiliar. The natural impulse was to call out for Mike or Rebecca or whom-the-hell-ever. He resisted that though, keeping as quiet as possible, setting his feet down softly as Fabergés. Inside the house, the curtains were closed over the windows, and though he could still see, nothing was sharp or clear. The Glock that had been holstered at his side found its way to his right hand. He was well-practiced, shooting ranges and otherwise, but in moments like this the gun always felt heavier than he remembered it. Breathing evenly, he crept through the house. Each room was as empty as the last.

The first floor was clear. Had he been wrong about hearing something inside when he rang the bell that first time? No, couldn't be. And besides, this was no time to start questioning himself. Better to take a decisive action, even if it turned out to be the wrong one, which they sometimes did. Still, far better that than being trapped by indecision like some long-dead insect in a prison of amber. That left the upstairs and the basement. *If I were hiding out,* he thought, *which is the better of the two?* Easier to hide in the basement, but the upstairs offered the advantage of a sort of built-in lookout from which to survey the comings and goings of the world outside. In his mind, upstairs was the logical choice.

But no, that was the detective talking. Michael Ventura, either of the couple really, wouldn't complicate the reasoning that far. The basement was the obvious, unthinking choice, and that was more their style. Although if it was just Mike and Rebecca ducking him, why the unhinged door in the back? Again he wanted to call out for someone, and again he decided against it. He carefully crept down the stairs. Half-windows lined the basement and provided a degree of natural lighting, but Drake drew his flashlight just the same and kept his gun trained wherever he shone it.

Hardly any sound at all down there, and Drake was acutely aware of his own breaths slowly moving into and out of his body. His footsteps were deliberate and imperceptible. At the foot of the stairs he saw the basement opened up to a capacious room. A massive TV ran the length of one of the walls with a wraparound couch running parallel to it. The rest of the room was largely barren except for a wet bar off to his right. Satisfied no one was hiding under the couch cushions, Drake clicked off the flashlight and moved on to the bar, his gun still drawn.

His heart pounded savagely. This was a heightened moment, and his senses rose to meet it. In fact, the basement was not as silent as he had thought; he heard for the first time the whisper-quiet hum of a top of the line air conditioner. Even the world outside the house was not without its contributions—a soft intermittent wind, the ever-present buzz of what must have been crickets. And still his breathing.

He inched along until he was flush against the bar and held there. Leaning back into the solid structure, he paused, listening with all he had. Nothing from the other side. His breaths were slow and measured. One... Two... On the unspoken *Three* he sprung from his hiding place like a leopard, gun drawn and pointed at the space before him. The empty space before him—empty and harmless. Letting out a long breath, he continued on his search of the basement.

Two doors lined the opposite hall, one on each side. The one on the right was open (and closer), the one on the left closed. Eight steps to the closer door, Drake swung to his right and surveyed the scene. A washer and a dryer stood against the wall, an open linen closet beyond them. Nowhere to hide in that room, so he moved on to the next, closing the door soundlessly behind him.

The nerves inside him cried out to throw the door open and see what was inside, like a child at Christmas tearing into the biggest present under the tree. But he quieted them and turned the door handle slowly enough that it would not click, pushed the door open the same way, and stepped through. Once inside, he looked over a spare bedroom. The room was windowless and sparsely decorated. Just an uninspired painting of a sailboat that clashed with the floral bedspread and a squat nightstand adorned with a small lamp.

No place to hide in this room either, except under the bed. Drake couldn't help but smile. Wasn't that where monsters always hid out? It could be studying his feet at that moment. Or, if his entrance had been as quiet as he hoped, it might not know he was in the room at all. *Or, dummy,* he thought to himself, *there's nothing under there at all.* The latter was the most likely he knew, but still, he had to be sure. The room was darker than he would have liked, far darker, but he didn't want to announce his presence by turning on the light.

So, much the way he had done when he was five years old, he snuck up alongside the bed and bent down in an effort to assuage the fears his rebellious subconscious dreamed up. At least now he could lead with the gun. With his pistol pointed at the space below the mattress, he jerked the bed skirt back in one quick motion.

"*Darkness there and nothing more,*" he said and scanned the length of the floor with his flashlight. The basement was clear. The main floor had been clear. And yet someone had been in the house when he arrived, he knew it in his bones. Only the upstairs remained. *The penthouse suite,* he thought.

Drake pulled at his shirt collar to let some air in, feeling like a character from the old cartoons. That didn't offer him much relief but he resolved to climb the stairs toward the top floor. The main floor appeared undisturbed since he came in, but just to be certain he circled back around to where he entered the house. Sure enough, the door leaned over the opening precisely as he had left it. That ruled out anyone disappearing out the back while he was canvassing the basement.

The real estate beyond the stairs was uncharted territory for Drake. The bedrooms would be up there, the master plus Claire's and her sister's old rooms at a minimum. But judging by the square footage of the main floor, he expected to find four rooms upstairs, maybe five. "Nothing succeeds like excess" might as well have been emblazoned on the Ventura family crest. Drake was inclined to resent this, but at the same time he couldn't help but admire the ostentatiousness of it all. The decor was expensive but stubbornly tasteless to his eye. It fit Mike and Rebecca well. Claire less so, he thought.

The steps were dark oak with an intricately-patterned blue Persian carpet running up the center of them. The first three led to a square landing after which the rest of the stairs climbed up toward the upper floor. Drake rested his left hand on the railing as he ascended, some subconscious attempt at establishing a totemistic bond with the house that wasn't quite successful. The air was quiet and still, and Drake could feel the beads of sweat standing out on his forehead. He half-wished for a bird to hit the window or a creak from the stairs, anything to reaffirm that he was still a real person in a real place. But the local avian population was unaccommodating and the construction of the house was immaculate, so he pressed on, silent as a statue.

Cresting the top of the stairs, he saw hallways stretching out in opposite directions like the flattened legs of a prostrate spider. Only four to deal with rather than the full eight. The one straight ahead went to the front of the house, he pegged that as leading to the master bedroom. The other three were anyone's guess. The girls' rooms, presumably, and then a guest bedroom, or a study perhaps? Michael Ventura wasn't the type to use a study, but he may have been the type to like having a study. For appearance's sake.

One path was as good as any of the others. The allure of the unknown led him to turn around and head toward the back of the house. What space would be reserved for the room farthest from Mike and Rebecca's bedroom, he wondered. Claire's bedroom if she was smart, and he knew she was. The hall wasn't especially long but the sense of anticipation made it feel that way. Soon Drake came upon a door that could only have once belonged to a teenage girl.

The white-painted wood was barely visible behind the collage of photos taped to it. Dozens of pictures were piled one on top of another, most of their edges obscured by one of the others. They must have spanned close to two decades. Mike and Rebecca looked so young in a couple of them. Drake couldn't believe he himself had ever been so young. But Claire was the star mostly, with friends and family, a border collie-looking dog he didn't recognize. All smiles and sun. No chronological or thematic groupings he could follow, but undeniable evidence of a life well-lived.

What looked like a closed door from several steps away now revealed itself to be ever so slightly ajar. Drake took one last look at the photo display, his eyes lingering sadly before leaning in to further inspect the door that rested gingerly against the frame. He rested the five fingers of his left hand against the door and pushed lightly, almost imperceptibly. The movement was slow but persistent, and after what felt like a lifetime he had the door open enough to slip into the room. Drake leaned his back against the door and led with his right shoulder and right foot so when he spun back to face the room, his right hand would be free to go to the gun if needed.

But it was all for nothing because when he stepped into the room his body froze and he could no longer command it. There on the bed, its back to him and seemingly unaware of his presence, was the monster. Dr. Fox, to his endless credit, insisted on not calling it that. The Individual, he said. But no, Drake thought, now that he was back in full view of this thing, that was woefully inadequate and wouldn't do. It would never be The Individual again as far as he was concerned. Monster. Golden sunlight poured in between the large window's pink curtains and reflected off the soft yellow walls. More photos inside the room picked up where the door display had left off and the scene would have been purely idyllic if not for the thing on the bed. The pastel surroundings emphasized its black coloring. Drake entered so silently, and the beast sat so unmoving, he would have thought it dead except for the subtle, almost glacial rising and falling of its breaths.

This was what tore the back door off its hinges, he was sure. But it had not disturbed anything else in the house. Just made its way up to this room, gently closed the door, and rested on the bed. Drake's hand was on his gun but he didn't draw it. To do so would have felt perverse somehow, introducing a weapon of such brutality into the serenity of this scene. Which is exactly what the monster was, he realized, as the pain from those injuries he sustained outside the Blue Valentine flared up anew. It didn't belong and its very presence was impossible to reconcile, like a hearse at a summer wedding.

In spite of all that, he didn't feel in danger, not really. The room was too warm, not only in temperature but in countenance, as though protected by an aura. *It's unaware,* he told himself, *completely defenseless.* A well-placed shot or three and he could finish all this. The whole ordeal, over. *No,* an inner voice answered back, *it can't be killed.* That was nonsense of course, anything could be killed, but the impulse was formidable.

All the while this was running through his head Drake was moving closer to the creature, ever so slowly, as though caught in the power of its gravitational pull. By now he was a little more than an arm's length away. He could be upon it in less than a second were he so motivated—he was decidedly not. And yet still he moved closer, close enough now to see the downward slope of the bed as it creased toward the weight resting on one side of it. Close enough to see individual black hairs standing up across its skin. The bedspread, like the walls, was an ebullient yellow and Drake was now close enough to see a few coarse individual hairs darkening the uniformity of the comforter.

The hair sample he somehow promised Fox, there it was, three inches from his hand now. The thing on the bed still hadn't noticed his presence. Asleep maybe? Steady as a watchmaker, Drake reached toward one of the stray lines of black that stood out against the yellow backdrop. Pinching his forefinger and his thumb together he snared it on the first try, then drew back his hand. *Like the world's highest stakes game of Jenga,* he thought, and he couldn't help but smile at the absurdity of where he was and what he was doing. The capture complete (to hell with Fox's blood sample), he drew his fingers back to his palm and his arm back to his body.

His mind was crying out to leave the room, the house, maybe the state, but he lingered, unable to pull his eyes away. He had the feeling of looking at a painting; he couldn't have been closer to the scene, but he felt powerless to affect it. The monster was undeniably of another world, yet there it was, right in front of him. There it was. As he stood there stuck in that limbo, he heard a car speed up the street in front of the house, the throaty rev of its engine shattering the silent dream he had been unable to shake free of. His head shot around the instant he heard it, a response buried deep in instinct, but his reaction wasn't as fast as the monster's. It too turned toward the sound, and toward Victor Drake.

His gun was up and trained on the monster before he even registered the fire of synapses that told him to raise it. The trigger was feather-light; his finger rested on it but not against it. The slightest pressure and the hammer would crash on the firing pin, starting a chain reaction that would end with a bullet propelled through the back of the monster's skull. His hands were stable and less than three feet separated the pair; even if he missed, he couldn't miss.

But again his finger didn't come down. The first meeting outside the bar had been so rushed, a panicked series of reactions rather than anything resembling conscious choices. Whatever he did next with the thing in front of him, still not moving, would surely be a choice. The beast eyed the gun quizzically, either unaware of or uncaring toward the threat it presented. Drake watched its massive blue eyes (hadn't they been black in the night?) scan him comprehensively. Something in those eyes. Not showing any aggression toward him, but not backing down either. Drake could feel his muscles crying out for deliverance and his arms began to tremble under the effort. The barrel of the gun stayed pinned between its eyes.

Years of training and a life on the margins prepared him to shoot without hesitation or second-guessing, but only when absolutely necessary. This didn't feel like that; danger was all, but that was nothing new. He decided he would not fire on it unless provoked. No sooner had he come to this conclusion than the monster took a quick step toward him. Now the only course of action was to use the gun as it had been designed. He jerked his hands upward and to the right and pulled off two shots in rapid succession. The bullets zipped past its left ear and embedded themselves harmlessly somewhere out of sight.

The move had been a gamble, but Drake comforted himself with the knowledge that if he guessed wrong he wouldn't be alive long enough to regret it. That he had not closed his eyes in the firing of the shots or in their aftermath surprised him; impressed him too, if he allowed himself that indulgence. If this was the end, he wanted to see it for what it was. Plenty of time to not see once he was in the ground.

As it happened, the end didn't come, not then. Instead the thundering sound of the shots, or maybe the respect that the bullets' profound physics commanded, froze the beast. It looked briefly to the holes in the ceiling and then back to Drake, its sad eyes searching.

"I've got eight more," Drake said. He wasn't sure the thing would understand the words but hoped his tone would carry the meaning well enough. "Stay where you are."

Keeping his right hand on the gun, he reached into his pocket with the left for his phone. Without taking his eyes from the monster he retrieved it and unlocked it with his fingerprint. A phone call could come later, to Fox or Claire, maybe even Cavillo, but his immediate priority was a picture. Some physical proof that this thing was more than a shared hallucination, and maybe the first step toward determining what the hell it was.

With his right hand holding the gun level, Drake brought the phone up into his field of vision. But before he could even look at it, the monster recoiled back toward the window with a shriek and leaped like a missile out toward the backyard. The sheer unexpectedness of the move caused Drake to drop his phone to the floor, and he could only watch helplessly as the weight of the creature crashed through the glass, leaving jagged shards scattered in its wake. Drake heard the sickening thud of its body hitting the ground outside and hurried to the window to survey the damage. Looking out, he saw the thing slowly bring itself to its feet two stories below, bright red blood shining against its deep black hair. The beast looked up to the window and met his eyes, howled again, and loped back into the woods on all fours, its movement somewhere between that of a wolf and a bear.

No sign of activity from the neighboring houses but a sound that loud wouldn't go unnoticed. Calls to the police would be made, curious neighbors investigating would probably even be there before the cops. Either way, Drake wanted no part of it and set out to make his exit unseen. He turned back to the window, the broken glass shone so brilliantly in the sun, and looked at the bright red blood that adorned the corners where the jumper had left its impression. The hair already acquired, he couldn't bring himself to leave without securing the blood. A high-resolution photo would have completed the trifecta but that could no longer be helped.

Nothing in his pockets to collect the sample with, so he scanned the bedroom for something that might suffice. Expensive-looking furniture, elegant decorations along the walls, no good, no good... He raced over to Claire's dresser piled with various jetsam and rifled through the stack, tossing things aside in his hurry. Finally he saw a pair of blue earrings sealed up in a tiny plastic bag. Discarding the earrings, he brought the bag over to the window and got as much of the liquid into it as he could. It was a frantic, untidy job and the final total didn't amount to much, but he hoped it would be enough. Resealing the bag and placing it next to the hair in his pocket, Drake finally descended the stairs and checked to see that he wasn't being watched before making his way out the back door unseen.

Police sirens sang out on the edge of his hearing and he could hear voices conversing closer than that, so he slipped into the woods and cut a path parallel to the houses until he was beyond the neighborhood and could exit the trees without anyone taking notice. It was tempting to hang around and see what the cops made of the crime scene, but that was asking for trouble. And furthermore he didn't have the time to spare. Evidence in hand, he got into his car and pulled out onto the street. Summoning the full power of his six cylinders, he sped off in the direction of Dr. Fox's cabin in the woods.

24

James passed the minutes, or hours, whichever they were, in a haze. He wanted to call Claire, talk to her at least, but pride was a powerful thing, and when wounded it became doubly so. She had been the one who pushed him away, over and over. The onus was on her to fix this, he decided, or not. That was an option too, maybe even the more likely one. Easy to overlook the fault lines when taking the bird's eye view. Harder to ignore upon a closer look, especially if those cracks were growing at the same time. All endings have their own unique feeling, he supposed, but this one (if that's what it was) didn't come easily. It all went by so fast; could it really be over so soon? And if so, what was the point of having lived it, if only to end with an absence?

Outside the early afternoon was bright, some Webster's-sanctioned ideal of summer, but James stayed inside. He hadn't slept much, had eaten even less, and felt reduced to observing his life as though it were some background noise movie of the week. His vague awareness of the plot and characters never rose to the point of investment. He wished he could direct the events, but the suggestion felt preposterous. Maybe a deus ex machina was on its way, maybe a falling curtain; he hardly cared which.

From the other room, his phone sang out its melody. Claire was his first thought, she was always his first hope when the thing rang, but he couldn't take that as granted anymore. More than likely it was someone else, someone who couldn't measure up. And so it was: Victor Drake. James wasn't sure he wanted to take the call but in the end the phone's insistence won out and he answered it.

"Hello?"

"James, Victor Drake."

"Yeah, you don't have to say that. I've got caller ID you know, everyone does," he started but decided that wasn't a conversation worth having. "What's up?"

"I'm going to give you an address. If you can, come now." An instant's pause. "If you can't, come now anyway."

The edge in Drake's voice did something to break the haze. Not entirely, but the impact left a spider-web of narrow cracks. "What's going on?" James asked but it was no use, Drake was already talking over him, delivering the address twice.

"No time, James. The address. Leave now and tell no one." The phone beeped to signify the end of the call and James was alone again.

At least a twenty-minute drive by the GPS directions, so he wasted no time in getting on the road. *Why not just tell me what's happening,* he thought with annoyance. Frustration was something anyway, far better than the apathy he had been sleepwalking through, and to that end he welcomed the return of feeling. He treated the speed limits as nebulous suggestions and tried to answer his own question as he drove.

As far as he could see, it came down to two possibilities. Either the conversation wasn't safe for the phone, or words were insufficient and Drake had something James needed to see. Maybe a combination of both. "Tell no one," he said. Who would James tell anyway? Not Claire, not after last night, but maybe Drake didn't know about that. After her, who else was even left? The mysterious stranger?

Although he had been unaware of its transition, at some point the scenery changed from suburban to rural. There were no other cars on this road, this winding corridor through the pines, and he followed it deeper into the woods. It was still summer, the sun had hours of life in front of it, but the shade of the trees darkened the ground and gave him the feeling that he had stepped, driven really, into another world. Some dimension parallel to the sunny green lawn he had left behind at his house.

To the right he noticed, it had to be, Drake's car pulled off to the side of a desolate stretch of road. Alarm threatened his thoughts; what had gone wrong? But no, James convinced himself, that must have been part of the plan, the abandoned car. Why, he couldn't say, but he knew enough to know this wasn't his wheelhouse. He could tell from Drake's voice on the phone that some crucial thing had occurred, but the man didn't sound panicked or at a loss for control. Resolute if anything, as though his spine were steel.

Maybe Drake decided to make the final leg of the journey on foot. Less conspicuous that way and easier to disappear into the forest should things go sideways. Was he planning on things going sideways? Probably not, but nice to have the contingency available if needed, right? James agreed with the voice in his head; it was comforting. Likely just an overabundance of caution. He followed the directions to a quaint cabin surrounded by a fortress of pine trees. Leaving his car, James walked up to the house and knocked on the door.

"Come in," an unfamiliar voice said from inside. James pushed on the door and found himself in a rustic-looking kitchen.

"In here," came a second voice from the room beyond, this one Victor Drake's. "Come on through, James."

James followed the voices and saw Drake and a portly old man sitting across from each with a third, empty chair off to their sides. Both men looked tired, haggard even. "James, Dr. Howard Fox," Drake said by way of introduction. "Have a seat."

James did as instructed and eyed them both uncertainly. "What's going on here?"

Drake sighed bitterly and pointed a raised hand toward the old man. "Take it away, Doc."

"It's a pleasure to meet you, James," Dr. Fox said warmly, getting up to shake his hand. "I only wish it were under better circumstances."

James nodded but didn't speak, hoping the man would say what he needed to say as quickly as possible.

"I work with Claire at the university, physics projects. I will be direct. James, what do you know about wormholes?" he asked.

If James had come in with a list of questions he didn't expect to be asked, that would have ranked right near the top. After a few seconds, he was able to formulate a response. "Like in space? I know they're in space. Or," he corrected himself, "I think they're in space."

"That's right," the doctor said. "And jumping through one would allow you to travel distances farther than light could travel in the same time. The basic idea of relativity then: the closer you get to the speed of light, the more time slows down." James' blank stare told him he would have to explain further. "All it would take," he paused to laugh at his own little joke, "all it would take, so the theory goes, to travel back in time from there is to exceed the speed of light. Or, failing that, simulate the same."

He drew a straight line on a piece of paper. "Imagine this is time. Now this is vastly oversimplified, but for our purposes will do. And we conceive of beginnings, middles, and ends. Starting here," he pointed to one end, "and progressing thuswise," he finished at the other end.

"Thuswise," Drake said with mock reverence but stopped talking after a disapproving look from Dr. Fox.

"Past, present, future," the professor continued. "But of course we know that's not how time works at all. Rather it is a fourth dimension, every bit as malleable as length, width, and depth if we had the right tools. Past and future are not some far-off, unreachable places. They are happening concurrently all around us, if only we were able to sidestep into the proper dimension. To solve the scientific riddle that, as far as we know, humans have never been able to unravel."

"Ok." James didn't see where this was going but didn't want to delay the reveal any longer by asking questions.

"Now imagine this." Dr. Fox folded the paper and poked the tip of his pen through to the other side. He unfolded the paper which now had two holes several inches apart. "If one could enter the hole here," he put the pen on the first hole, "they could come out here." He moved the pen to the second hole. "So relative to the time, as we perceive it, they went in, that person would come out—"

"In the future," James finished for him. He wasn't sure he believed it, didn't know the science well enough to say, but the old man had his attention now.

"Good," Dr. Fox said, "exactly right. What was more interesting, and verifiable, to us was if one could enter here," the pen went into the second hole, "and come out on the other side here."

It was a lot to take in. "You believe all this?" James asked Drake.

"All I know is I know enough to know I don't know enough to know how much I don't know about wormholes."

"I don't have the slightest idea what you just said." James turned back to Dr. Fox. "Continue."

"The challenge, well one of many, was getting someone into the wormhole, you understand. We are in the earliest stages of our infancy as a species in regard to space travel. Perhaps someday humans will be able to travel to one, if they even occur naturally, never mind the complications of what would happen to a person who did. But I'm getting ahead of myself. The first barrier to entry, we had no way of even getting to a wormhole."

"So they figured why not bring the wormhole to them," Drake said.

Fox nodded. "Project Horizon. A phoenix rising from the ashes of the Philadelphia Experiment, Gateway, and a dozen other failures that never made it public. The field's best and brightest, and that includes Claire. If we could create a wormhole under laboratory conditions, the first hurdle would be cleared. Dr. Beaumont... I will spare you the specifics, but after decades of calculations and trial and error, we achieved it—theoretically. To actually implement it and send someone through the portal would take a phenomenal amount of energy. More than we could ever generate ourselves. We would have to harness an outside source and from that... Well, there I go into the details again."

"What does this have to do with me?" James asked.

"Nothing. Well, not as such."

"Nonsense," Drake broke in. "He was the first one to see the monster, Doc, that's what got this whole thing started." He chose his next words carefully. "He saw what came through your portal."

Silence then, from all three men. "Allow me to proceed," Dr. Fox said. "If the first challenge was creating the entrance, the second challenge was calibrating the exit. Consider the complications: distant galaxies expanding faster than the speed of light, to say nothing of our own planet speeding through the universe at 67,000 miles per hour. Time and space were the two titans we had to tangle with, trial after trial after trial. Error after error after error. But Dr. Beaumont, the word genius doesn't begin to do him justice, was insatiable. And he recruited a fanatical team united under one shining purpose. Generations' worth of some of the world's most brilliant minds—myself among them, if I could be so bold—made it their lives' work and finally, impossibly, we had perfected everything.

"Past was easier than future, though not for the reasons you would think. Physics tells us a being of infinite mass traveling faster than the speed of light would, to our perception, travel back in time. The first part is impossible, of course, but Dr. Beaumont found a way to simulate its effects with the machine; he tricked the science, if you will, a masterstroke of invention. Not the first time he triumphed over the so-called limits of physical laws, I promise you. The second part, traveling faster than light, would be achieved, or again, simulated, by the portal. All we were missing was a large enough energy source to open the tunnel. Which brings me to August 27th, or thereabouts."

The date had no significance that James could see.

"What's August 27th?"

"A massive thunderstorm," Dr. Fox said. "Or, more specifically, the accompanying lightning. Do you have any idea of the energy in a single bolt?" James admitted he didn't. "Roughly one billion joules," Dr. Fox said. "That's billion with a B. Extrapolate that to even a medium-sized storm and we've easily surpassed a nuclear bomb. A storm the size of what we're expecting on the 27th? This will provide enough energy to make Bikini Atoll look like a cap gun.

"I was caught in a small storm once myself," Fox said. "I was running down a road in the countryside, and the thunderclouds rolled in so suddenly. Perhaps they had been in the forecast, I don't know. But I was not expecting them, and I was miles from shelter. The rain came first and turned the run pleasant. It had been such a hot day, you know how it gets in summer, and the cooler air was a most welcome respite.

"But then came the lightning. I had never seen it so close before. The sky had gone dark with clouds but the streaks of light brought my surroundings back to full brightness. I was so exposed and helpless out there, and the bolts struck all around me like falling bombs. I knew enough to get down on the ground, but what could have prepared me for the ferocity of that sound or the accompanying smell? Each strike cracked like a jackhammer in my ears. The landscape around me was so flat, I made as good a landing spot as any of the rest of it. I felt if the electricity didn't stop my heart, the force of those reverberations just might.

"My hairs stood on end and my skin tingled as I closed my eyes against the crisis and breathed in the burning, alien smell of ozone. Slowly, pauses came between the flashes and the roars, from simultaneous to upwards of a second. The storm was, at last, moving away. I survived, of course, but not untouched. The experience left me with a deep discomfort for open spaces and, what's worse, running died for me that day."

"Too much to even take in," James said, but it did nothing to slow down the stream of information.

"Forgive me," Dr. Fox said, "I've lost the plot. Where was I? Oh, right. So with the apparatus and energy source in place, the only thing missing was—"

"The traveler." James looked at Drake, who stared resolutely ahead and avoided meeting his eyes. His mind began to put two and two together but refused to come up with four. "But you must have gone through the proper safety channels, whatever laws govern these experiments."

Dr. Fox shook his head. "Not how these things work, not projects like Horizon. We couldn't afford the delays that would come with government oversight. We were in the shadows here, it was the only way. This was a sure thing."

"No such thing," Drake said from his chair. "That's your arrogance talking, and you see where it got you. You geniuses should have known that, but you weren't smart enough to recognize your fallibility. Fools," he added.

His assertion went unchallenged. "The traveler," Dr. Fox continued. "Someone fit enough and young enough so as to weather the journey, but also with an exacting knowledge of the project so as to report back and troubleshoot where needed." He lowered his head as though that would make for a sufficient apology. "There was only ever one candidate."

None of the three spoke her name but they all thought it just the same. "She knew what she was getting into," Dr. Fox said. "I loved her, but she knew."

"None of you knew!" Drake spat. "But it wasn't you crawling into that coffin."

For his part, James was still arranging the pieces. "Claire went into the machine," he said. Speaking it made it more real. He spoke as though waking from a dream. "When?"

"August 27th," Dr. Fox said.

"It's August 16th," James said, a flash of excitement lighting across his face. "So we still have time. We just don't let her get into the machine."

"That was my reaction, kid, till the doc set me straight. But you're missing the bigger part of the picture."

"She came back, which means she's already gone through the portal," Fox said. "That future has already happened, James. If we stopped her on the 27th, she would find another way to come back. Or else she wouldn't be here now."

"Be here now?"

"What we didn't know—how could we possibly have? What we didn't know was what traveling through the wormhole would do to a person on a molecular level. We had no reason to think..." His voice trailed off. "But it was uncharted territory of the highest degree."

"It warped her," Drake said bluntly. "Made her both more and less than human. Unrecognizable." James didn't fill the silence Drake left him. "The visitor from the gym, the monster we've been tracking... Claire went into the portal and that thing came out."

"That thing is Claire?" Full-on disbelief now; time travel had been easy to swallow by comparison. He laughed at the absurdity of the idea until Dr. Fox cut him off.

"I prefer not to think in those terms. The young lady went in and came out... changed. It's no longer her in any sense worth conceiving of."

"You're wrong," James said, though he knew the man of science must have known of what he spoke to present his conclusions with such certainty. And Drake seemed convinced as well. "Unless you saw it come through the portal, which you didn't because otherwise you would have known right away." He looked at Drake. "How else could he know?"

Dr. Fox answered. "Whatever the leap in space-time did, her DNA was unchanged. Your friend here obtained blood and hair samples this afternoon."

"Long story," Drake said.

"And the tests, conclusive beyond doubt. That 'man' you saw and what 'he' has become is, was, Claire."

"That's impossible. I don't believe you."

"Of course you don't," Dr. Fox said, but he pressed on. "Nonetheless, impossible is well behind us now, if it ever existed at all. The lightning tore open a hole in space-time, wrenching the laws of nature unrecognizable. Maybe even a trick of parallel universes. I daresay it seems so logical now with the benefit of hindsight, obvious even, that Claire would not pass through the portal unscathed... unchanged. And you," he directed the next part to Drake, "can spare me the lecture. We jeopardized an innocent girl's life on an unknown. Unconscionable, really, but we were so close. And we thought we knew, honest to God we did."

"Maybe you're being punished," Drake said after a time. "The whole lot of you Horizon bastards. You wanted to go playing God and He stepped in to show that maybe it's not so easy after all. I sure hope that doesn't count as a lecture. Hell, I've probably got it coming too, for one reason or another. Not sure about the kid here. Maybe we've all got it coming."

"'Any sufficiently advanced technology,' Arthur Clarke said, 'is indistinguishable from magic.' We're there," the physicist said. "We've been there since, what, airplanes? Radio? Further back, I'm sure."

"Electricity," Drake offered.

"Maybe so," Dr. Fox decided.

"It clears up a lot," Drake said, altering the direction of discussion. "Why she came to you and her parents in the first place, then tracked down Dr. Fox, why I found her at her old house. She's the only common thread. What we still don't know—have no way of knowing, I suppose—is how much of the brain in there is still Claire and how much is this new thing, this... other."

"Some proportion of each," Fox said, "but I couldn't hazard a guess as to how much of either. She still has the connections to her past Mr. Drake mentioned, but this thing is not Claire as we knew her."

James had gone silent so Drake tried to salvage what he could from the situation. "All we can control is what happens next."

"She's not getting in the machine," James said. "I'll burn the building to the ground if that's what it takes."

"If you do that," Dr. Fox was trying to sound more patient than he felt, "then whatever happens afterward is what sends her back in time. Nothing we do or don't do can prevent that now, as I've said. The Novikov self-consistency principle. Get beyond this childish conception that the future is not yet written. Naivete does us no good, no matter how pure your intentions."

Drake spoke next. "There's that story of the rich man from Baghdad who sent his servant to the market. The servant saw Death and felt it was there to take him, so he rode his master's horse far away, to Samarra. To avoid his future," he said pointedly. "The rich man tracked down Death in the market and asked why it threatened the servant. 'I didn't threaten him,' Death said, 'I was just surprised to see him in Baghdad. Because I have an appointment with him tonight in Samarra.'" He shrugged. "For what it's worth."

"Not much," James said. "Not much at all."

"Claire, though I don't think it makes sense to call this new thing by its old name—"

"How about The Individual?" Drake interjected but Fox ignored the jab.

"She came through as the thing you saw in the gym. As far as we can tell, that was the first sighting. Her first contact anyway. She was supposed to return to the lab, we would have been there to proceed accordingly, but on campus is damn close, considering."

"So you had been waiting for her, on the date you planned to send her back to." That much at least made sense to him. "And when she didn't show up, you must have thought the experiment was a failure? Or that you didn't go through with it."

"No," Dr. Fox said. "We considered, even planned on, the possibility of minor complications. After all that these men and women have invested into this project, there was never any question whether or not the plan would go forward. God Himself wasn't stopping us."

"I bet you're starting to wish He had," Drake said but then let up. "Sorry, there I go lecturing again."

"As I was saying, your visitor in the gym, that was our first brush with what came through the portal. Warped by the sounds of it and certainly not herself, but recognizable as human at least, able to communicate to some degree."

Drake picked it up from there. "Second time was the break-in at your house, although we know now it wasn't a break-in at all, right? No prints, another effect of the portal, we think. So then there's the roadside, you saw what looked like 'the man from the gym' but different. Some trick of the eye, where the figure seemed to jump in time, unconstrained by physical laws. Something happened in that portal, James. I don't know what or how, and it sounds like the brilliant doctor here doesn't have half a clue either, but looking back we were witnessing the transformation all along."

"Next was the bar," Dr. Fox said, "where she moved from you to me. No longer human to the eye as Mr. Drake can attest, no longer a creature of rational thought. Truthfully, I had my suspicions about the connection even then, but it didn't seem real. I wouldn't allow myself to face it. This is, if you don't mind me saying, where you are now. But I can no longer deny the evidence fits. I hate that it fits," he said, as emotional as he'd been since James entered. "But son," he said, "it fits."

"The final time was today, at Mike and Rebecca's house, in Claire's old bedroom," Drake said. "The doc asked for a hair and blood sample and I managed to get them. The DNA, as he said, is an exact match. It's ironclad." James shook his head but Drake soldiered on. "What we've got to decide together is where we go from here. For my part, I say it's too dangerous to leave alive. The threats on you, if that's what they were, the lingering hostility toward the people who worked on the project, never mind any innocents that get in the way. You saw what happened to the old woman in the car."

"I fought him on that point," Dr. Fox said. "At first anyway. The beast, for that's what it is now, I confess, could have eviscerated me, either of us, but it didn't. Although, as your friend points out, I likely would not have survived if he didn't come looking for me. I don't know that it's malicious. Your encounter with it today would suggest the opposite," he said to Drake, "but I agree it's dangerous. We as scientists unleashed this threat upon the world and owe it to everyone to neutralize the danger we created. I'm afraid that part is beyond debate. How we accomplish it remains an open question."

"The professor here thinks we can capture the thing, study it," Drake said. "I've got my doubts. After what I saw today, the way it hurled itself through that window, it won't come willingly. Maybe it could be tranquilized, led away in cuffs, but you'd be risking a lot of lives to do it. It's done well to stay hidden when it doesn't want to be seen but that won't keep up forever. Only a matter of time until this thing attracts the attention of some real authority. Better we resolve it ourselves; that's the cleanest way out now."

"What does Dr. Beaumont know?" James asked.

"That the project failed," Dr. Fox said. "Some suspicions beyond that, I'm sure, but he doesn't know Claire came back."

"So we tell him," James said, "and let the scientific genius figure out a way to bring the old Claire back. Send the monster back through the portal or something."

"Telling him would be the worst thing we could do," Dr. Fox explained. "This would reflect badly on Horizon, and therefore his solution would be to eliminate any trace of evidence that it ever happened at all. Beaumont would destroy the beast, probably as cruelly as possible."

"Just that good a guy?" Drake asked.

"For one, he would probably blame it, or Claire, for everything that went wrong in the first place; the alternative would be to admit an error on his part. Even worse, he could convince himself it almost worked, encouraging him to experiment further."

Drake interjected again. "He wouldn't be wrong on that last count either, would he? Your team sent someone back in time, to nearly the same place she left from. You're monsters for what you made of her, but the achievement is undeniable. Inspiring, some would say."

"Nightmare," Dr. Fox said. "You saw that for yourself clearly enough. Project Horizon must die before even worse follows."

"I'm going to tell Claire," James said at last. "She will believe me, listen to me."

Dr. Fox addressed Drake. "I told you he wouldn't understand. It's beyond his comprehension." And, to James, "I mean no offense, but I can see no reason to continue to try explaining. The possibility of saving her was ruled out the moment your stranger walked into the gym. No one knew it then, of course, but we had already lost. All you can control now is the time you have left with the real Claire, the days before the 27th. You should let Mr. Drake and I attend to the monster. I wager your emotions would only get in the way of what must be done."

"You mean kill her." The stun began to wear off now and James was building toward anger. "I'm not going to let that happen." The other two men gave him room to go on but he stopped there.

"It's not Claire anymore," Drake said. "So much less human than when you saw it. If we can, we'll take it peacefully; you have my word on that. If we can't..." He let the silence finish the thought. "Well, you have my word on that too."

"The only Claire that's left," Dr. Fox said, "is the one you've known all along. She is here until the 27th, James, and then gone forever. That's the choice in front of you, how to spend these last several days. With the young woman you love or in an unwinnable battle with the thing that came through the portal in her place." He sighed. "Enjoy the time with her that's left, son. That's all there is now."

"I've got to tell her," he said weakly. "I can't let her walk into this slaughter."

"She already has," Dr. Fox said. "And we've already ended her suffering, or not. We haven't perceived it yet, but it's already happened all the same. I know that's of no comfort."

That snapped something in James. He stood and stepped aggressively toward Fox, but Drake set a big hand on his chest and arrested his movement. "We're running out of time," he said. "That thing must have left a blood trail from the house, it was cut up so bad. The police weren't far behind and you know they'll track it if they can. It will be looking for refuge; we'll start with the places it's been before. In the meantime, you should find Claire. Your time is running out too."

A rustling sound then from outside, not loud but noticeable enough that all three instinctively turned their heads toward it. "The wind?" Dr. Fox asked, but Drake was already on his feet with his hand on his gun. James looked back and forth from one to the other and then to the back door, his row with the professor momentarily forgotten.

"Stay back," Drake told them and he crept toward the rear of the house. Ducking low he slowly raised himself up until he was looking through the window and out over the trees that stood like sentinels around the entrance to the cabin. Their branches swayed gently with the breeze but the scene was otherwise still. Drake looked behind him and saw Dr. Fox and James frozen where he left them.

"Wait here," he said, and opened the back door. Stepping outside was a respite he hadn't known he needed. The conversation inside the house had been heavy, of crushing importance, and their moods had followed. But outside, the air felt tropical and he could almost convince himself, if only for a moment, that the trouble he found himself in was outside his purview. He stood and let his stress unwind in the emancipating therapy of wind and sun. Under different circumstances it would have been ideal conditions to pass a lazy afternoon. The weight of the pistol in his hand reminded him this was anything but.

A vicious crashing sound from the front of the house tore through his self-fashioned asylum, leaving it shattered. He reacted instantly but his body couldn't move as swiftly as his mind. Throwing the door open, he saw the thing he least wanted but most expected. The beast burst through the front door of the house, the cuts from its dive through the window still glistening fresh and scarlet. James and Dr. Fox fell to the ground in the aftermath and they both gazed up at the intruder in helpless wonder. Had this thing been smart enough to draw Drake out and attack the vulnerability he left behind, or was that merely a stroke of luck on its part?

The savagery with which it made its latest entrance favored the latter, though he figured it didn't matter much in the immediacy of the moment. What he took for reflection, even sadness, at Michael and Rebecca's house, was now blind rage. The monster swung an arm out wide and knocked aside a floor length lamp like it wasn't even there. The lamp bent in two under the force of the blow and flashed out as its cord ripped from the wall. Natural lighting remained but the room was cast into a relative darkness, and Drake couldn't see the others as clearly as he would have liked.

Meanwhile, James laid on his back, unable to take in what he was seeing. The same emotions from that first day in the gym flooded back, amplified a thousand times over. That sick dread in the bottom of his stomach, like the very blood in his veins had turned toxic without warning. *We're doomed,* he thought, not just for the four of them in the room but for all the world. How could mankind ever recover from this? And since it couldn't, what had it all been for? His breaths were short and rapid, his lungs empty of air, but he hardly noticed. He couldn't tear his eyes from the monster, from what had once been Claire, let alone corral his thoughts toward coherent action.

Dr. Fox couldn't stop staring either, but he was past the point of panic that had gripped James. Instead, he rested on the floor almost casually, the picture of acceptance. He looked to neither Drake nor James, didn't acknowledge their presence at all, but rather studied the enormity of the creature—it had grown so much since that night outside the Blue Valentine!—like a monk with his sacred text. Perhaps he knew what was coming, and had known for a long time. Struggling against it would have been the height of futility. Men of science knew better than to waste energy.

Drake tried to divert its attention with a gunshot that sailed close over the monster's head. It went unacknowledged by its target, who had apparently not noticed James. The beast regarded Drake for a moment, dismissing him with a snarl. Bending at the waist, it reached down and grabbed ahold of Dr. Fox, its sickly yellow claws like razors at his throat. It shot back up to full height and lifted the old man off the ground until they were face to face, Fox hanging defenseless. His pale blue eyes had twinkled once, but no longer. Now, as the oxygen abandoned him, they bore into the eyes of his creation. Its eyes were crimson now and he realized with a detached acquiescence that they might be the last thing he would ever see. Those intractable and uncompromising eyes.

Drake took the shots he had avoided for so long, firing twice into the chest of the beast. The bullets found their target and the black fur trembled, but Dr. Fox stayed prisoner with his feet dangling high above the ground. The stick having proved ineffective, Drake tried for the carrot.

"Claire!" he called out. For the first time, the monster turned its head away from Fox and met his gaze. "I know you're in there somewhere, and this isn't you. Let him go." He hesitated then added, "We can save you, bring you back." It was a lie, that last part, but he felt it justified if it could save the professor.

Difficult to say in the dimmer light, and it could have been wishful thinking, but the red eyes seemed to flash to that familiar deep blue. The reprieve, if it existed at all, proved short-lived and passed by like a wisp of cloud. In its place, the ugly scowl returned and the monster let out a low-pitched growl. The growl turned to a roar and its attention returned to Dr. Fox, barely clinging to consciousness. He managed to raise an arm and push away at Drake and James.

"Go," he tried to gasp out but his lungs came up empty. At that the monster twisted its hand violently and the professor's neck made a terrible cracking sound. The life was out of his eyes before the rest of his face could acknowledge what happened. His head, forced off the natural axis of his spine, slumped lifelessly to the side.

James scurried back further behind his chair, trying but unable to scream. Drake's mouth had fallen open involuntarily but he moved the pistol up to the creature's head, his hands steady. Following the gun's trajectory to its logical conclusion, James sprung out from his hiding place and knocked Drake's arms off target. "No!" The creature bent over Dr. Fox, batting at his body like a cat with a dead mouse.

Drake grabbed James' upper arm and pulled him along toward the back of the house. "Idiot," he seethed. "I had it between the eyes. That was our chance." They rushed outside the house and into James' car.

"Keys," Drake demanded, and James passed them to him with trembling hands then hurried into the passenger seat.

"I couldn't let you do it," James said. "Not while there's a chance we can save her."

The car's engine fired and Drake slammed it into reverse before shifting into drive and tearing away from the house. "Weren't you paying attention in there?" His voice was as loud as James had ever heard it. "She's gone, James. That thing is left in her place, and the longer it's alive, the more people are going to get hurt or killed. I should have taken the damn thing out at Mike's house when I had the chance." His right fist shot forward and punched hard at the dashboard. "That man's death—his name was Howard, James—his death is on me. He was a damn fool, but he was hardly alone in that. Everything that man was, everything he would have become, it's all gone now, and that's on me. Anyone from here forward, that's on you."

No response from the passenger seat. James only turned to look out the car's back window, half-expecting to see the black fur and red eyes chasing the car. But the trail behind them was empty, and the trees that lined the road passed by so quickly he knew they hadn't been followed. Which was no great relief given that Claire knew where he lived, and apparently that was one part of her identity that survived passing through the wormhole.

Somewhere behind the hideous outside Drake couldn't see past, parts of Claire remained. And as long as that was true, all was not lost. He didn't know how he could possibly reverse the transformation, but he knew he would try. Certainly the first step had been to prevent Drake from burying those bullets into her brain.

James looked across the car at the house of a man behind the wheel. He had chosen Victor Drake for his competence—"resourceful," Claire said—hand-picked for him by Claire and her father. Now the dynamic shifted and the only chance he had at saving Claire was to outwit, outmuscle, and outmaneuver the man who had been his champion. The stakes would never be higher and any one misstep could prove catastrophic.

Game on, James thought.

25

Farther down the road they came upon Drake's car where he had left it on the side of the road. Drake pulled James' vehicle over and got out. "This is where we part ways," he said. "I wish you the best but after what you pulled back there, we're done working together. Go see Claire if you want, but don't contact me again unless it's an emergency. Goodbye, James." With that, he got into his car and drove off ahead. James thought of giving chase, to see where he was going, maybe even try to stop whatever he was planning, but the car was out of sight even before he could get into his driver's seat.

The man had made up his mind and James wasn't going to beat him in his domain anyway. The only chance was to outsmart him some other way. Two destinations sprung to mind. First was the lab and Dr. Beaumont. Where that conversation would lead he didn't know, but he wagered Drake wouldn't see it coming and that might be enough to disrupt whatever he was planning. Doing so might buy time for the transformed version of Claire, and maybe Dr. Beaumont had a way of reversing its effects. A part of him knew it was futile, but he wasn't sure his conscience could bear it if he didn't even try.

The second was Claire's apartment. They hadn't left things well but that hardly seemed important now. There was too much to lose to let the vanity of ego or fear of rejection get in the way. He wanted to run to her and tell her what he had seen, about the monster, and Dr. Fox, and everything else. But the others had tried to convince him doing so would only poison the time they had left together. If the future had indeed already happened, if it was as unstoppable as the passage of time itself, each remaining moment became valuable past the point of expressing. If he spent them pushing Claire away, he couldn't bear that thought either, regardless how noble the motivation behind it might be.

His SUV followed the roads as though driverless, running on pure automation. Without even recognizing it, he was heading for Claire's. That was the right move, he told himself, the only move. Along the way he passed a grocery store and stopped off to buy some flowers. Nothing fancy, it seemed a stupid gesture in the face of Armageddon, but one he wanted to make just the same. Her apartment was as he remembered it, he hadn't been there for several days now, and a sick feeling hit him when he realized how much simpler the circumstances had been when he used to visit. No visitor from the gym, no red-eyed monster, no expiration date hanging over them like a scythe. Just the two of them together in love. He knew then he couldn't confront her with the horrors of that afternoon. Rather, he resolved to do what he could to re-embrace that old dynamic, if only for a handful of days.

Up the stairs he had climbed so many times before to her

door. The doorbell made the same inviting chime it always had but it sounded hollow to him now, like it too was putting on a happy facade. Several seconds passed, James standing there with his sad bouquet and his eyes on the door. Finally a voice from the other side. "Who is it?"

"Claire, it's me," he said. "Can we talk?"

The door opened partway and she looked out at him from the crack. "Is everything all right?" she asked.

It was all he could do not to physically flinch at the question but his face didn't betray his feelings. "I'm sorry," he said and offered up the flowers. "Can I come in?"

Claire looked behind her. "Yeah," she said, "sorry, come in."

The door swung wide and James stepped through. He took his shoes off, force of habit, and sat down on the couch.

Claire took the flowers into the kitchen and joined him. "Thank you, they're beautiful," she said.

"It's very kind of you to lie," James said with a smile, and they laughed together. "Best I could do on short notice."

"How have you been?" she asked.

"Gave a lot of thought to how we left things, and the more I thought about it the worse I felt."

"Me too," she said. "But I'm not sure I can balance those two parts of my life right now. Maybe in the future, when we're on the other side of this project, we could try again. It's not fair to you, I know. I didn't realize what this commitment was doing to my personal life until it was too late."

"It's not too late," James said and took her hand. "I know it feels that way, and you're overwhelmed right now. I just," he had to word the next part delicately, "don't want to end it that way. I want to be with you through the project, whatever that looks like. But not resenting or missing each other."

Water rose in the deep blue eyes he had fallen so hard

for, a tough sight to take. "What are you doing tonight?" James said. "I thought we could sit on the beach, look at the stars the way we used to, figure out what comes next."

She shook her head. "I can't tonight, I'm sorry. This is what I mean. You hated always coming in second, and I understand. But for the next couple weeks the project has to come first."

"And then?"

"I don't know. And then maybe we try again." She wiped her eyes. "I'm no good for you right now, maybe not even for myself. No one would blame you if you wanted to take a break."

"That's not what I want," James insisted. It was difficult to justify his urgency without the benefit of the full picture—all that she knew and didn't think he did, all beyond that which he knew and she never would. He wondered if the transformation would hurt. Would she know what she came out as on the other side? He hoped not.

The silence hung between them until she finally said, "I'll make tonight work. I'm not sure for how long, but the southern stars in summer..." she said. "Sounds nice, don't you think?"

"'Nice' doesn't come close," James said. "Until tonight then. I'll be on my way."

He kissed her on the forehead then rose to his feet, heading for the door. "Thank you, James," she said. "I wish I had more to give."

"You're all I've ever needed," James said and stepped outside. He had no reason to believe that was the last goodbye, but if it was, he felt it a satisfying epitaph. The idea of visiting the Physics Building was in his mind again, but he wasn't sure that would make things better for Claire, and it might make them much worse. Another part of him wanted to see what Victor Drake was up to; Dr. Fox's death changed something in him, sharpened that edge. Drake would kill the monster or die trying, James was sure. Which one, he couldn't say. Maybe if he saved the creature and Claire still went through the portal... No, try as he might he couldn't see it through to a happy ending. All he could do was get the most out of the time that was left. A victory of degrees.

Ultimately, he decided he wasn't happy with how he left things with Drake either and headed in the direction of his office. Except even that decision didn't come without complications. Barely a half mile from Claire's, his phone rang, a local number he thought he remembered seeing but couldn't place. He answered it to find Detective Morley on the other end.

"I need you to come back to the station," Morley said.

"What for?"

"We've got your original story here, just a couple questions we need to clear up."

"Not a good time," James said. "Can't you ask them over the phone?"

"No. How soon can you be here?"

James felt the traffic around him closing in. "That's ridiculous. Am I under arrest? If not, have a good day."

Morley sighed. "We can do this the easy way or the hard way," he said. "Come by, I'll have you out of here in ten minutes. This goes the way I think it will, you're going to be able to put all this behind you today. For good."

That may have been a lie but James had to take the chance. "Fine," he said. "I'll be there in... fifteen minutes." He hung up without waiting for confirmation and picked up his speed. Give the cops what they needed and he could be back on the road to Drake's within half an hour. Overly optimistic maybe but he felt he was due for something to

break his way. It was just after 5:15 when he stepped into the
police station.

26

Drake watched James' vehicle recede in his rearview mirror as he sped up the road. The kid still might have been in danger, he couldn't tell anymore, but he hoped the monster would leave James in the clear. The creature's first interaction had been with James. Creepy (how could that thing not be) but non-violent, what had likely been an appeal for understanding in retrospect. From there it went to Mike and Rebecca's, probably seeking the same. Instead Mike responded with violence, because that's what he always did, and the monster returned in kind. Dr. Fox was a lead on Project Horizon and Drake had no doubt added himself to its list after this most recent encounter. Which was to say the creature's targets were limited to those who attacked it or, the far greater sin, created it. James was neither.

It was a sad thing, the way the dilemma unfolded itself, but Drake knew this abomination of time and space could not peacefully exist in the world in which it found itself. He would put it down humanely, like a beloved dog gone feral, but put it down he would. And then the story would be over. Claire would disappear in less than two weeks, and that was deeply tragic on an emotional level, but on a practical level the Horizon team would have a plan in place to account for such contingencies. Dr. Fox's murder would baffle the authorities (no tall order) and probably spur a series of paranormal theories alongside Bigfoot and chupacabra. Or, it wouldn't be the first time, they might cover up the details and let it pass from public interest quietly. If the Horizon people didn't scrub the murder too before the authorities were even made aware of it.

Within the hour he was back at his office. The gunshots were a last resort, but having been fired, they set up a promising trap. Now he was a target, which meant the monster would come for him; he hoped it would be soon. Had it already tried the basement laboratory or was it smart enough to stay away from there? From what little he knew of Dr. Beaumont, Drake was confident that his treatment of the poor thing would be anything but humane. He hoped this new version of Claire—no, it was still too hard to think of the beast in those terms—knew that much as well.

Claire knew where Drake's office was, so her twisted doppelganger would as well. *Well, let it come*, he thought, *and I'll be ready*. He had already made the mental preparations, had been doing so continuously for some time now, which left only the physical logistics. The creature had powers of limited transformation, which it could maybe control, and time manipulation, which it maybe couldn't. Unknown territory was an understatement, but the monster could be hurt. And if it could be hurt, it could be killed. The thought was like a bowling ball on his chest.

A couple hours of daylight left before the sun went down. Maybe the thing would come for him that night, maybe not for a week. But it would come, he was sure of that. He parked his car outside his office building and opened the door to the stairs, its bell chiming faintly. Heavier than he remembered it. Yes, he decided, the door had gotten much heavier in the past couple days; that was the more comforting explanation. Once inside he closed the door behind him, extinguishing most of the natural light and leaving only what filtered through a pair of small and grimy windows. Nonetheless, he knew the place well and could have made the climb in complete darkness.

At the top of the stairs he put his key into the lock and turned it until he heard the click, making sure to enter the office with his eyes up. The large window across from the entrance was right where he had left it, but a dark silhouette stood between him and the outside. The figure's finer features were obscured by the backlighting but the red eyes left no doubt who waited for him. Drake stepped inside and reached back to shut the office door, all the time keeping his eyes ahead.

"Right through the lock, hey?" he said by way of greeting. "One of your more useful tricks I'll bet." The man across from him (but not a man, not really), said nothing to that but fixed on Drake with its glowing arachnid eyes. "What took you so long?" Drake drew his gun as if it were an afterthought; the other watched this without reacting.

"Guess this has turned into something of a monologue then. You're a killer now, Claire." He watched the eyes for a reaction to the name but none came. "Meanwhile, James blames himself for the old woman, maybe the law will too, and he probably should. But there's no collision without the distraction, and there's no distraction without you, right?" He moved toward his desk, the gun still out in front of him. "You mind if I sit? Very good." The hulking black frame with the razor claws was in stasis for now but this other form's near-humanity was almost even more unsettling. Looking that way it could pass for a person, but it was no less a monster. Trying his best to set that aside, Drake continued.

"See where you are now? That's where James was the first time he told me the story. I was here of course," he said, lowering himself into the chair behind his desk. "Best to hear a story like that sitting down." The eyes were alert and watching and Drake realized he was afraid what might happen if he stopped talking. "I'd be lying if I said I believed all your boyfriend told me." He paused then; he had tripped himself up by talking to this thing like it was Claire. That felt like a dark joke without a punchline and he resolved not to do it again, moving quickly past it.

"Well, you can imagine the stories I've heard in a job like this after, what, almost twenty years? Believe me, I could tell you some stories. The thing is," he drew a cigarette and lit it, which the monster didn't seem to mind, "he laid it out pretty true. That first meeting, when you went to the gym, that part at least I chalked up to self-indulgent exaggeration. But... no, he got it pretty much right."

Finally his visitor spoke, its voice like the rustling of dead leaves. "Not long now."

It took a second but in time the phrase clicked. "That's what you said before, on the note," Drake said, nodding. "Scared the hell out of James, you know. I imagine he thought you were coming for him." He thought on that a moment longer. "And in a way you did, but that's not how you meant it, was it?"

"Not long now." It was difficult to assign a timbre to such a voice but the word that sprung to mind was simply Sad.

"A little over a week," Drake agreed. "Irreversible, isn't it?" The question was rhetorical and he didn't expect an answer, but he was disappointed all the same when one didn't come.

"You tried James, who was no help. And then your parents, who were even less help." He had slipped back into addressing Claire; he still didn't like it, but it felt like the one small kindness he could give her at that point. "What powers you gained having traveled through the portal, the shape-shifting and time manipulation were more than offset by the degraded ability to think straight, to communicate. So your dad attacked you, because that's what he does, and you reacted. May have been self-defense at that point or frustration, but I don't know that it matters much. Dead ends from the people who loved you most.

"Then there was the Horizon team, but that was never love, only utility. And when you came to terms with that, your anger needed a direction. Did you go after Beaumont? Seems like that would have been the play, but maybe he was too dangerous even for you. That building, those guards... Hell, that's probably nothing compared to what you've seen in there. Fox was an easier target, sure. You could have taken him that first night, could have taken me too. But you spared him. A battle of conscience maybe.

"And then," his cigarette was dying down, "you returned home, thinking of all you had been, all that would soon be lost forever. The anguish must have hit you like a steamroller. So back to Fox's to finish the job. And finish it you did, emphatically. In the process, a washed-up PI fires a couple shots that connect with all the force of mosquito bites. But he gets away, to the only escape he has in his life. Which you expected. So now," he held a hand out in front of him, "you're here to finish that job. Which I expected.

"That about sum it up?" Drake set his cigarette aside and looked into the red eyes staring out from that wrinkled and sullen face. "Except," he filled the silence quickly, "what happens next? Very soon you will have nothing left to lose, not even time. I couldn't even guess how many people it took to pull off honest-to-God time travel. Are you going to kill them all, the way you did Dr. Fox?" The gun which had been resting on the table found its way into his right hand and he trained it between the monster's eyes.

"Can't happen," Drake said. "Even if I were magnanimous enough to give myself up, and I'm not, those other people don't deserve what you did to Fox. Consequences, ok, but not that." For the first time since he entered, Drake got a reaction from across the table. The eyes narrowed and the mouth curled open in a grotesque snarl, giving him a glimpse of the serrated fangs. This was the third time he saw them but that didn't make them any easier to reconcile. "Which brings us to the point I've been avoiding," he continued. "Maybe I was hoping I could sidestep it, or it would pass me by, but I guess that's pretty silly, sitting here with you now. If you're past reasoning, then there's one way to stop you. Only one of us walks out of here, that's the endgame you signed up for when you came through that door, yeah?"

He would have liked to let the question hang in the air, give it the gravitas it merited, but he never got the chance. The transformation came down as suddenly and savagely as a bear trap. A cry of pain, an explosion of muscle and coarse black fur, and where the withered, sinewy figure had stood, the beast now towered. Drake's response was just as swift and by the time the monster jumped at him across the desk, he fired two shots in rapid succession. The barrel had been aimed between the thing's eyes but when it metamorphosed and leapt, the target had shifted. He had done his best to compensate but with so little warning the resulting shots didn't land quite where he had intended.

Still, they were close, not harmless body blows this time but direct hits to the unprotected face. One landed below the left eye, the other a couple inches higher and near the center of the forehead. The creature stumbled back under the power of the recoil and lay slumped against the wall, its bulky head sloped off to the side. Drake's hands were still on the gun and his mouth was set in a straight line, but he had to blink away the tears in his eyes. When he could see clearly again, he got up from his chair and approached the body that had gone still but for shallow, intermittent breaths.

Two small rivulets of blood ran down the lupine face. The crimson eyes were wide now, scared and uncomprehending. Its breathing slowed nearly to the point of stopping and its eyelids sank slowly. Drake knew there was nothing he could do or say, so he didn't try. Silence and a sympathetic witness seemed the most respectful things now, and he gave her what he could. An ugly wheezing sound persisted momentarily but trailed off as the lids closed. He thought that was the end, but for an instant they opened weakly, the eyes behind them a deep and brilliant blue. Then, at last, the breathing stopped and it lay dead.

Drake took a step back and tried to lower himself to the ground gradually. But the coordination that had served him so well seconds ago deserted him now and he fell backward awkwardly, hitting his back hard against the desk. It would hurt later he knew, but for now the shock overruled the pain. He sat there feeling the blood pulse through his body, his grip still tight on the Glock. No telling how long he would have stayed that way had the body not begun to change again. Within the space of a second the creature gave way to the decaying human form and then to Claire. Young, beautiful, and still.

And then it was gone, leaving only the empty air behind it. The two bullets dropped down from where they had lodged in the brain and clanked faintly on the hardwood floor. They lingered behind as the only evidence the interloper had ever been there at all. Drake stared where it had been, unable to pry his eyes from the nothingness as the shadows in the room steadily lengthened. After a long time the phone in his pocket vibrated, but he ignored it. The phone gave up and he continued to sit. Eventually he relented and got to his feet, finally letting the gun drop from his hand and onto the desk. He poured a glass of whiskey straight when the phone buzzed again.

This time he answered, not caring enough to look who was calling. "Go ahead," he said, his voice sounding unfamiliar to his own ears.

"Drake, I'm on my way over," James said. "I just left the police station. The old woman's family has sorted their side out and the police aren't pressing charges. I'm free..." He paused to allow a response but didn't get one so he moved on. "We need to talk about Claire."

"See you soon," Drake said and hung up.

27

The sound of footsteps climbing the wooden stairs and then Drake saw James walk through the door, not so much as a knock this time. He rushed in breathlessly, looking much older than he had just days before. "Any updates?"

"Have a seat," Drake said and gestured to the spot in front of his desk. James stayed standing but Drake held his silence until the other gave in.

"I saw Claire," James said, "and we're meeting tonight. Then I was on my way here, but that fat detective called, Morley, and he said I had to come in. Well I said the hell with him but then he said—"

"Slow down."

"Ok. The complication I told you about, with the woman's children and the shady lawyer... Apparently they resolved it and the police are content to call it an accident. Which it was."

"That's good news."

"What about the other news? Any sign of that thing? You

scared me the way you took off after what happened with Dr. Fox. I didn't know what was in your head. And," he prodded, "I guess I still don't."

Drake reached for the picture on his desk, the faded one of his office building, and passed it to James. "When do you think this was taken?"

James studied the weathered photograph. "When was the camera invented?" he asked. "I'd guess a week after that."

"It goes back," Drake agreed, replacing the frame on his desk. "Before you or me, that's for sure. And what do you feel when you look at that picture?"

"Right now I feel pretty damn annoyed. What does this have to do with anything? You still haven't answered my first question."

"You and I, Claire, anyone we've ever known, we don't exist in the world of this picture. Does that scare you, terrify you?"

"Of course not."

"See the sun there, and the sky, they seem to be all right. The people who built this place, they went about their lives just fine without any of us. And we're doing just fine without them. The people who will come after we've gone, whoever's sitting here 100 years from today, they're going to be fine too. Why should the world to come be any more concerning than the one in this picture? Life has never been about the individual. It's so much bigger than that."

"It's hardly a concern when we're dead," James said. "But it's hell on the ones we leave behind."

"I haven't got the faintest idea what happens to us after we die—and I don't believe anyone who says they do—but I find that reassuring, this idea that the world keeps turning. The show goes on no matter the significance of any one exit."

"Where's Claire? The future version, I mean."

"You said you didn't know what was in my head when we parted. Of course you did. I asked you the first time we met where your line was. Do you remember what we agreed on?"

James had to think back but yes, he did. "Carte blanche."

"As you say. The girl you loved went into that wormhole, James, but something else came back through it. It wasn't Claire anymore. The Claire you and I knew was gone when she went into that machine, through that portal. Putting the monster down was only a formality. That thing was past reason, it would have slaughtered those scientists and maybe others along the way. There was only one play. The sooner you accept that, the better this next part is going to go."

James leaned forward in the chair. "What next part?"

"It was self-defense if that helps," Drake said apologetically. "On my word, if I hadn't fired, you would've found me in the same condition they're going to find Dr. Fox. James," he said, looking hard into his eyes. "It was the only way."

James lowered his head and buried it in his hands. The bottle of whiskey was still on his desk so Drake got up and brought it to the freezer to give him the benefits of time and space. But he knew any amount of either would be insufficient, and eventually he returned to his chair behind the desk.

For a long time neither said anything. Normally the polite thing to do would have been to ask James if he was ok, but under the circumstances it was a stupid question, insulting even. Instead, he offered some unsolicited advice. That was probably insulting too, but by then there were no better cards left in his hand.

"Maximize the time you have left together. I will get a hold of Mike and Rebecca, tell them it's safe to come back. No details beyond that of course. Turns out they actually followed through on the isolation, by the way. A lesson to be had there about old dogs and new tricks maybe. Make sure her family gets some more memories with her before the 27th, too. Your curse is in knowing how near the end is; their curse is in not knowing."

He forced himself to go forward. "We build these little castles of impermanence, but time always wins in the end. When it does, maybe go somewhere new, somewhere free of all the associations here. This place is saturated in sentiment now. Your house, your job, every tree that lines every road is going to remind you of her. It's no good. The swampland of Florida, the woods of northern Michigan, life at sea. A radical departure and a new start, James. It's your only chance."

"And then what?" Red lines stood out on James' eyes and his voice sounded harsh. "She becomes a memory?"

"What the hell else would happen?" Drake initially matched his tone, then mellowed it. "That's all that ever happens, James, to anything. There's nothing on this earth you can hold forever, and you sure as hell can't take it with you." James didn't acknowledge that, wasn't even looking at him, but Drake knew he was listening. "You've got the now, which is all you've ever had."

"She will never grow old," James said, and Drake could feel his heartbreak from across the desk. He had no counterpoint. That line of thinking was distressing, so he pivoted to the practical. "I've run it over in my mind. Not the Why, that will take a lifetime, but the How. And the way I've got it figured, Horizon has planned for Claire's disappearance; it was inherent in the design of the experiment. When she doesn't come back, as far as they know, they will fake her death. Something well-orchestrated and foolproof, a can't-miss case for the police. Horizon will cover Fox's disappearance too. After that they may come for me, but I play dumb well enough, and by then you'll be gone. Which puts you and me in the clear on this. That's not the way you're thinking now, I know, but one of us has to be."

That was meant to be comforting but the logic came across as cold and uncaring. "You're too detached; it's not real to you," James said. "Not real enough anyway."

Unclear if James meant too detached from this particular situation or too detached as a general rule, but Drake didn't feel it was worth arguing either way.

"Nothing lasts forever," he repeated patiently. "That's a cliché and no grand insight. But it holds tremendous power, the way all obvious truths do. It's not fair that your time together is ending sooner than you'd like, so much sooner, but... it surely is." He felt he was rambling, reaching for something he couldn't quite grasp. "The only thing you can control is what you do with the time that's left. Spend it on some fool's errand that will drive her away? That how you want to go out?" He felt his ire rising again.

The frustration was not with James so much, his inability to understand, but the circumstances at large. Maybe the world entirely. How overwhelming everything seemed, and how small and weak he felt in comparison. "I've done what I can." He wished he could say more, do more. "You should go now." His closing words were ill-practiced and bordering on uncomfortable. "I'm sorry."

28

The mid-August sky was jet black, those southern stars as brilliant as promised. James paid them no attention, instead watching Claire and trying to hold on to each moment. They sat on a yellow blanket on the sand with the sound of crashing waves punctuating their conversation. They talked of small things and big things, but mostly small, and it seemed better that way. A gentle wind came down the coast and blew strands of dark hair across her face. She laughed and pushed them away, looking at James with those crystal blue eyes.

"This is nice," she said.

"The best."

The night took on the feeling of a pleasant dream, James thought, in that moment you realize it's a dream but try to will it to last. Which of course never works. He stared up at the sky helplessly, the innumerable tiny points of light and the vast dark spaces between them.

"How far away are the stars?" James asked. Such a basic

question, but he realized he had no idea what the answer was.

"It depends," Claire said. "There are so many. Light-years, anyway."

"What's that in miles?"

"Trillions," she said. "More than we can imagine." James nodded. "But then a lot of them are dead," Claire continued. "No way to tell which just by looking. Dead stars shine too."

James imagined a zoomed out cinematic shot, the two of them inconsequential and barely registrable under that eternity of empty blackness and distant fires.

"Does that make you feel more or less significant," he asked, "when you think about our place in all this?"

Claire was silent for a long time. The waves still crashed, and below them a baritone voice sang quietly through a speaker, weighing the possible existence of angels.

"More," she finally decided.

She yawned and put her head on his shoulder. He held her close. When the night of August 27th came, as it must, he would think of her. And watch the sky for lightning.

About the Author

Adam Dompierre holds a bachelor's degree in psychology from the University of Michigan and a master's degree in education from Augustana University. He has worked as a secondary English teacher since 2010.

Adam lives in northern Michigan with his girlfriend Riley, their dog Pilot, and their cat Max. In his free time, he enjoys playing guitar and tennis, though not simultaneously. *Wild Bolts Electric* is his first novel.

You can connect with me at:

🌐 https://www.adamdompierre.com

🔗 https://linktr.ee/adamdompierre

Subscribe to my free newsletter:

✉ https://www.adamdompierre.com/newsletter

Thank you for reading *Wild Bolts Electric.* If you enjoyed this book, please consider leaving a review on Amazon, Goodreads, or your platform of choice; it would really help me out. I appreciate your support!

All the best,

Adam

www.ingramcontent.com/pod-product-compliance
Lightning Source LLC
Chambersburg PA
CBHW020140310726
48970CB00006B/1954